D0711664

Meyer

© Stephen Dixon, 2007

Melville House Publishing
300 Observer Highway
Third Floor
Hoboken, NJ 07030

www.mhpbooks.com

First Melville House Printing: September 2007

Book Design: Blair & Hayes

Excerpts of *Meyer* have been published in the following magazines: *Avery Review, Bridge, Boulevard, Idaho Review, Lit, Meridian, New England Review, The Hopkins Review,* and *Vice.*

Library of Congress Cataloging-in-Publication Data

Dixon, Stephen, 1936-
  Meyer / Stephen Dixon.
    p. cm.
  ISBN 978-1-933633-30-5 (pbk.)
  1. Novelists--Fiction. 2. Fiction--Authorship--Fiction. I. Title.
  PS3554.I92M49 2007
  813'.54--dc22

                    2007027274

Meyer

Stephen Dixon

MELVILLEHOUSE PUBLISHING
HOBOKEN, NEW JERSEY

To my wife, Anne Frydman

1

"So what are you going to do now?" she says. "I don't know. Maybe bat out a poem. But I want to do something." He kisses her, gets out of bed and puts on his glasses, picks his clothes off the floor and puts them on, sits at his worktable in the room and takes the cover off the typewriter. She gets out of bed and goes into the bathroom and turns on the shower.

Let's see, he thinks; maybe something's in there. He starts typing: "Now is the time, beloved, that I love you the most. Think of it," and he subtracts eighty-two from a hundred and five, "twenty-three years, plus the three before we got married. Of all the women I've known, none has been anything like you. You are this, you are that. You do this to me, you do that. You, you, you." "Forget it," he says, and thinks what he's written is even a bit insulting, and pulls the paper out of the typewriter and puts the cover back on.

Shower's turned off. He thinks of her drying herself, naked. He knocks on the bathroom door. "Yes?" she says. "Can I come in?" "You can't use the other bathroom?" "It's not for that." "What's it for, then?" "I want to see you naked." "Oh, God. All right, come in."

He opens the door, looks at her naked. "Had enough?" she says. "Turn around." "This is silly, Meyer." "Please?" She turns around. "Bend over," he says. "Didn't we just do it? And if it's that important to you, wouldn't it be more comfortable in bed?" "This is how I want it. You bent over. Me behind you. And it's easier that way standing up here than crouched behind you on the bed." "All right," she says, "although it could also be dangerous doing it here. Don't slip." She grabs hold of the sink and bends over. He drops his pants. It doesn't take him long. "Boy, that was good for me," he says, "and so unusual for me, too, and so soon. Thanks," and kisses the back of her neck. "It was hardly anything for me but worrisome," she says, "but I'm glad you're finally satisfied. What are you going to do now?" "I think I'll try to bat out a story. Had no luck with the poem. Wasn't the right time or something. Quick first draft of a story, though—the time feels right for it." "How so?" "Not sure, but that's what I'm thinking. Sometimes you just know."

He pulls up his pants. They're wet from the water on the floor. He takes the pants off and wipes the floor with them, gets another pair from the closet and puts them on. She shuts the bathroom door and turns on the shower. Why would she want another one? he thinks. They weren't messy. Maybe she got a little sweaty. If he had known she was going to take one, he wouldn't have dried the floor. Oh, well. He goes into the kitchen and puts the wet pants in the washer, goes back to his worktable and puts paper in the typewriter and starts typing: "The quick brown fox got his hen. Don't be a jerk. Now is the time for this good man to write a story. Be serious." While he was in the bathroom, he now remembers, he got an idea for a story. He tries to think of it now. He was still behind her. She was still bent over. They'd just finished making love. Or he did. He was drooling on her shoulder. That could be why she's taking another shower. But she could have just wiped it off with a wet washrag. Anyway, the idea for the story was what? It just came to him then as ideas for writing often do right after he makes love. A boy. Something with a boy. And a bookstore. Got it, he thinks, and starts typing: "A boy in a huge bookstore was signing copies of a book of short-shorts and prose poems he'd written. He looked to be around twelve or thirteen. He was sitting behind a table stacked with copies of his book and more were in opened cartons on the floor. There were fifty or so people, all of them adults, waiting on line with copies of his book. Al, who'd had a few stories and poems in literary magazines the last twenty years but never a book published, walked up to the table and took a book. 'If you want that signed,' someone said, 'you have to get to the end of the line.' 'I just want to look at it; I don't want to buy it,' Al said. It was published by a major publisher. The jacket copy began with 'A youthful masterpiece, unlike anything ever written.' There were blurbs in back by well-known serious writers. One called the kid 'The real thing, besides being a literary phenom. The future of American literature is assured.'" Enough, he thinks, this is going nowhere, and he takes the two sheets out of the typewriter, tears them up with the poem he tried writing before, drops the pieces into the trashbasket under the table, and re-covers the typewriter.

His wife comes out of the bathroom. She's naked and she reaches for her bra on one of the bed pillows and puts it on. "I'm not sure how you'll take this," he says, "but can we make love again?" "I'm sorry," she says, "I have to get back to my work. And why would you want to? You need sex to shake some creative stuff out of you? Well, find another way." "It's been so long. Not the sex, of course, but my writing. Nothing's come for a month. I feel miserable if I don't have something to work on. I'm almost sure something will come if we make love again. It's worked in the past, though those times I didn't intentionally want to make love to get a writing idea going." "I told you; no." She gets her panties off the foot of the bed and puts them on. He grabs her arms, kisses her hard, tries to stick his tongue in her mouth but she keeps her lips closed, sits down on the bed and pulls her down to sit beside him and pulls her panties down from behind and rubs her buttocks. "It's not going to excite me," she says. "I'm not asking you to be excited, just to help me out one time. If it doesn't work, it'll be the last time I ask you for it like this. Not for life but for a long time. No, either way, if it works or doesn't, I promise this'll be the last time I ask you this for the rest of my life." "All right," she says, "but I'm not doing anything. I'll lie on my back and that's all, and I don't want it to go on forever." "Fine, because I think just you on your back is all I need."

She takes off her panties and gets on her back. He takes off his pants and undershorts. "Might as well take off my shirt too," he says, and takes it off and starts to pull off her bra. "The bra stays," she says, readjusting it. "But it's always better when we're both completely naked." "I say the bra stays, or I'm getting up." "Okay," and he lies beside her and tries kissing her. "No more kissing, either. You practically bit through my lip the last time, and I just don't feel like it." "Can I at least stroke your body a little, for my sake if not yours, and possibly you a little to me too?" "No. Just get it over with." "Okay," he says.

He gets on top of her. Tries. Barely gets excited. After about ten minutes of his trying, she says "I think we should stop. Or you stop, because I haven't been doing anything. It's getting—how can I put this—a bit tedious for me and it must be tiring for you." "Just a little more," he says, "and if nothing happens, I swear I'll stop."

He closes his eyes, thinks of being behind her in the bathroom, gets excited, gets inside her, but soon loses it and slips out. He holds onto her, keeps his eyes closed, tries to think of something to write about. Sees himself at his typewriter typing. Sees himself photocopying a new work in his department's office. Sees a boy of around eight, who looks a little like him at that age and then all of a sudden doesn't, holding a man's hand as they cross Eighth Avenue to the old Madison Square Garden. "This is so unusual," the boy thinks. "We never hold hands or go out alone together like this. And to a hockey game, to see my favorite team, the New York Rovers. He doesn't like any sports but boxing. How come he's taking me?" "Because he got two free tickets," the boy's mother said before he and his father left the apartment, "and there's nothing he hates more than to see something he got for free go to waste." So they're crossing the street. The light turns from green to yellow to red. His father's stopped and dropped the boy's hand. "Dad, what are you doing? The light's changed." His father stares past him, his eyes, it seems, open as wide as they can get. He grabs his chest with one hand and falls. Cars are coming. People on the sidewalks shout at them to get out of the street. "Dad, get up, we'll be killed." A car screeches to a stop about ten feet from them. A policeman runs toward them, holding up his hands to stop traffic coming both ways. He next sees himself sitting at his worktable and crying. The typewriter cover's off. His wife asks "What's wrong?" "Madison Square Garden," he says. "Oh, I'm sorry. But if you can put it down on paper, maybe you'll get it out of your system." "I can't write about it. What's there to write? I'm crossing the street with my father. For the first time in my life he's taking me to a sports event. We once went to a movie alone together, also with free tickets, and that was the only other time I can remember being out alone with him except when he took me to manufacturers of boys' clothes to get a jacket or winter coat or two pairs of pants, all wholesale. He has a heart attack in the middle of the street in front of the Garden. A policeman asks me my name and phone number so he can call my mother, but I don't know them. I forget them. I can't speak, in fact. Then he asks me to write them down and hands me a pad and pencil. I can't write. My hands feel paralyzed. My tongue too. They take my father away in an ambulance. 'He was dead before he hit the ground,' I hear a doctor tell someone. A policeman drives me to a police station. They got my father's name and address from his wallet and call my mother. She comes to pick me up and we go to the hospital, where there are some things she has to attend to, she says. She asks me do I want to see him one last time before the funeral? I don't say anything or move my head. She leaves me and I stay with a nurse. While we're going home in a taxi, she says 'I'm very sorry I said those things about Dad before you left the house today.' I just stare at her. 'That he was only taking you to the game because he got free tickets and felt he had to use them, even though he didn't care for hockey. That he was cheap that way. I said it out of anger. Your dad and I had a fight earlier this morning. Nothing unusual, but a much bigger one. That was probably another reason he wanted to get out of the house. That and because he knew you'd love to see the game. Now he's dead and you're in shock. Please come out of it, my darling,' she says. 'I need to have you to talk to. Believe me, it's as much of a shock to me as it is to you.' And that was that. I couldn't speak for months, or just didn't. Didn't leave the house, wouldn't go to the funeral, never once opened a comic book or turned on any of my favorite radio shows, barely ate. Mostly moped in my room, stared at the fifty or so university pennants that lined the four walls near the ceiling. My sisters tried to bring me out of it—no doubt at my mother's urging—but nothing worked.

Then one afternoon I snapped out of it. It was like, earlier in my life, when I suddenly stopped stuttering after about three years, but without even knowing it. I got off my bed, went into the kitchen, sat down at the table and started helping my mother shell peas. Then she said 'Set the table for dinner, please?' and I said 'Sure,' so I began to speak again. Monosyllables at first; then whole sentences. Began to write again—meaning using a pencil and pen in school and doing my homework. I also began drawing again—mostly airplane battles; you have to understand this was during World War II. Nothing there that's interesting, though. I think I should give up entirely on this incident," and he puts the cover back on the typewriter.

His wife nudges him. He rolls off her. "I'm sorry, I think I must have fallen asleep," she says. "I didn't think I was that tired before you started doing it, but I only got a few hours sleep last night." "Why, something upsetting you?" "No, I just had difficulty falling asleep. So, did anything come of it?" "Of what?" he says. "Writing ideas. Anything surface that you like?" "Nothing much." She gets up. "Don't worry," she says, "I'm not going to take another shower. I don't know why I did the second time. Possibly because I was in the bathroom, no clothes on, and forgot I'd just taken a shower." She puts on her panties. "So, what are you going to do now?" she says. He's still lying on his back. "I don't know. No story, no poem, and no ideas for one. I don't know. Maybe just nap."

2

What now? Off the bed. Gets off the bed, puts his clothes on, gets his jacket, watch cap and muffler off the coat rack in the living room and leaves the house. Why leave? Just to do something. Walk, exercise, fresh air, see things. You never know. Also: Work ideas come to him outside better than in. Not so, but they do come, and one's what he wants now. Has his memobook and pen? Feels his jacket pocket. Yes. "Don't forget to close the storm door tight," his wife said from her study as he was going out. "It's ten degrees." Ten? Cold. Is he dressed for it? He'll find out soon enough. But by then he might be some distance from the house and won't want to come back for more clothes. So, what is it, cold? Not so much. Ten degrees? Maybe one time today or it hasn't gone down to that yet. Now it's fifteen, twenty, and no wind, so not bad. Clothes he has on are plenty.

Walks. Did he shut the storm door tight? Forgot to. When he comes back she might complain. "You didn't shut the storm door as I asked you to. It was a simple request. What is it with you?" What is it with him? Maybe he did shut it tight and forgot he had. Did he? Forgets. He does things so quickly, without thinking. He'll find out when he gets back. Door might be ajar. That so, he won't ask. If she says, he'll know.

Walks. Forgot his gloves. No big deal; he'll keep his hands in his jacket pockets. Five minutes into the walk: that house there. Woman lived in it he found attractive. Found? Thought. Found and thought. First saw her digging out her driveway on a day colder than this. Ten degrees, maybe a little below. Where was her husband to help her with the snow or do it, as he would, himself? Well, he does it partly for the exercise, for on those days the Y's closed. Little boy was with her. Shoveling with a child's snow shovel, saying "Am I helping good?" He stopped, said "Lot of snow to dig out." They'd had a storm the previous day that dumped fourteen inches. "Can I give you a hand?" "No, thanks; I'll manage," she said. Nice smile. "Two can work better than one, if you have an extra shovel." "We are two," the boy said. "Then three can work better than two." "This one and my son's shovel are all we have," she said. "Then let me shovel with yours for a few minutes while you take a break." Smile, complexion, cheeks ruddy from the cold, wavy hair coming out of her ski cap, lovely cultured voice. Cultured? Intelligent voice? Just a nice soft voice, no trace of a regional accent. She said "Okay, if you insist." "I am sort of insisting, aren't I. Well, you looked bushed." He said that? Doesn't think so. Thinks he just said "Good," but felt he'd gone too far. She gave him her shovel. He shoveled. "What's your son's name?" "Mike," the boy said. "That's right, you'd think I would have learned by now, having had kids that young once. Ask them directly. So what's your name, Mike?" "He's funny," Mike said to her. "Mine's Meyer. Meyer, Mike. Close. I always wanted to be called something like Mike, or even 'Mike.' But you can't shorten my name. Meyer's always Meyer. You wouldn't want to trade names, though, would you?" "What's he mean?" "Oh, don't mind me; I'm talking silly." Shoveled. After a few minutes, she said "We're almost to the street. I can finish up." Maybe she isn't married, he thought, or is separated and has no man to shovel the driveway for her. And all that talk about names, how come she didn't give hers. She doesn't want to. Don't push it. "Give me two more minutes," he said, "and you'll be all dug out." "My husband's plane was grounded in Pittsburgh and I wanted the driveway cleared when he drove back from the airport tonight. "Well, you've done it," reaching the cleared street. "Now, a little here, there, widening it a bit so the car gets through, and finito," and he banged the shovel on the ground to get the snow off the scoop, and handed it to her. "Thank you," she said, "but I owe you something." "No, I'm a neighbor, about eight houses down. Neighbors don't take money for digging out driveways for neighbors." "I meant a hot chocolate or tea. It's freezing cold out and you did it without gloves. I never should have let you, or loaned you my mittens and kept my hands in my pockets while you shoveled." "God, forgot them and didn't even realize it. Something I never do, forgetting them when it's this cold. Didn't forget my boots, though, so shows I'm not totally out of it. Okay, my hands are cold, so a hot drink would be nice. Thanks." They all went into the house. Mike quickly took his outerclothes off and disappeared. From the mudroom, as she later called it, Meyer could see the dining and living rooms. Lots of books on the coffee and side tables. Floor-to-ceiling bookcases covered two walls and maybe others he couldn't see, furniture not lavish or gaudy and room not excessively neat. An uncovered typewriter on the dining room table with sheets of clean paper beside it. He pointed to it and said "Who uses that?" "I do, mostly for letters. My husband's a computer whiz and practically holds his nose whenever he passes my typewriter. I'm exaggerating." "I also use a typewriter," he said, "and more than for letters. We've got to be the only two people in the entire community who do." "Then you have to let me know where you get yours serviced. I can't find anybody and mine hasn't been cleaned since college." "Will do, and also where to get typewriter ribbon and those white-out correction tabs if you're having a problem getting those too." "I type so little, the three extra ribbons I have amount to a lifetime supply for me, and I just let my mistakes go." She took off her cap and coat and shook them out. Left the scarf on. "I'm tracking up your nice room here with my boots," he said, "and I'm certainly not going to go inside with them." "Take them off, and don't worry about this floor. This is our pretentiously named mudroom. We inherited the name from the elderly couple who lived here for thirty years. Smacks of something out of a Jane Austen novel, where streets were filled with horse manure and mud. I'd prefer calling it our entrance room, but the name's stuck." Took off her boots. She had a good figure. Sizable breasts, small waist, no fat anywhere, slim legs, he could see in the tight jeans she was wearing; firm behind. He hung his jacket, coat and muffler on the peg next to hers. "I don't see Michael's boots," she said. "Michael, come back here, your boots," and the kid came running back. "They were stuck," he said, and sat on the floor and she pulled them off. "Your socks are wet," she said, and Michael said "I don't care. Call me when the hot chocolate's ready," and went inside. He grabbed her. No he didn't. She caught him eyeing her body when she hung up Michael's muffler and coat, which he'd left on the floor. "Excuse me," Meyer said. "For what?" "Nothing," he said. Then he took her hand. No he didn't. He touched her shoulder. She said "What are you doing?" He grabbed the two ends of the scarf around her neck and pulled her to him. She said "What on earth are you doing?" She pushed his hands away from the scarf and said "I think not. You also better go." She let him kiss her—she even closed her eyes during it—and then pushed him away and said "I don't like this. No more, and you have to go." She did none of that. She said "So let's have some hot chocolate," and they went into the kitchen in their socks. She boiled water. When she was at the kitchen counter pouring it into three mugs with powdered chocolate in them, he came up behind her, put his arms around her and fondled her breasts. She pushed her behind into his crotch and turned around and kissed him. He put his hand down the back of her pants. They did none of that. She called out "Michael, your hot chocolate's ready"—his was made with warmed milk, theirs with boiled water. "Do you have marshmallows for mine?" Michael said. "We're all out, sweetie." "Can I have sugar in it, then?" "That'd make it too sweet. And you already have cookies. —Sure you don't want one?" she said to Meyer, holding out the tin, and he said "No, thanks." They all drank their hot chocolates. Then he got up and said "I should go," and she said "Thank you again." She walked him to the mudroom. He put on his boots, coat, muffler and cap. "May I loan you a pair of my husband's gloves? He has several—if you're ever by here again you can put them in our mailbox—and one size fits all." "I'll be all right; and I don't want to risk losing them. Nice meeting you," and they shook hands and he left. He turned around when he got about ten feet from the door. She was looking at him through the door window. He waved; she smiled and motioned for him to come back. He pointed to himself and mouthed "Me?" She mouthed or said "Yes." He walked back to the house and she quickly closed the door once he was inside. They hugged and kissed. No they didn't. They just kissed and she grabbed his hand and opened a door in the mudroom that led to the playroom downstairs. At the top of the door—probably that high up so Michael wouldn't be able to reach it—was a hook, which she latched. She led him downstairs and unrolled a futon. No she didn't. He headed home. What a doll, he thought as he walked. And what a drip she must have thought him. Insisting on helping her dig out her driveway when it was obvious she didn't want him to and could easily finish the job herself. And when he started shoveling, her son stopped. The boy wanted to shovel alongside his mother and show her he was being helpful. Why couldn't he have just waved to her when he walked past her driveway? Maybe said something like "Some snow we had," and even "Can I be of any help?" and when she said no, to just continue walking.

Gets home. His wife says "You didn't shut the storm door tight when you left." "I'm sorry. My mind, you know. Short-term memory is a thing of the past for me." "That's a good one, I think." "Actually, it just turned out that way," he says. "I meant to say something else, of which I forget now, but thanks." "Your hands must be freezing, with no gloves. Let me feel them." She takes his hands. "Oh, boy; cold." "Feel my lips." "Okay," she says, "I'll bite. I mean, I won't bite, but I will feel them." They kiss, hug. Oh, Sandra, he thinks, what a doll. He puts his hand inside the back of her pants and feels her buttocks. No he doesn't. Front. No. Feels her breasts. Doesn't, or not with his hand, for he can feel them against his chest. They kiss again, a long one, and she says "That was nice; what I needed to get through the rest of the afternoon," and stands on her tiptoes to kiss his nose and goes back to her study to work. He goes into the bedroom, takes the cover off the typewriter and puts two sheets of writing paper in. He writes "I made love today with a beautiful neighbor I'd never met before and don't even know the name of, and my wife has no idea I did." No, he thinks. Writes: "I fell in love today with a neighbor and I don't know how to tell my wife." No. Writes: "My hands are still cold. I can barely type.

Should've borrowed the gloves the woman offered, but that would mean I'd have to return them and I don't want to risk seeing her again. Not true; I do." No.

Sits back, the front chair legs off the floor a few inches, and keeps himself from falling backwards by holding the edge of the table with one hand. He did once see her shoveling snow, two years ago, and she was very pretty and charming and seemed intelligent. Did shovel about twelve feet of her driveway till it connected to the cleared street, and it was way below freezing out and he had no gloves on and he did have a hot chocolate with her after in her kitchen. Strange of her, though, he now thinks, inviting him in when she didn't know him. Or just very trusting and generous of her. Anyway, not something he'd want Sandra to do. Accepting some guy's offer to help shovel the driveway out, okay. Never saw her again, and he thinks he would have recognized her if he'd bumped into her in the local market or at a concert, let's say, but saw her son playing in their front yard a couple of times when he drove past. Last time he saw him, there was also a dog. About six months after he shoveled snow for her, he walked by her house and saw a huge moving van in the driveway and movers carrying furniture and boxes into the house. He doesn't recall seeing a For Sale sign out front, so they must have sold the house without putting it on the market.

3

Thinks: Write a memoir. Never done that. Not even started one, and leans forward and begins. "He was born, lived and is now almost dead. Something with his chest. In it, with it, but he knows he's on his last leg." Ridiculous: chest, leg. "He knows he's finished. Won't go to his doctor for it. Knows what the doctor will say. He'll put him in a hospital and he'll die there or be released after a couple of weeks and die at home. Has had the illness a year now, feels weaker every day, doesn't know what he's going to do about it." What's he mean there? Strike the last line out, and he moves the paper up two spaces and crosses the last sentence out with a pen and also the entire "last leg" line.

Resumes typing: "He's very sick, that's all. Doesn't want to die but knows he will in a few weeks. That's how bad off he is. How advanced his illness is. He's going to miss so much. His wife:

cuddling up in bed with her at night. Though in ways she'll be glad he's gone because his coughs and hacking and spitting into paper towels after won't keep her up as they have the past year. His kids. But they've been out of the house a few years. But he'll miss them, what does he think? Misses them now. And they'll miss him, won't they? Sure, because he's been a good father, caring and thoughtful and uncritical and free with the money, so for a while they will miss him and then maybe only when they sporadically or periodically remember him or talk about him together or with their mother. Loves when they visit or he and his wife visit them. Though actually, because of his illness, it's become difficult for him to travel. And how can he miss them if he's dead, even though he knows what he meant to say? And this was supposed to be a memoir, so what's he doing going so much off the subject like this?"

Raises the paper, strikes the last two lines out. Thinks: Maybe he should strike everything out, or just make it easy for himself and put new paper in and get rid of what he's written so far. But something could come of what he's written, so keep it for now and just go on.

Lowers the paper and resumes typing: "I was born. Of course you were born. Don't be a nitwit. Strike all of the last part out." Done. Now resume the memoir. Resumes: "He's not sick. Was just pretending he was. The line came to him and he ran with it. Ridiculous to do so." Strikes all of that last part out too. Resume. Memoir. Write one. Start one, he means. Writes: "I come from a family of eight. Actually, ten, with my parents. I was the third boy

and youngest child. My father died by the time I was born, so I
actually come from a family of nine. Killed by a cab as he crossed
the street to the hospital where my mother was in labor with me.
They didn't tell her of his death till after I was born, thinking it
would complicate the delivery. Not true, any of that, except I do
come from a family of ten and was the third boy and youngest son
and my father did die in a street but not by being hit by a cab. Not
true either, other than my father dying in the street. So why'd I put
the rest of it in? Seemed more interesting than the truth." No good.
Tears the paper out. He was down to the end of the page anyway
and rips the paper up and drops the pieces into the trashbasket
under the worktable.

He still want to write a memoir? He'll give it another try.
Puts new paper in, but the platen only moves a little when he tries
rolling the paper into it. Knows, without seeing it, what the problem
is. Piece of paper from one of the two sheets he just pulled out got
stuck in the platen. Takes the sheets out, rolls the platen back and
forth several times and sees the torn paper. With tweezers he keeps
on the window ledge above the worktable for situations like this, he
pulls the paper out. On it is typed "godalmighty, already," which
had to come from the written side of one of the two old manuscript
pages he uses the clean sides of for his first drafts, since it wasn't
from anything he just wrote. Thinks: Which of his manuscripts did
it come from? Can't remember.

Sticks the two sheets back in, rolls them into the platen and
writes "I was born, lived and now want to die. Isn't so. A striking

first line for an amateur. I'm the amateur and shouldn't be, as I've been writing almost without stop for more than forty years." How many exactly? Started writing seriously when he was twenty-three—a woman had broken up with him and to help get over it he sat down at a typewriter at work—he was a newsman, in DC, so it also could have been in either the House or Senate press galleries, or whatever they're called—God, he's forgetting everything; the places where newsmen write their stories in the Capitol—and wrote the first draft of a story about the breakup. Never was able to sell that story or anything else he wrote the next four or five years. Couldn't even give them away to little magazines. Anyway, started writing seriously at twenty-three, so forty-five years. Writes: "…almost without stop for forty-five years. So, amateur at memoir, then." Not good. In fact, dreadful. Don't even bother striking out everything you wrote here or tearing out the page. Certainly don't tear. Piece of paper could get stuck again. Just start the memoir again on this page, but in a new paragraph.

Pulls the paper out and puts two new second sheets in. Oops, wasn't going to do that, but it's done, so start. Writes: "He was born. Not that, but last child, third one, one of eight kids, only one still alive." He could write about his brothers and sisters (hates the word "siblings," though it is shorter), because each one was unusual and had a strong influence on him in different ways, but wants to start with his birth, so later. Could even start with his parents and grandparents—they also had unusual lives—but that'd take some research, and again, he wants to start with his birth. To start it on

a dime, so to speak, but not with the line "He" or "I was born."
Grandparents came over from Eastern Europe in the late-19th
century and settled on the Lower East Side. His parents were born
in tenements there—their parents couldn't afford hospitals. Mother
was a showgirl when they met, father an actor—had eight children,
five of whom died—two by suicide—before they died themselves.
He was the last born. Said that. It was a difficult birth, his mother
said. He was born in a taxi. This is true, not in there to make the
memoir more interesting. His father had left for work that morning
and couldn't be located. He was a salesman and on his rounds in the
Garment Center. Textiles, mostly for linings of women's jackets and
coats. Said his acting skills helped his selling spiel. His mother was
seven and a half months pregnant with him—her other children
were all born full term—when suddenly, while she was on one knee
in front of the opened oven basting two chickens for the day-after-
tomorrow's dinner—she said she usually cooked that far ahead
because of all the other work she had to do—when she recognized
the signs. She tried calling her obstetrician but the phone was dead.
Went to a neighbor's apartment to call and was told that phone
service was out in the whole neighborhood. Something to do with
a water main break that affected the phone lines. Till this day he
doesn't see the connection—the subway system, he could see not
operating because of flooding—but that's what she said the neighbor
told her and his father said he read about it in the paper the next
day. She said she thought at the time Get to the hospital, pronto, so
she left the younger kids with the neighbor whose phone she'd tried

to use, hailed a cab outside, was helped into it by the super of their building, and told the cabby to take her to the lying-in entrance of New York Hospital, where the previous seven kids were born and she and his father and one of his sisters died in the main building years later. Halfway there, she started giving birth. By the time the cab pulled up to the hospital, he was completely out and she was bleeding a lot. She remembered the cabby screaming at her "You stupid bitch; look what you're doing to my cab." He honked his horn till help came out of the building. The cord was cut in the cab so they could treat her immediately. He was fine, but his mother almost died from loss of blood. His father was finally located and came to the hospital that night. He'd skipped his salesman rounds that afternoon to take in a Broadway matinee and after it to have a drink with some old actor buddies. So it was a Wednesday he was born, since the Garment Center was always closed Saturdays. The cabby sued his parents for damages to his cab and won. They had to pay out of their own pockets, as none of their insurance policies covered it. Later on his father would say to him "Know what your being born cost me? Twenty times as much as the others, so more than twice as much as all of them combined. Only teasing you," he'd always add, "but why were you in such a damn hurry?" Week after he was born, he and his mother went home. His father had had a bad month selling, and most of his income was off commissions, so they took two city buses, parallel route and crosstown, and he convinced both drivers to let his wife on free. Thus his birth. Now get to his death.

Knows he's got something wrong with him. Feels it inside his chest. But he can't stand going to doctors or hospitals, so he lives with whatever it is. One day, he gets out of bed and falls. He never gets up again. This is the way he sees it happening. He's in a coma for three days and then dies. Either the plugs are pulled or he dies despite the best efforts to save him. It's what he thought: his chest, his lungs. Bronchitis became acute pneumonia. Whatever it's called. His system couldn't fight it anymore. However it happened. His wife and kids are devastated for a week or more. Though his wife likes that she's now able to sleep peacefully and undisturbed. Before, for a couple of years, his coughing and hacking and constant turning over in bed to try to find a comfortable sleeping position kept her up. Even when she asked him to sleep in one of the two vacant bedrooms, his hacking kept her up. Even with both doors closed—hers and the one in the room he slept in. She would have put in earplugs while she slept, but she wanted to be able to hear him if he called out to her or was in some sort of distress. She soon meets another man. His wife and he used to get subscription tickets to about eight concerts a season and always sat in the same orchestra seats in their city's symphonic hall. He used to say "It's our one big luxury." He especially liked getting to the hall an hour before the concert began and having tapas and a martini at the martini and food bars in the lobby. But because of his coughing, they couldn't go anymore. People in the seats around them would shush him and during intermission or after the concert, complained to him about his coughing. "If you know you're going to be this big a nuisance," one person said, "why come?" "Good question," he said, "but the subscription cost me a fortune." The last time they went, someone from management told him if he couldn't control his coughing or do it in the lobby during the concert but not near the auditorium doors, she'd have to ask him to leave. He did what she said, but his coughing in the lobby by the ticket entrance was so loud that she asked him to do it outside. They gave the rest of their tickets to a music conservatory so its students could use them. His wife said if she couldn't go with him or one of their kids, who visited them a few times a year, she didn't want to go at all. He said "What a waste of good money. 'Good money.' That was one of my father's expressions, though he also said 'All money's good,' and I don't think I ever used it before." She said "It wouldn't be a waste of anything if you'd seen a doctor and had treated whatever's causing the coughing." "You know me," he said; "intransigent." A month after he dies, she gets subscription tickets for the five remaining concerts that season. She sits next to the same man at each concert. They talk about what's on the program and, during the intermission of the third concert she goes to, have a glass of wine at the hall's wine bar. He takes her phone number after the last concert and calls her the next day and they start seeing each other. In a few weeks they're sleeping together almost every night—the man's a widower with two grown children—and eventually he moves out of his small apartment into her house and they marry. Again, this is the way he sees it happening. She's very happy with the man. His kids like him too and are glad their mother has someone again. The kids marry too, have children, do well in their professions: One's a cellist in a highly regarded string quartet and occasionally gives solo recitals here and abroad and the other sings lieder and opera in some of the major opera houses and music halls and has toured Europe several times. All this will be part of the memoir. Sort of a postscript to his life. In addition: He was cremated, which was what he wanted—never put it in writing but told his wife many times. "No ceremony, religious or otherwise, and no guests. Just you and the kids, if you want, and dump my ashes down the nearest hole." His ashes are buried in a steel box in their front yard. A tree's planted on top of the box or right beside it. A flowering cherry tree. He always wanted one on their property and never got around to buying it. He wanted a mature one so he could see it flower the next spring. Actually, he once did buy one—years ago—and kept it in the carport with its roots in a tub of water, but it died because he waited too long to plant it. A year after he dies, his wife sells the house and she and her husband buy an apartment in the city.

4

Let's say if she goes, he thinks, what would he do then? Last night
in bed she said "I'm feeling dizzy." She was on her side facing him;
her night table light was off. He was reading and had put a shirt
over his lamp shade so as little light as possible would reach her.
He said "But you're lying down; how can you be dizzy?" "I'm still
dizzy," she said. "My head is spinning; I don't feel well." "So what
do you want me to do?" "Hold me," she said, and he said "But I'm
resting for the first time all day and reading. —Okay, of course."
He looked at the page number, would try to memorize it, and then
thought You'll never, and put an old envelope on the page he was
reading, closed the book, put it on his night table and said "How can
I hold you if you're facing me? You'll have to turn over." She turned
on her other side and he held her. "You should probably shut the
light," she said. "Are you feeling better?" "A little, but please shut

the light." He shut off the light and went back to holding her. Soon he was asleep. In the morning—sometime while he was sleeping he had stopped holding her—he said to her in bed "How do you feel now?" "Do you mean am I still dizzy? Yes, but much better. Your holding me helped."

He gets up from his worktable and goes into the kitchen to get a celery stalk out of the refrigerator. "Ah, forget it, you're not really hungry," he tells himself. "You just want to do something." Goes into the living room and sits in the easy chair—the chair he always sits in when he reads in this room, unless the cat's sleeping there; then he reads on the couch—but doesn't turn the floor lamp on. If he wanted to read, there's a magazine and book he left on the side table last night. He also sits in the chair when he wants to listen to music here, but he doesn't get up to turn the radio on or put a CD in. Actually, one's already in from the last time he used the player—three late Schubert piano sonatas, which he wouldn't mind hearing again, even though he heard them two nights ago—but he doesn't get up to cross the room and press the buttons to start it. He just wants to sit and think about what if she's sick, very sick? What if she gets so sick she dies? What happens then? What does he do? How will he take it in and later feel? What will he do after? He imagines her dying. She's dizzy every night; this is what he imagines. He has to hold her in bed every night for weeks. She's also getting dizzy in the day. She's examined by their doctor. He sends her to a specialist. She has lots of tests. The results aren't good. More tests and then treatments. She gets much worse and is taken to a hospital and dies there. He's holding her hand when she dies and then holds it with both hands a few minutes before he lets it go. He kisses her forehead and rings the nurses' station. She dies at home. She wants to die there—she never said that but this is what he imagines her saying when she gets very sick and thinks she'll die. To die at home just with him and the kids by her. "Every day she's getting weaker," her doctor's said. "There's no cure or stopping it; it's going to happen soon," and it does and she's gone. He and the kids hug and cry and say things like "I can't believe it.... Mommy's gone.... Your mother gone.... She was so healthy up till a few months ago, or seemed so. What are we going to do without her?" Kids stay with him a few days, though after the first day he tells them he doesn't need anybody around, but if they're staying for their own reasons, that's fine. They go back to the cities they live in. There's no funeral or service or memorial. She's cremated—what she once said she wanted done with her body after all the usable parts had been donated—and anyway, he has no cemetery plot and doesn't want to buy one, for he also wants to be cremated when the time comes. He picks up her ashes in a box a few days after the cremation and brings them home. The box, covered by a towel, is kept on the floor in the coat closet, and that summer—this is what she asked him to do, he imagines—he distributes them, making sure no one's around to see him do it, over the wild blueberry field behind the house they've been renting for two months every summer the last seventeen years. He stays alone in the house that summer except for a week in August when the kids come up. The house has been great but is a shell to him now, he thinks, and he tells the landlord he won't be renting it anymore.

Or it's slow; several years. He quits his job or takes a leave of absence from it so he can take care of her. He learns to give injections, catheterize her, transfer her from bed to wheelchair and then back to bed, clean her after messy bowel movements, everything. He hires caregivers for three hours every weekday to give him time to shop for things they need and to write a little and nap. He wants to do most of the work himself, feels nobody else could be as gentle with her. Besides, caregivers aren't covered by their medical insurance and he doesn't have much money saved. She says things like "You're wasting your life on me." He always says things like "I was meant to do it and it's not wasting my life at all. It's the best thing I can do. Sounds hokey, I know, and fake, but it's the truth." She lets him make love to her about once a month. "Please," he says, "it's what I could really use. It won't take long, I'll be very careful with you, and if it hurts even a little bit, say so, and I'll stop." He has to do it in a way where he doesn't move her legs. One night she suddenly starts shrieking. He turns on his night table light. "I need the big painkiller," she says; "I need it quick." He injects her. It doesn't help much. "I can't give you anymore," he says; "it'll kill you." An ambulance takes her to the hospital early that morning. She dies a few hours later. The kids don't get to the hospital in time to see her go.

He pours himself coffee out of the thermos. Made it an hour ago. Goes back to the easy chair and sits. His wife walks through the room. He says "How do you feel now?" She says "Still a little dizzy. I'm going to call Dr. Angelino about it. It's been going on too many nights and now in the days too sometimes, and today a bad headache with it." "Did you take an aspirin?" "Two," she says, "but of something stronger, and they didn't do anything for it," and leaves the room, probably to go to her study.

Or she could die one night when there was no sign before she had anything wrong with her that bad. They go to bed. About twenty minutes later, she says "Hold me, I'm feeling dizzy again." He doesn't mind closing his book, since he just finished reading a long chapter, and shuts off his night table light. She's on her side, facing away from him, and he holds her from behind. Short while later, she says "I feel a little better already; thank you." "You're welcome." He gets an erection, rubs it against her. "What do you say," he says, "—that is, if you're feeling up to it? Privilege of a husband and advantage of this position and all that?" "I don't feel much like it, but if you do, go ahead. But from behind. I don't want to move. And after it, you can hold me again." He pulls down her panties, has to sit up to get them over her feet. Pulls up her nightshirt till it's above her breasts, moves her legs a little, sticks it in, and in a couple of minutes is done. "Too fast," he says, "though it was good. I really appreciate it and wish you could have enjoyed it too." "Still too dizzy to. Could you help me with my panties? I don't know if I can find them and put them on." He turns on his light, finds her panties, puts them on her, pulls down her nightshirt, shuts the light, wedges his forehead into the back of her neck and holds her from behind. "Still not feeling well?" he says a minute later. No answer. She must be asleep, he thinks. He continues to hold her and is soon asleep. He gets up around seven the next morning. Had his back to her when he awoke. She's in the same position she fell asleep in, which doesn't mean she didn't turn over a few times at night and ended up in that position. He washes and shaves in the hallway bathroom so not to disturb her, dresses, feeds the cat and lets it out, gets the newspapers from the driveway, makes coffee, has toast with a slice of soy cheese on top of it, sits in the easy chair and reads one of the newspapers with his second mug of coffee. At 8:30 he goes into the room to wake her because she doesn't like to sleep past that. "Sweetheart," he says, "it's 8:30." She doesn't respond. "Want to sleep another ten minutes?" Nothing. Gets close to her. She's fast asleep, he thinks, but making no noise. Usually she makes noises early in the morning: snoring, heavy breathing. Well, let her sleep another fifteen minutes, he thinks. He sits in the easy chair with the second newspaper and reads the first page and a couple of stories that continue inside the paper. Then he goes into their room; it's almost nine. She'll want to get up even if she is in a deep sleep. She might even complain to him why he didn't get her up sooner. She does, he'll say "You were sleeping so soundly; I didn't have the heart to wake you. And what's another half-hour?" She's still sleeping. He touches her shoulder. She doesn't stir. Feels her forehead. It's wet and cold. Shakes her shoulder and says "Sandra, get up, it's past nine." Nothing. "Oh, no," he says. Gets her on her back and puts his ear to her mouth. No sound, and no air coming out. Pulls back the covers and puts his hand under her nightshirt to feel her chest; can't find a beat. Wrists, temples; nothing, and her feet are freezing, though her chest seemed normal. Pulls up her nightshirt and puts his ear where he thinks her heart is. Can't hear anything. Moves his ear around on her chest. By now he thinks she's in a deep coma or dead. Shakes her hard, yells her name, pinches her thighs and cheeks. She doesn't move. A needle, he thinks: no, no needle. "Oh, please, please," he says, "wake up or give some sign you're alive." Dials 911 from the phone on the dresser, never taking his eyes off her. After the call, he pulls her nightshirt down and pulls the covers up to her neck. An EMS team from the fire department comes. Police. A fireman checks her for pulse and heartbeat and breathing and looks in her mouth and opens her eyes and feels her neck and ankles and toes and says she's dead. Someone from the county medical examiner's office comes and certifies she's dead. He's asked lots of questions by this man, is told his wife will have to be autopsied, "since she died so suddenly, and without, you're saying, being sick when she went to sleep, except for dizziness and a headache," and is then questioned by a policewoman. Calls the kids; reaches one and she says she'll call the other. Calls Sandra's father in New York. She's put in a long black bag, zippered and taken away for the autopsy. Several days later she's delivered to a crematorium facility he got from an ad in the newspaper. "Call some other," his sister says on the phone, "or I'll do it for you from here. Since you want the minimum amount of service, maybe one's a lot cheaper." He says "The price seems fair enough and I don't want to shop around or have anyone haggle for me." A week later, their doctor, after getting the autopsy report, explains to him what killed her and why there were no warnings except for headache and her dizziness in bed.

But his original point, he tells himself, was: What happens to him if she dies? He needs the money, so he goes back to work after a couple of weeks. He tells his colleagues and the office staff "Please don't offer your condolences. Don't speak of her, either. I'm all right, the kids are holding up, and that's all I want to say about it." He doesn't want to see any friends and tells his sister not to visit him, when she offers to. "Another time, perhaps, but I'm not ready for it yet. Yes, you're right, I just want to mourn on my own." Two of his wife's friends come to the house uninvited with cooked food for him. He says at the door "I don't want to see anyone, unless I have to, like at work, and I can take care of myself alone. But thank you. It smells good, what you made, so please take it home and give it to your families." After they leave, he puts a note on the kitchen storm door and another on what's considered the front door but is almost never used: "To my kind friends and neighbors. My not coming to the door doesn't mean I didn't hear the bell ring or am not in. I know you mean well, I appreciate it to no end, but I'm not up to seeing anyone but my daughters for even a quick visit and I don't know when I'll be." When his kids come, which they do about once a month, taking the same train down together from different cities, he makes them dinner or tells them to get takeout from whatever restaurant they want and he'll pay. "Nothing for me, though. I'm happy just eating buttered rye or sourdough toast and raw vegetables." He reads a lot: novels, newspapers, two weekly magazines, and poetry from Sandra's personal library. Buys a lot of CDs—mostly Renaissance and Baroque choral works and sad chamber music—and listens to it while he drinks two or three martinis and some wine, and reads. He's usually tight by the time he goes to bed at night, and on weekends he takes one or two naps a day. About six months after she dies, friends call saying they know a woman they think he might want to meet. He says "Too soon." Keeps saying to these offers "Too soon." Then says "You know what? I'd rather not. It's too late for me. I met Sandra when I was forty-two. I'm now sixty-eight. I don't want to start in with someone new. Nor do I want to try having sex with anyone else. She's still too much part of my memory and I think that's the way it'll always be. I'm not lonely, or not that much, but I make do. I read, I listen to music, occasionally rent a movie, although I've got to admit it's no fun watching it alone, so I know it's something I'll stop doing soon. I also take long walks and work out at the Y, where, believe me, even for a guy my age there are plenty of women there if I wanted to hook up with someone, and also at work. Smart women, some very attractive women, but not for me. And I have Sleek, the cat, who's a great companion. When he dies, and he's getting old, maybe I'll regret not having anyone else. And of course, whenever I want to speak to someone on the phone, there are my kids." He got rid of all her clothes a few weeks after she died but keeps a number of photos of her around the house. One in her hospital room where she's holding their first daughter the day she was born. Another with her mother and the kids in Maine, all of them looking cheerful and healthy. Another with him, a kid on each of their laps. One of her the summer before they met: walking on a beach followed by her two Siamese cats, who were sisters and lived with them a few years before they died. Sometimes he cries when he looks at one of these photos. He lights a candle for her on her birthday. Another one for the day she died. A third on their wedding anniversary. Does this for years. Then adds a fourth: the day they met—Thanksgiving Day, when he by chance stood behind her in a crowd watching the parade go down Central Park West, so always on that Thursday. The candles are special memorial ones he has to go into the city to get and which last twenty-four hours. Were they happy together? he thinks. Relatively so. No, they were mostly happy, and often were very happy together. Kissed a lot. Continued to hold hands in movie theaters. Got into fights—a few a year that never lasted long because he was always at fault and didn't like keeping bad feelings between them, so quickly apologized. She broke up with him nine months after they started seeing each other, saying they'd gone as far as they could as a couple, she was approaching an age where she had to think of getting married again and having children and he wasn't the right person for that. Called him three months later—they hadn't had any contact till then—and said she missed him and did he want to have coffee and talk: She'd understand if he didn't? So, a few setbacks, sure. But for the most part they were very good to each other and shared a love of literature and serious music and such, and of course their children, who are wonderful, have always been wonderful; never a problem with them or in how they wanted to bring them up. And their sex was usually very good and she was always generous with it too when he wanted it, and she always let him do it, or almost always, when she wasn't in the mood. She was great, he thinks. He loved her deeply, that's what he'd think if she died. And she loved him. He knows it.

5

Sitting in the easy chair, he thinks: This is how it can happen. He comes back from shoveling snow, says to his wife "Boy, that was work, but it's all done. I think I'll take a shower and then rest awhile." She says "You should. But I told you not to shovel it all at once. Healthy as you are, you're too old for that. Do some of it, rest, some more of it, rest, and then go back out and finish the job. It's a long driveway, there's been lots of snow, and it's Sunday—we're not going anywhere today—so there was no reason to finish it so fast." "You're right," he says, "but you know me: I like to get things over with," and goes into their bedroom. He starts taking off his shirt and then thinks: Forget the shower for now. Too exhausted for even that, and he lies on the bed, takes the book he's been reading at night in bed off his night table, and after reading half a page he feels himself getting sleepy. Good, I'm tired enough for a nap, and

Stephen Dixon

puts the book down, shuts his eyes and falls asleep. He doesn't wake up. Heart attack; it was shoveling an hour straight that did it. His wife finds him. EMS tries to revive him. The kids and his sister are called. He's cremated; ashes are left at the crematory, which is what he once told his wife, "and on this I'm serious now," he wanted done with them. "Don't even think of buying the metal box they'll want to sell you to put some of the ashes in. Let them all go out with the extras of everybody else's from that day or week. It's too morbid for you to take any of mine home, and I also don't want to stick you with the task of getting rid of them."

Which reminds him: He needs to shovel the driveway and the path to it from the kitchen door. He gets up, puts on his boots and outdoor clothes, tells his wife he's going to shovel the snow: "I've been putting it off." She says "You ought to get a neighborhood kid to do it." "You know any? Like changing a flat tire, I feel I've done more than my share in my life and I don't want to change another." "I don't get your point." "Sure you do." "Just say it without any metaphorical assistance." "Shoveling snow. I wish there was a triple-A service for it. Call up, you wait in the warm house for them, they come in an hour or two, and it's done professionally and quick. I've shoveled this Gargantuan driveway the last twelve winters. Actually, though, since I can't get to the Y today because of the snow, it's a good substitute exercise, so I really shouldn't complain about it." "Promise me you won't shovel it at one time. Halfway done—even less than that, because there's a ton of snow out there—come in, make yourself tea, rest up. Then, if you want, go back to it, but

46

again, slowly, with lots of breaks outside, and not all at once."
"Gotcha."

He goes outside and starts shoveling. Ten to twelve inches fell last night and early morning. Soft snow, not so hard to shovel. Shovels half the driveway and stops. Rest like she says, he thinks. Even go in like she says. You're sweating and your heart's going a little fast and you should drink some water. He leans on the shovel handle and looks around. Not so cold out, and it's still as beautiful as it was this morning. No matter how much he hates it when it snows this hard, because of the work it forces him to do, it's still beautiful. Looking out the dining room window earlier today and seeing the snow on every branch and bush and tree crotch, or whatever the part's called where the branch meets the trunk, he thought It's a cliché but true so nothing to do about it: It's winter wonderland outside, he can't deny it. When his wife woke up later, he opened the curtains of the long window facing their bed and said "You have to look outside and do it before the wind blows the snow off the trees. It's gorgeous out. As beautiful a snowfall as I think I've ever seen. Must be some combination of meteorological phenomena—temperature close to the ground, temperature high in the sky, dampness of the air in between, and so on—to produce such a snow." She raised herself up in bed to look out the window. "My goodness," she said, "—gorgeous. There's no denying it. Absolutely phenomenal." "That's what I thought too," he said, "and almost with the exact same words. Maybe that's the effect a great snowfall has on you. Leaves you at a loss for original descriptions of it, which is also a thought I had when I first saw it."

Resumes shoveling. In about twenty minutes he reaches the end of the driveway. A plowtruck going up the street past it had left a huge mound of snow, blocking the entrance. Maybe eighteen inches, he thinks, and it'll be wet heavy snow, he bets. But get it done because you know you'll have to do it sometime, and probably better now than later. Later it might be hardened into ice or something close to it. Tries pushing through it with the shovel, but it won't be pushed. So, shovels it. When the entrance to the street is cleared, he thinks "Good, finished," even though the cleared driveway could be widened by about a foot on both sides so their van won't have any trouble getting through. Pretty narrow now. Later, he thinks, and heads back to the house. He's tired and his back hurts and he feels clammy from all his sweating. But do it now and he won't have to put on his boots again to come out and finish it. He can rest inside after, shower, change his clothes—not only his shirt but his pants because the bottoms are wet—make coffee or tea or a grapefruit juice and vodka, read the paper and listen to music and maybe even induce his wife to making love.

He shovels about a foot off both sides of the driveway from the carport to the street. Takes off his boots in front of the kitchen door, bangs them on the ground to get the snow off, gets the travel section of the Sunday *Times* off the dryer right by the door and puts it on the floor and the boots on it. Hangs up his outside clothes on the coatrack in the living room, the gloves sticking out of the pegs so they'll dry faster. "That wasn't as easy as I thought it'd be," he says to his wife in her study. "I'm not complaining. It had to be done, and better now when the snow's still soft. But two heavy snowfalls in four days—in some places I didn't know where to shovel it." "I can see the effect on you," she says. "Lower half of your face is a dark red. It's not worth doing if it's going to exhaust you." "I want to get to the store later," he says. "I'd walk, but I don't think I'll feel like it. And I have to get to work tomorrow—that joint never closes because of snow—so what was the alternative?" "Not to do it all at once, that's what I'm saying. Anyway, it's done?" "Done, and it did me in." "Next time with so much snow, let's hire someone to plow it." "They're so costly." "One time," she says, "we can afford it. Would it be worth it to save you from collapsing?" "Who's collapsing? We've time till the next big storm, if it ever comes, so I'll think about it. Meanwhile, I'm going to shower and look at my red face and maybe rest up." "Good. You should."

He goes into the bedroom, takes off his shirt and thinks should he jump into the shower or wipe his underarms and chest and back with the shirt, put another one on, rest a little on the bed, and then shower? The wet pants aren't so wet that they bother him. Socks, though, and takes them off. Nah, even the shower now seems like an effort. But the warm water will make his body feel good. And a shower always makes him feel better and less tired. After he rests, he thinks.

He puts on a clean shirt and lies on the bed. So this is how it could happen, he thinks. Oops. Forgot to look at his face. The color's probably gone by now anyway. But this is how it could happen, he thinks. Instead of a shower, he rested. If he hadn't rested, he wouldn't have got the heart attack. Resting can do it. Shower would have kept him active, made his body feel better. Then he wouldn't have even needed to rest after it. He would have driven or walked to the market, got some prepared food for tonight—their paella is a special all week and his wife loves it—and got enough food for the next few days. They need lettuce, scallions, mushrooms, yogurt, bread, cranberry juice for her, food for the cat. He shuts his eyes. No, you can really die this way, he thinks. You exerted yourself too much, shoveling. But say he did die, what would happen? It'd be terrible when his wife found him. He can't even imagine how badly the kids would take it. Of course his wife would be very sad too. But she's still quite pretty and has a good body and is very intelligent, so he's sure friends would be introducing her to all sorts of eligible men and she'd hook up with someone in a year or so. The kids would recover. The cat would miss him. No kidding, he would. He's the one Sleek talks to most, and he knows Sleek understands sometimes what he's saying to him. "Sleek, get off the bed," and he always gets off. Sleek can be deep in the woods in Maine around their rented house and when he yells "Sleek, come home, it's getting dark," he bounds out and runs to the porch or screen door he's yelling from. Just then, Sleek meows as he comes into the room. Then makes the same gurglelike sound he always makes as he prepares to jump on the bed, and jumps on it and quickly settles down and cuddles up to him. "Just what I need," he says. He won't want to disturb Sleek, and he'll get tired and close his eyes and fall asleep and get a heart attack and die. "Sorry, my man," and pushes him to the side, gets up, takes his clothes off and goes into the bathroom to shower.

6

He comes out of the shower and thinks "Oh, darn, what day is today? Did I miss it?" Quickly dries himself and runs through the living room to the kitchen and looks at the newspaper there. February 6th, he sees, Thanks goodness, and his wife says "What are you doing with no clothes on? Aren't you cold?" "No. Or only a little. Doesn't matter." "And you're wet—your legs and back." "Am I? Thought I dried myself completely. Today's the third anniversary of my mother's death." "Today? February 5th?" "It's the sixth." "I thought she died on the fifth. I remember thinking then, and other times: two-five. Twenty-five. Not twenty-six." "It was the sixth, believe me, and today's the sixth." "Three years," she says. "Doesn't seem that long ago, though that's what people always say. Are you going to light a memorial candle for her?" and he says "I only have one left. They're so tough to get. I have to go to Pikesville for them, so I'll save it for her birthday next month. That way, I'll light it soon as I get up and have it the whole day. Here, half the day's gone already." "I can understand. And finish drying. You'll catch a cold." "You don't get one that way."

He goes back to the bedroom, gets the towel off the bed and dries his legs and back. When he first got into the shower and was waiting for the water to warm up, he thought maybe he could lure his wife to the bedroom after he dried himself. Yell out, or go into the living room to yell it, because sounds don't carry well from this room to the front of the house, "Sandra, care to take a break?" Now he doesn't feel like it. How could he. Three years. He was sitting up in bed reading a book when the call came. His wife was in the bathroom and said through the door "Can you get it? It's not that I don't have my portable, but I don't like to answer the phone when I'm on the potty." It was his sister with what she said was very bad news: "Mom's been taken to the hospital and they don't think she's going to survive the night. You better get on a train, though there's no guarantee she'll be alive when you get here."

Maybe he will light the candle. No, save it for her birthday. And get dressed. Gets dressed and goes into the living room and sits down to read a book he left on the chair's side table last night. Phone rings in the bedroom and his wife's study. He can hear his wife running the faucet in the kitchen. Phone rings again. "Could you get it before the answering machine picks it up?" he yells to her. "I don't feel like talking to anyone." "Oh, you're in there? I thought you were in back." She answers the phone in her study. "It's for you," she yells to him. "Your sister." "I told you, I don't want to speak to anyone." Then he thinks: It's probably about their mother. He goes into the bedroom and picks up the phone. "Meyer's on," his wife says. "Nice talking to you, Naomi," and hangs up. "Hi," he says. "Why didn't you want to come to the phone?" Naomi says. "You don't know?" "How would I? I don't live in your house, eavesdrop on your conversations or know your thoughts." "Today's the third anniversary of Mom's death." "I thought March 6th." "February." "I'm almost sure it was March." "February." "If you say so," she says. "You sound very positive, and you'd remember." "I have it written down in my datebook for that year, the day she died." "You still have that book from three years ago? What, for tax purposes, in case you get audited and have to show it to them like a diary for certain things?" "No," he says. "Because it has phone numbers and addresses in it I haven't transferred to this year's datebook." "Why don't you transfer them, or just get a regular address book?" "I have one but it's for the most part filled up. As for transferring them to later datebooks: not enough space; I'm also too lazy to; and I know where these numbers are in the '02 book: all in the front. But other things are in it too. PIN numbers, for instance." "You keep your PIN numbers out like that? They could be stolen, the important ones. Where do you keep those datebooks, for I supposed you also have your '03 and '04 books for the same purpose?" "I do. From '01, which is when most of the popular letters of the address book filled up, to '05. They're wrapped together, along with my checkbook—this way I don't have to look in different places for them—in a single rubber band, and they're all about the same size. And I always know where they are when I want them: in the canvas shopping bag I carry my students' papers and other stuff to school." "Your checkbook too? You're really asking for trouble. Anyway, it'd seem the effort of transferring these numbers and the still-current old-address-book entries into a new address book would be worth it, since you'll be carrying around a growing pile of these books the rest of your life. As for the PIN numbers and other important IDs like that, I know what I'd do, but do as you wish. As Mom used to say: 'I already interfered enough.' By the way, what do you do on her anniversary? Much as I loved her, I don't do anything. Besides, I thought it was on March 6th, so if I had done anything, it would have been on the wrong day." "For the last two years, I lit a memorial candle. I only have one left, though. And since I only just realized—maybe fifteen minutes ago—it's her anniversary, I feel it's too late in the day for it. I'll light it on her birthday." "That one I know is in March, but I always forget which day." "The eleventh." "I'll remember it. I'm in fact writing it down now on a piece of paper stuck to the refrigerator door, and will do something that day for her. Maybe light a candle like you." "You have a place in the city where you get them? If you do, could you pick up a few for me?" "You're talking about the *Yahrzeit* kind, right?" she says. "The ones in the glass that last a whole day?" "Yeah. Like Mom used to light for her parents and then Dad and Rosalie." "There's a store near me on First Avenue that sells them and other Jewish things." "I live in a Gentile neighborhood," he says "and the nearest store that carries them is a twenty-minute ride away." "I'll get you a few. When you next coming to New York?" He says he doesn't know and then "Look, I don't mean to cut you off, but I was in the midst of doing something and have to get back to it," and she says "Wait, I haven't told you why I called. Charlotte's getting married." "To the guy you don't like?" "I never said I didn't like him. I just said his family is very strange and I only hoped it didn't rub off on him. Father who hasn't left the house in ten years? Sister who has several illegitimate kids, each by a different man and none more than a year apart? Brother who served time for selling cocaine and carrying a gun? Mother seemed relatively sane, by what Billy's said, but she died when he was twelve. He's a sweet boy, has always treated me nice, so I expect I'll come to appreciate him as a son-in-law. Just thought you'd want to know of the engagement and offer your congratulations. Your only niece, and she's thirty-seven, so it's long overdue." "Congratulations. Will there be a big wedding? Sorry, but you know how I hate large social functions." "All depends on how much her father's willing to cough up; I know I can't afford it. Besides, who said you'd be invited?" "Good, it's better if I'm not. These days, they usually go on for an entire weekend, and I can't give up that much time." "You know, next time I'm going to speak to Sandra about something like this. Because I'm sure she'd like to come to it no matter how large it is and wouldn't like you refusing for you both. Anyway, it's probably a year off. Goodbye, my dear brother. I love you, even if you can be annoying." "Same here," he says, "about the first part."

He now understands where that dream of his mother came from two nights ago. In it, someone sat down next to him in a symphony hall. His wife wasn't with him. He took his left arm off the armrest to make room for the arm of the person who just sat down and saw it was his mother. "How strange, you being here," he said, and she said "Why so?" "Quickly, Mom, and I'm happy as a lark to see you, but tell me what it was like." "What was what like?" she said, and he said "Death, of course." "How should I know?" Dream ended with that. First time since she died that she spoke to him in one. But it'll be dark soon, he thinks, and puts on his sneakers and sweatshirt, says to his wife in the kitchen "Charlotte got engaged to that Billy guy we met at Naomi's Christmas party. There's going to be a wedding in a year I won't want to go to," and goes outside for a short run. "When there's ice and snow on the ground?" she says before the door closes. "Don't be crazy."

He showers. Dries himself and before he starts dressing in the bedroom, his wife comes in and says "Like to take a break?" "You bet," he says, or "Why not?" She takes off her clothes and they get on the bed. "Are you dry," she says, "because your back and legs still look wet?" He stands up, dries the parts she said, and gets back on the bed. Or he's already on it, completely dry, and watches her take off her clothes. Or he helps her take them off. Or he showers and goes into the bedroom to dress and thinks he'd like his wife to come in right now and say "Like to take a break?" He'd say "I was about to dress and try to get some work in, but all right." Or "I was about to go for a short run." "In these conditions, when there's so much ice and snow on the ground? You could slip and break a bone. But if you don't want to make love," she could say, "that's all right." But she comes in and says "Like to take a break? If you don't, or have something else you want to do, like get some more work in or go for a run, even if conditions outside aren't the best for it, don't let me stop you. There's always another time." "No, I don't ever want to refuse you," and she says "You can refuse. I have. Not 'refuse,' so much, but just said I didn't feel like it now or it wasn't the right time." "You never said it that much." "Oh, no? Well, I guess that's good." He gets on the bed. "I'm dry, by the way," he says, "so don't worry." She starts to undress. Or he thinks, after he comes out of the shower and is drying himself, how can he get his wife to make love? It's been a week. Maybe longer. After she showered and shampooed, which she does once a week—shampoos—usually on Mondays, it seems, so he'll say six days ago. Does he want to make love? He's sure he will. Just thinking about it is making him excited, so he'll obviously get more excited once they start doing it. Yes, he wants to. "Sandra," he could yell from the hallway outside their bedroom, "do you think you'd like to take a break?" Because it'd look ridiculous, going out naked to wherever she is—probably in her study—and asking if she wants to take a break or "make love." Or he could yell from the hallway "Sandra, could you come back here, please?" If she says "What for?" he'll say "I want to show you something." If she says "You can't show it to me out here?" he'll say

"I've just showered and have no clothes on and am still a bit wet and the house feels cold," or better: "No, it can only be shown back here." If she comes into the bedroom and says "What is it you want to show me?" he'll say "Obviously, or maybe not that obviously, it was an excuse to get you back here without my first getting dressed. And it isn't, which you might be thinking, anything referring to my penis, when I said 'to show you'; I'm not *that* adolescent. I just wanted to ask if you'd like to take a break." If she says "Why did you think you needed an excuse? If you wanted to make love, you should have just said so. All I could say is yes, no, or later," he'll say "I didn't think it right, yelling that to the front of the house. Anyway, since you've given me license to, maybe next time I will. So, do you want to?" He goes into the hallway and yells "Sandra, could you come back here, please? I want to show you something." "What?" she yells from the kitchen, it seems, but it could also be from her study. "I said, Could you come back here?" "I still can't hear you. Why don't you tell me in the kitchen?" "I can hear you but you can't hear me?" "What?" "Forget it," he yells. "Forget what?" "Nothing. It's not important. He'll wait till tonight. But he might have drunk too much by then—he usually does, starting around six—and not get much of an erection. That's what's happened the last few months at night when they've made love. It's always better in the morning or afternoon, which is why he'd like to do it now. It's his age, he supposes—that it's finally caught up on him in this area—but also that he's tired at night, even if he's taken a nap that day, and the drink. As for prescribed drugs to help it, he's wary

of what harm they might do to other parts of him. Last month
when his wife was going through the vitamin catalog she gets—he'd
gotten the mail from the mailbox and looked through the catalog
when he was back in the house—he said "I see there's something in
the men's products section called horny goat weed. Silly name, but
could you order me a bottle when you next phone in your order?
It's not very expensive." She looked it up in the catalog and read
the description and said "Why do you want it? You think you have
a problem?" "No, or nothing I can't resolve myself. But I thought
if it makes the sex better, why not try it? I wouldn't take it every
time. Maybe once a month or so, and I might find out the first time
that it doesn't work." She said "It has herbs in it I never heard of.
Mucana pruriens. Polypodium vulgare. From Peru or someplace. If
I were you I'd stay away from it. Sometimes these medicinal herbs
can be more dangerous than their synthetic equivalents. If you
think you have a problem now and then, but more so than normal,
not to worry, my darling—I'm sure it'll go away. Don't drink so
much at night or take such longs naps an hour or two before you
go to sleep."

He comes out of the shower and for some reason thinks of
the time he went to a brothel in Paris. Not "for some reason." He
was drying his crotch and got a slight erection from it and played
with himself to see if it'd get harder. It didn't and it felt good doing
it, but he stopped because he wanted to save it for making love
later. Then he thought about when he was much younger and there
was no problem. Time he was in a Paris brothel, for instance, and

the woman took off her skirt and panties and lay on the bed and opened her legs and patted her thighs and said in French "Come in, come in, you're ready." He was undressed and said in French—it was his first trip to Europe; he'd boned up on his college French before he left and attended conversation classes twice a day on the student ship—"Could you take off your top too?" She said in French "You want the shirt off? Strange boy." She took it off. "And the brassiere?" "The brassiere?" she said in French. "No. For that you must pay more." "I can't pay more. I'm a poor student and I have little money and I think I paid more than I can afford. I want to feel your breasts when we make love." "You want to feel my breasts? You want to make love with your hands?" "Not if you don't want me to," he said, "though it's true I'd like it. But if not that, then just with my chest against yours when I'm on top." "You want to be on top? Go on top. But go on top now, because you're wasting my time." "Please take off your brassiere." "For more money," she said, "I will. Did I wash you?" "You washed me." "Perhaps I should wash you again or you wash yourself. You're strange and I think strange men need to be washed two times." "I'm not strange. What man wouldn't want the whole naked body rather than only half of one?" "Many men," she said. "Besides, I don't have pretty breasts, so why would you want my brassiere off?" "Your breasts look very pretty. But okay, if you don't want to take off your brassiere, do as you like." "You want the brassiere off that much, all right. No more arguments." She took it off. They made love. This was in the afternoon. He came back to the same street that night and made love with a different prostitute. She was much younger than the first one and he was very excited when he followed her upstairs to her room. She played with him a little. He said "No more. I'm ready to go and I don't want to spoil it," and got on top of her and did it in about twenty seconds. Same thing in Amsterdam the next summer when he was co-leader of a student bicycle-and-bus tour of Europe. To get the job, he told the tour company he was twenty-five, when he was twenty-one, a Ph.D. student in history at Columbia and spoke fluent French and could get along in German and Italian. It was evening. Someone at the youth hostel his group was staying at gave directions to the red-light district. He stopped beneath a second-story window, where a woman in a two-piece bathing suit motioned for him to come up. Several other prostitutes in other buildings had motioned to him from their windows, but she was the most attractive and looked the youngest. No problem with her taking off the top of her bathing suit. She'd come to the door in a bathrobe, took it off and was naked. Then he walked around Amsterdam, had a few of those little fruit-flavored gin drinks that cost about a dime each in Dutch money, got sexually excited again and went back to the red-light district. The same woman was at the window and waved to him hello—she didn't speak English or French and he didn't know any Dutch—and he gestured with his hand he wanted to come up. She looked surprised. This time she came to the door in her bathing suit, he gave her the same amount of guilders he had before, and she took her suit off and got on the bed. So: twice in about an hour. But nothing unusual for him then.

The woman he was in love with when he was twenty-two—she was his age, an actress, and had her own apartment—they'd do it two, three, once four times in a night, but at least once every night for months except for the first day or two of her period or when one of them was ill. He remembers when they did it four times because he said after "I've never done it so many times in a night. Even in an entire day." He doesn't remember when they did it three times in one night or an entire day, but he thinks they must have if they once did it four. After his remark, she said she was beginning to hurt down there, "so that's definitely it for today and probably tomorrow as well." He said "Don't worry. I've done it enough, too, and my penis is also sore and was barely able to stay up the last time." With his wife, their first ten years or so together, they did it twice a night a number of times. He doubts they ever did it three times in one night or an entire day, but they only started going together when he was forty-two. For the next ten years of their marriage, it was around every other night, instead of almost every night, and rarely twice a night, and sometimes they did it two or three nights straight and then nothing for a couple of days. Now it's once, at the most, twice a week, and he's never fully erect. Enough to stuff it in almost all the time, but if he can't, he rubs the tip against her vagina or a little inside it till he gets off that way. He's never said anything to her about it and she's never brought it up, so he wonders if she's even aware of it. In fact, last week when they made love, she said "Look at us; still going at it after twenty-five years." She was on her back, smiling at him after he got off her, obviously very pleased, even proud. "Yeah, it's great," he said. "I hope it goes on forever. I can't imagine what it'd be like, not being able to do it." "You won't have to worry," she said.

He puts on his boxer shorts, is about to put on his socks, but goes into the bathroom and takes his penis out of the fly and pulls on it. Much as he pulls and strokes it, nothing much happens. Years ago there was never that problem; he could masturbate a few times a day if he wanted to. Right up to the time he met Sandra, when he didn't see the need for it anymore and has maybe done it ten times in the last twenty-five years. He puts on his clothes and goes into her study. "Hi," he says. "Hi," she says. "Work going well?" he says. "Very well, thanks." "Good. I'm going to make myself coffee. Long as I'm boiling water, like a decaf?" "No, thanks." "Tea?" "I'm really too busy to drink anything now, and I'd be afraid of spilling it on my keyboard." "I get the message," he says. "What message?" "Oh, just the message. I'm glad your work's going so well. I won't disturb you," and he shuts the door and lights the burner under the tea kettle.

7

The water boils. He makes coffee, dumps the cone filter into the trash can, washes the cone holder and hangs it on its hook under the shelf above the stove, says to his wife in her study "Sure you don't want a tea or decaf? The water's boiled." She says "I heard it. No, thanks. And if you take your coffee back to the bedroom, please be careful. The carpet's already got too many stains." "You think it's from my coffee?" and she says "That or wine." "Wine? When do I take that in back?" He dumps out a little of the coffee so there'll be less chance he'll spill it, and goes in back. Looks at the carpet near the bedroom door. Several large dark spots, but he doesn't remember spilling coffee on it. But it had to be him; she never brings food or drinks in back, and he brings a lot of coffee here, since this is mainly where he works. Maybe it's cat piss. Gets on his knees and puts his nose right up to the largest stain. Doesn't smell of cat piss or coffee. If it were cat piss, it'd smell, even after a few weeks, he's almost sure of it. Actually, he would have smelled it the same day the cat pissed and without having to bend down to it. Coffee he's not so sure it'd still smell once it dried, even a stain this size, about four by ten inches. Crawls on the carpet to another stain and smells. Coffee? Presses his nose into the stain. Coffee; faint odor of it, so it must be more recent. But how could he not remember spilling it? All three stains near the door and another on the other side of it in the hallway must be from his coffee. Same dark color and they look as if they were made from a liquid that had fallen from a few feet up and splashed. When he was a kid—probably up till the time he was nine or ten—he spilled food a lot, even more than his younger sister, and she was often very sick and didn't have good control of her hands. Remembers sitting at the dinner table with his parents and sisters and being told by his mother sometimes "Look down, Meyer, and what do you see?" He'd look and see food around his chair. Like the coffee, he didn't know how it got there, but never said it wasn't his. His older sister saying a few times it's her turn to sweep tonight but it's not fair because all of the mess is his. He once said at the table "I know where the mess comes from. A food fairy who pushes food off our forks and plates when we're not looking and then kicks it all over to my side." Remembers that, and his parents laughing at it, because for years after his father would kid him about the food fairy still making a mess under his chair. "When is the fairy guy of yours going to stop hounding you?" And his mother, one of the last times he took her out to lunch. Her hands and head shook and she'd spilled some of her food on the table and in her lap and she said "Sorry I'm such a klutz today. So unlike me. Maybe it's the work of your food fairy who followed us here." As a kid, checking the floor around his sisters' and parents' chairs after the meal, especially when it was his turn to sweep. Nothing there. At most, a kernel or two of rice or a pea, if it wasn't his and had rolled under one of their chairs. But around his chair? Always lots of food of whatever he ate that meal, but not once remembering dropping any of it. From now on he'll be extra careful with his coffee mug when he walks it from the kitchen to the bedroom, and also, if there's anything left—even a few drops—when he brings it back.

Wants to work on something but doesn't know what. Has a file folder on his worktable of obituaries he's cut out of the *Times* and *Sun* the last twenty-five years: people he's had even the slightest personal contact with starting when he was a boy. Carried it from their last two residences in Baltimore: apartment they lived in when they were first married and had their kids, then a small brick row house they owned before they moved to this one-story, surrounded by trees, out here. Never used anyone in the folder for his fiction, which was its purpose, but has opened it a number of times when he had nothing to write about to see if anything was there. Earliest person he knew in it was his elementary school principal who died about twenty years ago. "Lemonhead Lisson" they used to call him behind his back. He was short, stocky and bald—not a single hair on top and only a thin fringe on the sides and in back—and his skull seemed polished it shined so much. "Your principal is your pal," he said to the students at school assemblies over the years—same line every time. "That's also a useful way of knowing how to spell the word and not get it mixed up with the 'rule' or 'standard' principle, especially of good behavior." Only real encounter with him was the time he got caught with some other boys making snowballs in their homeroom—got the snow off a windowsill after their teacher told the class to stay seated and be on its best behavior while she was out of the room for a minute—and was sent to his office. He bawled them out and put them on detention for a week. They had to sit the whole time in the anteroom to his offices, doing math and grammar exercises he gave them and writing essays on why they think they misbehaved and remaining silent and not even using body language to one another and only getting up with permission from his secretary to go to the boys' room for a maximum of three minutes twice a day.

Opens the folder, finds the principal's obituary. Short one, no photo, only got written up, no doubt, because he eventually became superintendent of schools for New York City. Princeton, decorated soldier in World War II, six children and fourteen grandchildren, died of lung cancer after having the superintendent's job for less than a year. Obituary on top of the pile is last one he put in: Sonya West. He was a radio news reporter covering the Democratic National Convention in L.A. in 1960. Tall, lean, long dark hair, high cheekbones, long neck, expressive eyes, full lips, really beautiful. Eight years older than he according to the article.

He'd seen her in a few movies, mostly westerns—one, one of his favorites at the time, with John Wayne—when he was in his teens. Party in some big donor's mansion in Beverly Hills. Must have been two hundred people there. Huge pool shaped like a whale, the fins being the wading area for children; buffet tables around it with food and drink. Senators, congressmen, governors; he knew lots of them from working the Hill in Washington. A couple of the top candidates for the presidential nomination and all the men who'd like to be the running mate. Many well-known actors and actresses and television and print newsmen. *The* party that night, which is why his news service sent him: get a slew of interviews on tape. He thought there was a chance he could pick her up and leave with her or at least get her phone number. He was twenty-four, a good-looking kid, full head of curly hair, well-built and -groomed and smartly dressed, nothing like the slob he is today, and he spoke well, much better than he does now. Maybe good speech—certainly glibness does—had something to do with confidence. Didn't know she was married at the time—didn't even think of it, but the obituary, which he hadn't read till now, says she married an actor she'd met on her first film and was still married to him when she died from complications after surgery and that they lost their only child when the boy was six. Would knowing she was married have stopped him? Probably not, unless the guy was nearby. He would have looked around, made sure this familiar actor was far enough away, and made his move fast. He'd interviewed a number of politicians on his tape recorder already and went over to her when she was getting a canapé off a buffet table. She seemed to be alone. "Miss West," he said, "—Meyer Ostrower of Radio News Press. I wondered—" and she said "Radio News what?" and he said "Press." We're a news service, like UP and Reuters, but for radio stations around the country." "Never heard of it, I'm sorry." "We cover Washington for some of the biggest stations. WNEW in New York. WGN in Chicago and KHOU in Houston and several smaller stations in California. I wanted to know if you'd mind granting me an interview, which we'll feed to about fifty stations tonight and will be used tomorrow morning. That's why I'm lugging around all this equipment. Just, what the Democratic Party means to you, whom you'd like to see or you think is going to get the nomination, what you think the platform should've contained, things like that." "I'm here, aren't I, so of course I support the Democrats. Really, I'm not someone you should be interviewing. There's Mort Sahl. He knows politics ten times more than me, and he's funny. Thanks for asking, though," and she turned back to the table, forked a piece of smoked salmon onto a cracker, waved to two women a few feet away and went over to them. He eyed her the next half an hour, did a couple more interviews with senators, and then thought maybe his approach wasn't right. Possibly he came off as too young and obvious. Whatever it was, she wasn't interested in him, that's for sure, but maybe he could get her to be. What could he do that'd be different than before? He'll come up with something at the time. "Be right back," she seemed to say by her gesture to a woman she was talking to, and went over to one of the wine tables. He walked up to her and said "Miss West, Meyer Ostrower again. My apologies for disturbing you a second time, but I've spoken to my boss—the news director of our news service—and he said he'd absolutely love for you to say just a few words into the mike on tonight's goings-on or anything you wish." "Just a few words? He can't think much of me, I guess, or know much about me either." "Oh, no. He's an ardent admirer of your work, he said, and he meant only a few if only a few is all you want to say. But as much as you want if that's what you want." He smiled. "I came here with plenty of spare tapes," pointing to his shoulder bag. "I'm sorry," she said, "but this is an off-night for me. No acting, no showboating, and certainly no pontificating on subjects I know only a little about and couldn't articulate well besides. It's a beautiful night, the air smells lovely, and the company is of an unusual high quality for this city and quite stimulating, and being interviewed isn't what I want to do now or think of as an enjoyable activity anytime. My thanks to you and your news director for asking, though," and he said "If you could just say that about the stimulating company here, it'd be enough, believe me." "No is no. C'mon, bub, give it some air," and she reached for her glass of wine on the table. "All right," he said, "if it's not too great an imposition, I'll be frank with you." "I knew this was coming," she said with her back to him. "Excuse me," and she turned a little ways to him, "but I'd like you to leave me alone. If not, I'll ask the host, Jerry Sinclair, to have you escorted out of here. Freedom of the press can go too far, know what I mean? I didn't come to this event to be hit on by a reporter." He looked around. Some guests nearby and the bartender were of course looking at them. "That wasn't my intention at all," he said to her. "In language I want to make as clear and honest as I can to you—" "Bullshit," and she put her glass down and walked away. She left soon after with a couple and what seemed like their young daughter. He went to the fence surrounding the grounds and house and looked between two boards. A valet pulled up in a huge Mercedes, the man slipped him a bill and got behind the wheel, the girl beside him and the women in back. "Rich bastards," he said very low into the fence. He left a few minutes later. Had nobody else to interview—neither of the major candidates there would give him one, even the one he used to interview off the Senate floor—and also wanted to get to the radio studio his news service was working out of and edit the tapes and get it on the main feeder tape for an early-morning transmission to their headquarters in DC. He waited at the bus stop about five streets away—his company gave him cab money but he liked to take public transportation, tell them he took cabs, and keep the difference. Bus came in an hour and he got on it with his forty-plus pounds of equipment—heavy tape recorder, mike and foldup stand, box of tapes and extension cords and book to read on the bus—and took it to Center City, if that's what it's called, L.A. Nah, no material there, or not much to work with— he's done it long enough to know that. Probably nothing in the other obits, either. Goes through them quickly, never gets to the end. Chairman of the House Foreign Affairs Committee whom he interviewed a lot: a doctor, pockmarked, big beefy guy with a gravelly voice and who was very nice to him, but so what? A literary agent, maybe the most successful of her day—the Sixties and Seventies—and with a beautiful name. She represented a friend of his who recommended him to her. She turned him down, a pleasant keep-up-the-good-work rejection letter to him, but saying to his friend—why the guy told him this he never understood—that he was a no-talent of great pretension, with no chance of publication in the mainstream and only a slight one with the littles. An Indiana senator—a freshman at the time—who gave him a Christmas gift of six highball glasses, no doubt because he interviewed him on a wide range of political and legislative subjects every third week and excerpts of these interviews went out to the only two 50-kilowatt radio stations in his state. He asked his boss "Should I give the glasses back? Isn't it something like payola?" and his boss said "Keep them. It's one peanut compared to what some newsmen get." The dean of the diplomatic corps, as he was called—the ambassador from Nicaragua—whom he interviewed just once but who every time he saw him at some function and once at a museum, gave him a big smile and wave. The director of an art colony he went to for a month one summer, who said to him on the last day of his stay "I didn't like you at first, but you grew on me." The mother of a girl he dated when he was seventeen—a prominent bathing suit designer—but he'd already written about that family and its tragedies, and because he didn't disguise them, except by changing their names and address on Riverside Drive and what article of clothing the mother designed, regrets it today. A friend's father—

once the biggest women's sweater manufacturer in New York and a great philanthropist—whole floors and lobbies of hospitals in the city are named after him and his wife and parents because of what he gave—who died at a hundred and one. Never met the father but heard stories about him from his son—dropping a million dollars at a racetrack in one day, renting a private jet to see a musical in London, private dinners with Presidents Johnson and Nixon, still running his business and sleeping with some of his showroom models when he was well into his nineties. But the son's a writer, so it's his material and he'd probably get upset if he used it. Dumps the obituary of Sonya West and then the rest of the folder into the trashbasket under his worktable. Slim chance he'll ever use any of them, and it'll make a little room on top.

He runs for about three minutes, stops, says to himself "Admit it; you hate running. It's so freaking boring and eventually kills the legs and knees." Then in his head: Been doing it for forty years—the end's been coming for a long time—but this was the last, and walks back to the house. This is nice, he thinks. You can see and really smell things when you walk. "I'm going to the gym, use the exercise bike there from now on," he says to his wife when he gets in the house. "Hell with running; it's such a bore." "You wouldn't want to try one of those Walkman things and listen to music and talk shows while you run?" "I hate talk shows, unless they're about literature, which they almost never are, and especially hate them when they're about some writer's new book." "And when someone's bashing the president, you don't like that?" "Yeah, but they always have someone on the same show who's defending him. Nope, with my luck I'd get lost in the music or that rare discussion I'd be interested in, wander too far into the road, wouldn't hear a car coming because of the headphones, and get killed." "Doesn't sound like you," she says, "although the cynicism about other writers does, but it's up to you. Oh, by the way, Sylvester called while you were out and said, if you have time, call him." "I don't want to speak to anyone on the phone but our daughters, and even there, I'd rather you spoke to them and told me what they said. I've become terrible, I know." He puts into a plastic shopping bag a tank top, shorts, towel, washrag, and a book and today's Op-Ed pages of the *Times* for when he's on the bike, kisses his wife goodbye and drives to the Y a couple of miles away. He goes there three to four times a week to work out with the free weights and on the strength machines. He uses the machines—the chest press, which he gauges his strength on, he couldn't press above 110 pounds, when the last few times he got it to 135—rides the bike for thirty minutes, showers and dresses and leaves the locker room feeling healthy and good. In the corridor, heading to the lobby, a pregnant woman's in front of him with a couple of three- or four-year-olds and is pushing a small carriage with a baby's arm hanging out of it. He hustles ahead and holds the door open, for her and the two boys, who he now sees are identical twins. She goes through it without thanking him or even looking at him. Jesus, he thinks, be polite, will ya? I just made life a weeny-bit easier for you. She stops in the lobby to put the baby's arm back in the carriage and to make sure the boys' coats are buttoned, and then heads for the vestibule. He's already there, waiting for her with the door open, and then gets the one to the outside. She pushes the carriage through both, the twins behind her, again doesn't say thanks, but this time she looks sort of angrily at him. Odd behavior, he thinks, looking away. For what he do? Helped her twice; three times, actually. She knows the doors didn't open on their own. Maybe she's had it rough today with the three kids or it has something to do with her pregnancy. But anger? He doesn't get it. Walks past her and gets in his car in the crowded lot. Starts it up, looks through the rear window, check the side mirrors—car on his right parked too near his, because he knows there was plenty of room there when he left his car—nothing behind him and he backs up. Hears a woman scream, then a bump against the back of his car. He brakes, turns the motor off, looks behind him, stomach suddenly icing up. It's the same woman, a few feet behind his car, screaming hysterically. No, he couldn't have, he thinks. The carriage? One of the boys? Oh, my God. It's impossible. He checked the mirrors, looked through the rear window, nobody was there. If he hit or ran over one of her kids, he's finished. Please don't let anything be wrong. Then tells himself he has to deal with it, he can't just sit here, and gets out of the car. It didn't happen but was close. He started to back out slowly. "Watch it," someone shouted. Saw in the rearview mirror the same woman pulling one of her boys out of the way of his car. He stopped, put the car in park and the hand brake on, kept the motor running. How'd that happen? he thought. He'd looked; no one was back there. How stupid could he be? Maybe he didn't look in the rearview mirror while he was backing out and the kid ran up to his car or was already there but below viewing level of the rear window when he looked through it. Something, but he almost ran over a kid. Woman's now by the van next to his car on his side, pressing the twins against the closed sliding door. She gives him a much angrier look than before. This one he can understand. Even if it was partly her fault—didn't stop the boy from running up to his car or being behind it when someone was in the driver's seat, let's say—she has a right to be angry. Not "a right"; just he could see why she'd be and lay all the blame on him. He should have looked again and again in the lot packed with cars, especially when backing out of tight spot and he knows kids are around. He'd told himself this plenty of times but too often forgets to do it. The carriage, he thinks. Turns the motor off, looks out back and in the side mirrors and sees the handle of it sticking out behind the van. Now what's he supposed to do? Tell her to move the carriage, of course. But get out to tell her and also to apologize? Say nothing about how she should have had her kids under better control—she'd flip out if he said it—but just that it was stupid of him not to have been more careful and he's sorry, very sorry. She'd never accept his apology. A puss like that doesn't go from scorn to forgiveness in seconds. And if he got out of the car she might strike him. Looks at her through his closed window and she gives him a dirty look and then says "Are you nuts?" He doesn't hear it but reads it on her lips. "What the hell's wrong with you? Do you like going around killing a kid?" "I'm sorry, I'm sorry," he says. She shakes her head, then sticks her middle finger up at him. Oh, great, he thinks, so classy. Well, maybe I can understand what's behind that gesture too. But had enough? Can I go? Starts up the car, makes sure she's got her boys pressed up against the van, which must be hers or she'd be gone from here by now—how's that for coincidence and luck, having her parked beside him? Then remembers the carriage and turns the motor off and rolls down his window and says "Maybe you should get everyone in the van first. I'll wait here till you do." "It's not mine," she says. "I wanted to stay here as long as I could to show you what an asshole you are." "Then maybe you should move the baby carriage; it's sticking out," and she says "I'll move it when I like." She goes behind the van with the boys, pushes the carriage out of the way and stands there staring at him while holding a shoulder of each boy. He backs out very slowly, has to look her way to know the boys aren't near the car, and drives off. Driving home, he thinks Jesus, that was close. What would I have done if I'd have hit one of her kids? Forget the woman; I feel awful, just awful. Home, he thinks should he tell his wife? No; doesn't want to scare her and he knows just about what she'd say. "Listen, when you're in a parking lot—any kind of parking lot, not just one with kids—you have to be extra careful backing out. Driving forward out of a space is much simpler. For just think how you'd feel now if you had hit some poor kid and what your life would be like from then on if you had killed or maimed him."

8

Damn, he thinks, forgot to drink the coffee. Now it's probably cold. Sips it; cold. Goes to the kitchen with it. Should he make more? Just reheat this; it'll taste okay and give him a needed quick lift. Pours the coffee into a saucepan and lights a low flame under it so it doesn't boil. Thinks of going into the living room to get last Sunday *Times* book review section off the wood pile so he'll have something to read while the coffee's reheating. No, stay here. Don't get distracted, or the coffee, low as the flame is, will burn. Ought to be a way to get tea-kettle-type whistles on pots and pans to signal when the coffee's warm or the dish is done. Burned how many pots and pans and how much food the last few years because he forgot he was cooking or warming up something. "Meyer," his wife would yell from her study or somewhere deeper in the house—she smells things long before he does—"you have something on the stove?" And after he runs into the kitchen from wherever he is and turns the burner off: "You can't leave food cooking like that if you don't put in sufficient water or oil." Stays by the stove till the coffee starts moving. Shuts off the burner, pours the coffee back into the mug—sips it; right temperature but tastes a little bitter—and goes in back with it and sets it down on the worktable and sits. Now drink it before it gets cold again; you can't reheat coffee twice. Lifts the mug. His three right middle fingers suddenly stiffen and curl on their own around the mug handle, and trying to grab the mug with the other hand, he spills some of the coffee on his lap.

So now it's getting to the hands, huh? he thinks, putting the mug down and squeezing the fingers with his left hand till they straighten out and don't hurt. Almost every night in bed for a few minutes he has arthritic pain in his legs and also usually when he gets out of a car or stands up after sitting awhile in a chair. There are over-the-counter medicines for it, but he doesn't trust anything for any ailment but aspirin. "If it helps, as it does for me," his sister's said—glucosamine or -cosamate is what she takes two to three times a day—"why not use it?" But he thinks it'll affect his urinary tract, making his penis burn when he pees, as has just about every over-the-counter cold and cough medicine he's used, and possibly also make it even more difficult to get a good erection. Who knows, but why chance it, especially when it takes a few weeks to become effective, she's said, which means a few weeks for his system to get rid of it if he then decided he wanted to stop taking it. Anyway: the coffee. None got on the carpet, so just stay here and work.

Starts to type—a line out of nowhere he'll never use: "The old man moaned"—and then thinks No, coffee's soaked through to his boxer shorts and feels uncomfortable. Gets up and shuts the door, sits on the bed to take off his pants and shorts. Why'd he shut the door? Who's going to come in but his wife? Habit from when his daughters were around. Wipes his legs with the shorts, notices the two-inch-long scar near the top of his right thigh. Not too far from where his penis would have been if it had been hanging that way and was as long as it is today, a thought he never had before and winces away. Summer; Goetz's Bungalow Colony near New Paltz. Forty-three was the last year they went, so he was five or six, at the most seven. Family had started going there a few years before he was born. He was most likely conceived there, a thought he had before. They stayed—his mother, sisters and he—all of July and August. His father came up weekends. Two bedrooms, his older sister in the tiny one and his younger sister and he on foldup cots in the living room or, if the night was warm, in the screened-in porch. Costume parade at the colony's day camp, and his mother and aunt, who was staying with them—where'd she sleep? Probably on the living room couch—urged him to go as a girl. "Your features and physique are perfect for it." He didn't like the idea, but they said the winner of the best costume for a boy gets a dollar as a prize. So he let them put lipstick and rouge on his face, tie a ribbon in his hair, and help him get into a sun dress of his older sister's. They said he looks more beautiful than any girl. "See for yourself in the bathroom." He stood on a stool in front of the medicine chest and looked in the mirror. He looks like a sissy, he thought, and washed off the makeup, took the dress and ribbon off and went back to the kitchen and said he only wanted to go as a ghost. That's what he dressed as last Halloween at a Saturday morning costume contest at the Beacon Theater near their building, where, because the eye slits in the sheet were too thin, he had trouble seeing and walked the wrong way on stage and fell into the pit. Two scars from that one, on his chin and knee. His mother said they hadn't any sheets to spare here and for sure none to cut holes in, so he said he wasn't going to camp that day, not even to watch the parade. "Cutting off your nose again," she said. He hung around the house that afternoon, later went to a friend's bungalow and the friend took him to the cellar and showed him his father's tools. The hand drill looked interesting, the crazy zig-zag shape of the handle. He sat down and tried using it on a board he placed over his legs. The board slipped and the bit went into his thigh. He bled a lot, the friend said he'd get help, but he said "Don't tell anyone; I'll get in trouble," and wrapped a rag around the gash, tied it tight with his handkerchief, and started home. He collapsed on the way, was taken to a hospital and screamed so hard at the thought of a needle going in and out of his skin that the doctor couldn't sew up the wound. That's why the scar, though it's shrunk by half, is as long as it is.

Same with the scar on the left side of his head, right above his ear. He was around ten, waiting his turn at bat in a stickball game on his block, when the batter swung the broomstick at the ball and hit him in the head. He was taken to Roosevelt Emergency, told the gash needed several stitches—it won't hurt; they'll freeze the part they'll sew and the sutures will keep the scar from being big—but he said "I don't care how big the scar is, I don't want a needle in my head."

Around eight other scars in his head. He once counted them but forgot the number. One when a friend threw a hatchet at a tree in Central Park. He was standing too close to the tree and the boy's aim was bad—or maybe it was good; kids did things like that at that age—and the blunt end of the blade hit him above the right ear. He was twelve and because the stickball scar always showed for about a week after he got a haircut, even when he told the barber not to cut too much hair over it, he thought girls would be turned off by two long scars on opposite sides of his head, so he let the doctor sew it up.

Another time he had a water fight in his kitchen with a couple of friends. It was Friday or Saturday night, not long after the hatchet accident. His younger sister must have been in her room, the rest of the family was out and not expected back soon, and his friends had promised to keep the fight short and help him clean up the mess after. He doesn't remember there being any object to the fight other than to soak the other guys, and because they'd done this before in someone else's kitchen and the fight had got out of hand, there were rules. You could wear a raincoat, you couldn't throw water at the same person twice in a row, the sink faucet, where you filled up your glass, was neutral territory up till the count of five, and when one person said he'd had enough, the fight was immediately over for all of them. He was ducking one throw and his head smashed the glass in the boy's hand. The boy's finger was sliced through to the bone. He was able to get most of the glass pieces out of his head, but a few slivers were left that he and the uninjured boy couldn't pull out with tweezers. So with the other boy's hand and his head wrapped in dishtowels, they took a bus to Roosevelt to be treated. One of the cuts—must have been the deepest—ended up being a small C-shaped scar at the top of his head. It never showed, even when he had a crew cut, but has since he went bald.

He was around thirteen, sledding down Eagle Hill in Central Park. A boy on a sled was about to cut in front of him, so he swerved left without seeing where he was steering, and his head, just above where his widow's peak came to a point, went into the runner of another kid's sled.

He was twenty-two, working in DC, and a girl he had just told that it'd be best if they stopped seeing each other, said "You're telling me this right after you get laid?" and when he turned away from her, slammed the side of his head with his guitar. "You see," he said, "you see," bleeding from the ear and head and going into the kitchen for paper towels, "that's the reason. You say and do whatever you please, and you're nuts. Get dressed and get the hell out of here." She started crying. He came back into the bedroom, one hand stanching the wounds with the towels, and handed her her coat and bag and book and pushed her out of the apartment. She called a few minutes later and said she was in a phone booth down the street and was worried about him and he should go to a hospital's Emergency, and he said "What, and wait for three hours before they finally take me? I'm okay except for a few splinters I can't reach in the back of my head, but I'll get them." "I can help you," she said, and he said "Not a chance. Don't be concerned about me ever again, you hear? It just makes me so sad to do the things to you I do, and God knows what it must be like for you," and hung up.

He was twenty-seven, at Stanford University on a writing fellowship, heading home through a eucalyptus grove on a campus bike path. He'd drunk too much at a party and had left his flashlight at it, but there seemed to be enough moonlight to see where he was riding. He hit a cement pole, which was in the middle of an intersection to keep cars off the paths, and flipped over his bike and landed on his side. He broke a shoulder and cracked his head open. It was an expensive bike and not his, so with his good arm he dragged it back to his apartment and called a friend to take him to a hospital. He sued Stanford, claiming the pole should have had a reflector on it. The university said the pole did but his bike had broken it in the crash, and he lost the suit and had to pay the university's court costs.

He was in his thirties and trying to fish a paperclip out from under his typewriter keys with a fork. It was a big Royal table model, not the smaller standard Hermes he uses today, so it stood higher, which might have been why he had the accident. He'd bent down too far to see into the typewriter's carriage and the line space lever went into his upper eyelid. There was no blood or cut, just a swelling and discoloring for about a week, but it left a small white scar when the wound healed. The scar can only be seen when he raises his head back.

A year or so later, he saw on his street late at night a robbery taking place: a man with his hands on his head and his back to another man, who was going through his pockets. Or maybe it's an undercover cop going through the pockets of a suspected criminal, he thought. He didn't know if he should interfere—neither of them had seen him—but then thought he couldn't just let a guy get robbed, if that was it, and maybe worse, and yelled from about thirty feet away "Hey, is everything all right there?" The guy going through the pockets said "Yes, everything's under control; I'm a police officer." "No, he's not," the other man said. "He's got a weapon and he's robbing me." "Let the guy alone, will ya?" Meyer said. "I'm not leaving here till you do." The robber stuck the man's wallet into his jacket's side pocket and walked over to Meyer and said "Don't you know when to mind your own business?" "It is my business. You can't just go around robbing some poor guy. Give him his wallet back." "You want his wallet? Okay," and he reached into his jacket pocket, but it was the opposite side pocket of the one he stuck the wallet in, and Meyer turned to run away. The guy hit him over the head with something hard, and he went down. Then he stood over him and hit him on the head a few more times. The man who'd been robbed said "Stop that, you'll kill him, he was only trying to help me. Police! Police!" he yelled, and the robber, according to the man, took Meyer's wallet out of his pants pocket and casually walked away.

He was in his fifties, standing on a stepladder in their previous house to take down some window curtains to be cleaned. There was a hook in the ceiling for a hanging plant, and he climbed up the ladder too far to reach the curtain rod, and his head went into it.

Just the other week he was on the same stepladder, reaching as high as he could to stick a book in one of their floor-to-ceiling bookcases. It was the hardcover edition of the complete works of Isaac Babel, more than a thousand pages. He'd squeezed the book between two other Babel books and was getting off the ladder, when the book popped out and the pointy end of the cover hit him just to the side of his right eye. He washed the cut in the bathroom and, pressing gauze to it, went into his wife's study and said "I've just been beaned by Babel, your second favorite writer, if I'm not mistaken—Chekhov being the first—and I know it's going to leave a scar."

9

Feels vulnerable today. Did yesterday, too. Tomorrow he'll probably also feel vulnerable. No, he will, definitely; doesn't go away so fast. Doesn't know where it comes from. Knows the symptoms, though. When he's outside, walking to the mailbox, let's say, he walks with his head down, eyes on the driveway. When he gets there and a car passes, he turns away from the road. Doesn't want to see anybody. Feels weak, too. Maybe that's the reason or a result of it. Stuff he used to do and liked doing—trimming trees, raking leaves—he can't do as quickly anymore and gets tired faster than before. Meaning... meaning what? That's another thing. His mind. Isn't what it used to be. It's just not as fast. He doesn't articulate well what he wants to say. Which is another thing. He was never glib or articulate or succinct. But now it's worse. He even stutters sometimes, something he hasn't done since he was a kid, when he stuttered for years. Where even his pediatrician would say to him during his annual exam "M-M-Meyer st-st-still c-c-can't st-st-stop st-st-st-stuttering, r-r-right?" probably think it'd make him self-conscious of it and get him to stop. Till once after he said it—Meyer, by then, had stopped stuttering sometime before; he didn't know when or how; he just knows he was in the back seat of their car, heading to the country, and realized he wasn't stuttering anymore—and he said "Dr. Baron, I've no idea what you're talking about. Could you speak more clearly?" For a while a good story for laughs in the family. His mother even brought it up when she was around ninety, after not mentioning it for what could be fifty or sixty years. "I don't know why I just thought of this, but do you remember your pediatrician Dr. Baron and how he used to kid you?" "You mean with his st-st-stuttering r-r-remarks?" She laughed and said "It was wrong of him to do that, of course, and I should have said something. But it doesn't seem to have done any harm." But where was he? That's another thing. Gets off the track, or whatever the expression is. Loses, he's saying, what he started out saying and also can't remember the right words and expressions. Also his looks. His neck. It's gotten like an old man's. That's the best way to put it, or will have to do for now, since he doesn't think he'd be able to describe it more clearly, or just better. But his looks shouldn't bother him. After all, he's getting old, so what of it? But he just doesn't look... he means, he just doesn't like the way he looks, and hasn't for about a year. He looks tired, haggard, gaunt, withdrawn. Not "withdrawn," but something. Anyway, everything like that's been making him feel vulnerable. Something—a sound behind him, which could be as soft as a pine cone dropping from a tree onto his carport—and he jumps. Scared. He was almost never like that: jumpy, scared. Now he doesn't feel he can fight off an attacker, or something jumping at him, like a dog. Doesn't think his reflexes are quick enough anymore—they're not, so say so—for him to dart out of the way or swipe at whatever's attacking him before it hits or bites him. Okay, exaggerated examples—attackers, dogs—but what he's saying, and he's trying hard as he can to be concise and clear, is that all this makes him feel vulnerable. Both, and which he knows he's said, but maybe that's the only way to get the point across. Pains in his stomach. Probably just from the last night's drinking, but he gets worried. Thinks: He's at the age where guys get stomach cancer, liver or pancreatic cancer, or some other serious diseases there. Pains in his chest: Thinks it's a heart attack or warning of one. Runs down his driveway to get the newspapers left there, and his legs hurt; they never did for so short a run. What's it mean? If it isn't arthritis or the sciatica he sometimes gets, he doesn't know. Other things. He forgets what. Of course his eyesight. Which has been getting worse for years, and now the early stages of glaucoma, or whatever the other one is, where he has trouble driving at night because of the other cars' headlights. And his hair, which in the last year he's lost all of what was left on top and the rest had gone from gray to almost white. But this isn't the first time in the last few months he's had these thoughts about his vulnerability. There! A good complete thought—articulately thought, if that can be an expression. Anyway… anyway, what? Just anyway, anyway, anyway, he isn't—but don't say it, but he wants to say it and can't think of any other way to say it, so he'll say it—the man—the person—the human being he was a year ago. He feels he's fading, body and brain fading, and because he feels this way… oh, enough. He just wants to get in bed, under a blanket, nap, forget everything while he naps. But he has to go to work. He gathers his things, puts on his shoes and jacket and says to his wife "Well, I gotta go. It's getting late and I hate being late for class." "Of course," she says. "But you feeling all right?" "No," he says. "I'm feeling vulnerable. Have I ever admitted that to you before? No. Very vulnerable." "Why?" "I'm not sure. Or I don't know. One or the other. But I haven't time to go in to it," and kisses her and goes. "My keys," he says in the car. "And my wallet. What the hell's wrong with me?" and goes back and says "Can you believe it?" "You forgot your keys," she says. "Not only my keys, but my wallet. Keys I would've known about before I left because I couldn't leave without them, right?" "You mean, 'couldn't start the car'?" "Right. That's what I meant. But my wallet. I would've been halfway to school, or got there, or even in the classroom and discovered I didn't have my wallet, and would've thought not that I forgot it but that I lost it along the way. If I was still in the car, I would've stopped, looked for it, and then driven back to get it and been a good twenty minutes late for class. But if I was in my class, I would've given the kids a ten-minute break and retraced my steps from the classroom to the car and not found the wallet." "Then you would call me, wouldn't you? Or done that first and asked if it was where you always leave it, on the shelf above the stove." "Right. But would I have thought to do that. I would've worried. Because I'm so damn vulnerable today, I probably would've started panicking. Lost wallet, all the cards in it—driver's license, two credit cards, school ID, which gets me into the parking lot, and so on. Anyway, what I'm saying is my vulnerability would've made me worry rather than be practical." "It's getting late, Meyer." "You're right. I don't want to get to class, see a roomful of students who've been waiting for me for ten minutes, and have to apologize, though nothing's wrong with apologizing. Oh, I don't know what I'm saying." "Yes you do. Everything's going to be fine. Now go, and drive safely." "That too. I get in the car, I sometimes think I'm going to get in a crash because I'm not paying attention. I gotta do something about it. Bye," and he kisses her, gets the keys off the hook by the door, gets in the car, starts it up and thinks You idiot. Your wallet. He goes back and gets it and says to his wife "Can you believe it?" and holds up the wallet. "I'm sorry, I should have reminded you," and he says "No, no; I should've reminded myself. It's everything I've been saying," and gets back in the car and thinks I can't go to school today. I won't speak or remember well. I'll seem unprepared. The kids will stare at me and give each other glances about my lousy teaching and during the break and after class talk about it. One day in my twenty-five years in the department I can call in sick when I'm not sick and stay home, and he goes inside the house. "What did you forget now?" his wife says. "Nothing. I just can't go to school, that's all, and not because I'm sick," and goes to their bedroom and picks up the phone.

10

Nobody really calls him anymore, he thinks, lying on the bed and looking at the phones on the dresser. Regular receiver kind and portable. Headset for the portable—they used to call it a receiver till their daughters corrected them out of it—is with his wife in her study. The calls are almost always for her. His nephew calls, though, about once a month, to speak to them both: how they are and what they've been doing and from him to learn some more history of Meyer's family: "Mom doesn't even know the names of half your aunts and cousins, while you seem to have remembered everything." But nobody else except the roofer, for instance, saying he'd like to drop by this Tuesday to check the job his men did on his carport and if it's satisfactory and Meyer has no complaints, to pick up the balance he owes him. Someone from Purple Heart calls about every other month to say their truck will be in his area in two weeks and does he have any items to donate? He usually does. Likes to reduce their belongings as much as he can, so gives away lots of clothes: his and what his wife and kids no longer need and just about all of his dead mother-in-law's, which his father-in-law sent to them thinking his daughter and grandkids might want. And other things they don't need anymore: books they'll never read or reread, cheap silverware and old dishes and pot covers and useless odds and ends that just clutter up the place and LPs they now have the same pieces on CDs, and so on. Someone from the Fraternal Order of Police calls about three times a year for a donation and he always tells him "I take no solicitations on the phone. Send the request through the mail," even though he knows he'll dump it when it comes. "Maybe you didn't hear," the guy always says, "it's for the Fraternal Order of Police, and sending a request takes time and postage, when I can give you where to send here." And Meyer will say—happens every time when he gets the call; if his wife gets it, she always pledges ten dollars and takes down the address—"Excuse me, I'm going to hang up now. I told you, I don't like soliciting calls, and I don't even know what your organization does, nor do I have time to find out," and hangs up. Who else calls? Of course his daughters, about every third day, if they or one of them hasn't called them. Sometimes his wife calls when she's about to leave from wherever she is and does he need anything along the way? or she's at the car-service place with her car and it's going to take an hour more than she thought. Students call. Because he doesn't use a computer, he tells them to call instead of e-mail to the on-line address his university insisted he get and be posted, or whatever the right term for that is, so his students and advisees can reach him. If he does get an e-mail from them, he has his wife—it's her computer it comes in on—write back for him "Please, no e-mails, ever. Phone me at work or home," and give both numbers. So he gets a few calls a week from them and mostly at home, but they're not what he's referring to in his nobody-really-calls-him-anymore line. Also, the administrative assistant in his department with questions like what will his office hours be next semester? Or the chair's trying to schedule a faculty meeting this Friday, what are the best times he can attend? Occasionally he gets calls from writers he knew but lost contact with, wanting to know if he knows of a good literary agent, or they saw a review of his new book and does he think his publisher would be a good place for him to send to? And from writers he doesn't know though might have heard of and a couple of them he's read, calling to say they have a new novel or story collection coming out and could he arrange a reading at his school? To the literary agent calls: "Haven't used one in years. They could never do anything for me, so I had to sell everything myself." About his new publisher: "Why not? With the stuff we do, any publisher taking a chance with us is a good publisher. But don't ask me to speak to my editor about you. She'd see through that move in a second. Just query her and say you're my friend." As for arranging a reading: "The reading series is booked for the next two years," when it never is. He's actually on his department's reading-series committee, which if it accepted someone he suggested—so he never suggests anyone—he'd have to introduce the writer at the reading and go to it, two things he tries to avoid doing. He used to get calls from two good friends and call them regularly too. One, a few years younger than he, died of a stroke three years ago—just got out of bed and dropped—and the other, around the same age as he, showed signs of Alzheimer's five years ago and now hasn't a clue who Meyer is, so he's even stopped visiting him at the nursing home he's in. Last time he went, his friend said "Who are you? What do you want? My blood? Get out of here," and swung at him. Looks at the phone again. Thinks maybe if he stares at it long and hard enough it'll ring and the call will be for him. But an important call, not a student or the administrative assistant or the pest-control company wanting him to renew his contract. His editor, for instance: sale of his last book to a foreign or paperback publisher—something like that. He stares at the phone and then thinks this is silly. And then: You're being silly. And then: Phone's not going to ring. It rings. At least not for me. His wife answers it in her study. Can't hear what she's saying. But she picked it up on the second ring and isn't yelling out "Meyer, it's for you." Maybe the doors to her study are shut. Still, he'd hear her yelling through them. It's a small house, on one level, and their rooms aren't that far from each other. No, it's for her, or something like the pest-control representative that she can handle as well as he. If it is that company he hopes she remembers what he told her: "They did barely nothing for us for the money—same problems returned—so tell them to get lost." Or maybe the caller hung up before she answered the phone—that could be it too. Turns away from the phone, puts his hands under his head, thinks It's not that I'm complaining about any of this. It's just what happens. If it wasn't for his daughters and nephew, nobody would really call. Regularly, he means, people he has conversations with, and those three, as he said, are calling to speak to them both. If he lived in New York he'd call his nephew now and invite him and his girlfriend out to dinner. Ask his wife first if she wanted to go to dinner with his nephew and his girlfriend one of these nights, and then call his nephew. What a sweet kid he is. Oh, yes, his sister—his nephew's mother—calls him every so often, just as he calls her every so often. So people do call. Just not as many as it used to be years—maybe three, maybe five—ago. Nowhere near.

11

He thinks: She sees him through the kitchen window taking off his clothes to put in the washer. It's night, past twelve; his wife's in bed, going to sleep. Their young neighbor, who lives by herself since she got divorced a year ago, shares a driveway with them till it goes past their house and only goes to hers. He thinks: He's taking off his clothes, first the shirt, then the sweatpants—he isn't wearing undershorts; the pants feel better without them—and his neighbor's just rolled her garbage can down the driveway to leave at the end of it for the morning trash pickup. Walking back to her house, she looks through the kitchen window—he doubts she intended to spy on him; probably just saw a light go on in the kitchen and looked that way—and saw him taking off his clothes. He'd planned to go to the bedroom naked, after he dumped the clothes into the washer, and put tomorrow's long-sleeve T-shirt over his night table light to make it easier for his wife to fall asleep, and if she was already asleep, so the light wouldn't wake her. He'd been in the living room the last few hours, reading and drinking and napping and listening to music and for about a half hour, because his wife wanted one, trying to get a fire started with wet wood. After covering the lamp he'd planned to get into his side of the bed and read a biography he's been reading in bed the last two months, no more than five to six pages a night, when he gets too sleepy to read, and then shut the light, snuggle up to his wife, rub her buttocks if she has her back to him, her thighs if she's on her side facing him or on her back, put his hand under her nightshirt no matter which way she's facing and feel her breasts—she lets him about every other night and always, or almost, says okay if he says "All right?" or "Please?" or "Just for a few seconds," or something like "These are my sleeping pillows—I can't fall asleep without them." But tonight, in the kitchen, he turns on the light—his wife had turned it off when she went to bed—and takes off his pants and shirt and socks and puts them in the washer for tomorrow's wash. It's more than half filled, so he knows there'll be one. He doesn't know his neighbor is watching him. He hadn't heard her drag her huge trash can down the driveway to place it, as she always does, next to his two smaller cans. If he had heard her can rolling on its wheels, he wouldn't have taken off his pants and shirt, or would have taken them off without turning on the kitchen light and dropped them into the washer with the socks. That way, since there's no light in the kitchen from the street or sky, he wouldn't have been seen. But she saw him standing in the room naked and putting the clothes in the washer and thought Jesus, for an old guy, he hasn't got a bad body. In fact, it's pretty good, almost a flat stomach and his muscles are big and hard and he's got a nice-sized cock too in what looks like the relaxed position. But his body is more muscular and youthful than she ever imagined. She goes to his door. He's at the sink now standing in front of the window she saw him through, running the water and then putting a glass under the tap, filling it and drinking it down. He always has a glass of water before going to bed at night, and if he's drunk a lot of alcohol, two or three glasses of water—best way to avoid a hangover, he's found—and usually another glass in the middle of the night. She rings the kitchen doorbell. It doesn't work—hasn't for a few weeks and he knows he has to call in someone to fix it—so she then raps on the door window. He's startled, puts the glass down without drinking the second water and looks at the door. "Hi," she seems to say, and is smiling. He thinks: Is she nuts? I've nothing on, can't she see? She points to him and then to her chest and presses her hands together and holds them out flat and moves them up and down in quick motions. He looks for something to cover himself with. Dishtowel hanging on the refrigerator door handle, but it's too small. Looks at her. "Open up," she mouths, and he backs his way into his wife's study with his hands covering his genitals and shuts the door. Goes through the study to his older daughter's bedroom, out that to the hallway to his bedroom, looks at his wife—she's sleeping—puts his bathrobe on and goes through the living room to the kitchen, hoping she still isn't there. If she is, what will he say?

"I apologize for exposing myself like that. It was a complete accident. I didn't think anybody would be outside so late, but did you come to the door because something's wrong and you need help?" He unlocks the door and opens it. "Hi," she says. "Hello." "I saw you through the window there before and I have to confess something you might not want to hear, but I'm not one for holding back, so here goes...." Puts the pants, shirt and socks into the washer, shuts the light, turns the light on in the dining room and lowers the thermostat to sixty-six, shuts the light and goes into the hallway bathroom and looks in the medicine chest mirror. My body, he thinks—God, it's become so old. I'm always controlling how much I eat, haven't had a slice of bread for weeks so I can lose weight and haven't eaten desserts in months and never ate much of them and drink lots of water—couple of quarts a day, maybe—to fill me up, and I still have an ugly paunch. Can't be the water. Has to be something to do with age—the body going through some natural settling. And my chest. I go to the Y four to five times a week and exercise for an hour or so on the weight machines and stationary bike and though my arms are muscular and hard, bigger than they were when I got married, my chest sags like an old man's. Where'd that strange fantasy with Vicki come from? Never thought of her before in that way, and I know she'd never act like that. What could I have been thinking that a woman so young would be attracted to my body, admire my cock, would be anything but repulsed or simply turned off seeing me naked? Sandra's never said anything about the changes in my body, the chest hair and much of the pubic hair turning gray, the beginning of a turkey neck, and so on. And I never say anything about the changes in her body, which haven't been much. She still has no gray hairs, or maybe just a few in front, though the blond hair when I first met her is now, except for her eyebrows, light brown. She hasn't gained weight or developed a paunch, her legs and butt are still pretty good, her breasts seem a little larger and have fallen somewhat but are still attractive, and her face and neck show no signs of aging, either. Well, she is nine years younger than me. Anyway, don't take your clothes off in the kitchen no matter how late at night unless the light's off and they're also off in the rooms on either side of it. That's what I learned from that scene I imagined, and also don't think you'll ever have the body you once had or even close to it except the upper arms, besides… besides what? Nothing. It's ridiculous looking in the mirror except to shave. Everything's changed, you're getting old, in ways you're already old, and nothing you do—no exercise, no diet—will bring any of it back or do anything to stop it. That's a dumb thought. Go to sleep. Washes his face, brushes his teeth, flosses, uses the water pick, brushes his hair a few strokes—don't need a mirror for that—goes into the bedroom, puts his pen, watch and handkerchief on his night table, gets tomorrow's long-sleeve T-shirt out of a dresser drawer and drapes it over his lampshade, gets in bed, picks up his book and opens it to the pages a strip of torn paper's sticking out between, tries to remember which paragraph he was reading when he started dozing off last night, can't and just starts reading the first complete sentence on the left page. "Don't you want to go to sleep?"

his wife says, on her side with her back to him. "Light keeping you up?" "No, I can fall back asleep. Just thought it'd give us a chance to snuggle." "I'll shut the light if you let me put my hand inside your shirt." "Only if you turn off the light now." "If I read a couple more pages and then shut off the light?" "Outside, not inside." "But the deal is I can keep my hand inside your shirt till we're both asleep, right?" "Okay." He puts the book down, moves his two pillows closer to hers, shuts the light and snuggles up to her and puts his hand inside her shirt and fondles and then holds her left breast and then the right one and then both with one hand and feels himself going to sleep. Her last words to him, or last he hears, are "That's better, isn't it?"

12

He's in Central Park with his mother again. He isn't but imagines
he is, mostly from memory. She says "Something on your mind?
You look so pensive." She often said that. At her apartment or in a
Columbus Avenue restaurant he'd taken her to for lunch and in
Central Park when he'd wheeled her to a gazebo-like foodstand
overlooking Sheep Meadow. He says "Nothing." That's what he
just about always said. She was right; something always was on his
mind when she'd say that and he no doubt did look pensive. He
likes that she used the word "pensive." And she usually said "Well,
that's what you look like, as if something's troubling you. Is
anything?" Now he says "Plenty's on my mind," and she says
"What? Do you want to tell me? You don't have to, you know. I
don't mean to pry, but sometimes it's good getting whatever's
bothering you off your chest." "You," he says. "I worry about you.

I'm so sorry I can't come to the city more to see you." "That's all right. The women who look after me are very nice. They're not the best company—our interests are too different. I can't discuss books with them or interesting articles and columns in the *Times* and I don't like the television programs they watch—soap operas, or some sanctimonious host with moronic guests. I used to love the radio soaps, a hundred years ago, but these I can't stand and are often lewd and vulgar. But it's good to have pleasant people always around, even if not to talk to." "I worry about your health." "I'll be all right. I'm old, I'm infirm, I'm frequently sick, but I always recover. I don't sleep well at night. I'm usually tired. I ache and have bedsores from sitting in this chair so much and not being able to exercise and not turned enough in bed. But who's complaining, as your dad liked to say. Just seeing you every two or three weeks is all I really need, and your sister I see a lot too, so I have enough company." "I worry that you're depressed," and she says "How can I not be? This isn't living, it's existing. I sit in my room all day and barely speak to anyone. I sit and my head goes back to better times with your father, although my life with him wasn't great, and your stepfather and my children and being young and having a good time and going to school, and those sorts of things." No, she wouldn't say that or much of any of it. What would she say? "This is existing, not living." Said it many times. But they're in the park. He wheeled her there from her apartment a few blocks away. It's a nice day; a bit breezy, but mild, sunny. He offers to give her his baseball cap to wear, but she says "How often do I get out and let the sun shine on my face? What am I going to do at my age, die of skin cancer? First you got to get it, and I'd die of any number of other things before it became fatal. Don't worry, I'll be fine." He says "Like to stop off at the old place for a sandwich?" and she says "I had my lunch. It wasn't food I liked but it was filling; the girl cooks with too many spices. But a dessert would be nice. And if they serve beer, I'll have that too." "They serve beer." He doesn't like drinking so early himself—six is when he normally starts—but gets her the best foreign beer they have—"Japanese; made out of rice," and she says "Good; it'll be easy on my stomach"—and a slice of pound cake and he has coffee and a small piece of her cake. They take a table outside. She says "You look pensive. Is anything wrong?" and he says "No, why do you say that?" "Because of your face. You look like the whole world's on your shoulders." "Really, I'm just thinking about my work," he lies. "The school?" and he says "No, the other." "How is it going?" "It's going well. It always goes well. You know me, I don't stop. Sometimes I wish I could. Lately, it's been keeping me up at night. So I'm a little tired, that's all, but I'll be all right." "You're fortunate you have something you like to do that always keeps you busy." They sit silently for a while. Staring out at the meadow and people playing Frisbee on it and people walking and jogging and bicycling and rollerblading past them and some stopping at the food stand. "How's the beer?" he finally says. "It could be better. To be honest, and I should've said something before you bought it, but I like American beer better than foreign. This one's too rich, not as refreshing. But it is cold, which I like.

This is a good place." He wheels her into the park. "It's a nice day," he says, as he pushes the wheelchair. "Just the right temperature." "What's that?" she says. "I can't hear you when you talk behind me. That accident I had as a young girl." He knows what it is—she's told him the story several times—but he stops pushing her, brakes the chair and comes around in front of her and says "What accident?" "I never told you?" "If you did, I forgot." "Don't give me that; you've got a memory like a steel trap. But I'll tell you again. But push me. I'm too conspicuous sitting here in the middle of the path. You can hear while you're pushing me, can't you?" and then she tells him how she once talked back to a grade school teacher and the teacher slapped her in the left ear. "It busted something inside—I forget the name of what—and I lost most of my hearing in that ear and five years later the hearing in the ear went totally deaf." "Was the teacher reprimanded?" and she says "What?" He stops pushing, leans over her right shoulder and says "Was the teacher reprimanded?" "They weren't then. I told my parents what happened and they said I deserved to get slapped. That was before I realized I lost most of my hearing in that ear. Then when they learned how much hearing I lost, my mother said they should complain to the principal. But my father said no, I talked back to a person of authority, and a teacher, no less, so even if it resulted in my going deaf, I still deserved what I got. And teachers, he said, make so little money. You don't want to do anything to get them fired and force them to go on relief." He pushes her to the food stand. "So what'll you have?" and she says "Just a ginger ale, and in a mug with a handle this time, so I can hold it, and perhaps a cruller." "Would you take a pound cake?" and she says "That'd be nice too, if they don't have the other thing I wanted." He gets coffee for himself and a ginger ale and pound cake for her. She says, after they don't speak for a while, "Your expression—it's so pensive, as if you're carrying all the troubles of the world. Anything the matter?" "Not a thing, really." She doesn't look well, he's worried about her health, but to distract her and make conversation, so she won't think she's boring him, he asks questions he's asked and she's answered a few times; he can't think of any new ones to ask. "What was Dad like when you first met?" and she says "Haven't I already told you that? He was happy-go-lucky, handsome and slim, not like the roly-poly he became after we married, and gave the impression he was a big spender, when in fact he was very cheap." Who introduced them? Why did the family move from Brooklyn to Manhattan? Why did her father object so strenuously to her being a showgirl? "What's the story about you and the Duke of Windsor when you danced in the Scandals?" "Now that one I know I told you before." "You did, but not for a long time and I've forgotten a lot of it," and she says "You're not going to write about it and use my real name, are you, at least not till I'm dead?" and he says "No, and don't talk about your death." "Why? You've got to start facing facts. I can't live forever. Anyway, to change the subject, since it's now obvious to me why you're being so pensive; my condition; I must look like I'm on my last leg—I'll tell you, if I can remember straight. He wasn't the Duke of Windsor then. He was the Prince of

Wales. He was going to be the king of England. That I don't have to tell you, because you majored in history in college, right? But did you know he was a lush? That they don't put in your history books. He was in New York and went to a performance of the Scandals—I forget which year, '24 or '25, the two Scandals I was in—and wanted to be introduced to me after the show. I got a note to that effect from a high American official chaperoning him. I didn't want anything to do with him. Let's say he had a reputation and I knew what he was after and I wasn't going to be part of it—I wanted to remain a virgin till I got married—so I asked Mr. White—we always called him that, never 'George'—if I could leave through the lobby that night rather than the stage door." "Didn't the prince also send you flowers?" "Oh, yes. He already had them and a heart-shaped box of chocolates in the dressing room I shared with a dozen other girls. They all said to go out with him. That he's so handsome and elegant and he'll take me to the finest places and maybe give me his jeweled stickpin, which they heard he had a habit of doing. I'm not sure if they meant what I think by that. Half of them were good girls but the other half had rich boyfriends who paid their rent and gave them bracelets and clothes and things. In other words, they were being kept. So I gave the flowers and candy to two of my friends among the dancers and slipped out through the lobby, which we were never allowed to do—only the headliners of the show were—except for me that night. Mr. White, you have to understand, was a gentleman and very protective of his younger more innocent girls." "So, if you had played your cards right, you could have been the Duchess of Windsor or the Princess of Wales." "Just the Duchess of Windsor. But not a chance. He never would have married a Jewish girl, not that that influenced me. Sleep with them—that was okay." Another time in the park. He gets her an Orangina and a turkey sandwich—"I'm suddenly hungry," she says, "which is a good thing, right?—appetite"—and a toasted bagel and butter and coffee for himself. "Take the other half of my sandwich," she says. "You gobbled down that bagel as if there was no tomorrow." "I'm fine. The bagel was more than adequate." "Please, it'll only go to waste." "No, really, you have it all, Mom. I know you can finish it and I'm glad you're eating." "It is good, the sandwich." She eats, he drinks. She says, after sipping the Orangina through a straw, "I'm glad you introduced me to this drink. It's much more refreshing than ginger ale." "I'm glad you like it. The bottle's small, so if you want another, I'll get it." "One's enough, thanks." Then, after a long pause: "Is there anything bothering you you want to talk about? You look so pensive, troubled." She wants him to talk. That if they don't, she'll think he thinks they've nothing to talk about but food. So think of something to say, he thinks. "Just, we're a little short of dough these days—all of a sudden, so many expenses—but not to worry; we'll make out." "Can I give you some? I'm not the richest person alive, but everything I have is yours and your sister's." "Of course not. You have just enough to keep you going. That also worries me. What happens if you run out of your savings or have to cash in your stocks or bonds or whatever is it you have? Who'll pay for your caregivers? Not Medicare. So I feel I need to make more money to help you out in the future if you need it." "I have enough," she says. "Between Social Security and your stepfather leaving me in pretty good straits. Not enough to give a lot away, quite honestly, but enough to live fairly comfortably. Anyway, that's all that's disturbing you? Just money?" "That's all. Just money," and he smiles and drinks his coffee. She finishes her sandwich, drinks her Orangina. They sit this way for a few minutes, watching people pass. I should ask her something, he thinks. So she won't feel uncomfortable. But something I never asked her before. "When you were a girl, what did you want to be most?" "You mean professionally? An architect. But there were no Jewish women architects then and very few men ones. Then I wanted to be a physician. I had the aptitude for it and I loved helping people. But my father said women shouldn't be doctors." "But women were becoming doctors then, no?" "That's what I told him. He said even if that was true, it'd be too expensive to send me to medical school. So I said I'd work to save enough money—this was when I was in high school, you understand—and pay for medical school myself. That's when he put his foot down. 'I forbid you to go to medical school,' he said. 'Not only that,' he added, 'you'd make an abominable doctor.'" "What an awful thing to say," he says. "And he used the word 'abominable'?" "Yes. And I couldn't stand up to him when he was so adamantly against it. If I had—my father ruled the roost in our house—he would've slapped me and I'd have lost the hearing in my other ear. Then I certainly couldn't become a doctor. No deaf doctors, I'm sure." "Oh, I'm sure there are," he says, "but maybe not then. But how'd you lose the hearing in your left ear?" "I've told you." "Something about a teacher?" "You know it was. I talked back. I had a big mouth and was very brazen then. If it happened today, that teacher would be canned. But corporal punishment was permitted when I was a girl." "It was even when I was in school. P.S. 87. Teachers slapped our hands with rulers and pointers and pulled on our ears." "No." "It's true. But I don't think I ever told you." They're silent. He says "What was Irwin like when you first met him?" "Not as handsome or funny as your father." "Did he like books as much as you?" "You remember him. Never read anything but newspapers and his dental journals. In some ways, though, he was a better father than your real father—more attentive. He used to help you with your science and math homework and taught you how to swim and things, and he was also a much better provider." "You would have made it on your own if you hadn't remarried, not that I was ever unhappy that you and Irwin got hitched." "I could have. I worked hard at everything I did and was considered smart and a fast learner and I was very pretty and had good legs. That wouldn't have hurt. Now I'm an old hag." "What are you talking about? You're still very beautiful for your age. Men might not stop in their tracks and turn around to look at you anymore, or maybe I'm wrong; maybe they still do." "Oh, you're nice," she says, patting his cheek. "You know just what to say to me. One of the reasons I love going out with you to the park." He wheels her into the park. At the food stand, over Orangina and coffee and a cruller he bought at a bakery at the train station, she says he looks pensive; is something disturbing him he'd like to talk about? "Truth is; I feel awful I can't come in to see you more." "I wish you could," she says, "but I understand the problem. Your life is in Baltimore now. But I treasure the times you do visit me, and you also call a lot." He starts to cry. "What's this? You're too old to shed tears over such a thing. I'm fine, I'll be all right. I have nice girls looking after me. Some aren't girls. One's only ten years younger than I am, but strong as an ox. And your sister comes around fairly often. We don't go out to lunch or to the park as I do with you, but she brings me food and we have long talks. Don't be sad. Try to be happy. It's good for your health, they say, and if you're feeling good, then I feel much healthier." "That can't be true, he says. "It's not, but I thought I'd say it to take your mind off things. What I wanted to say was if you're in a good mood when I'm with you, then I am too." They sit at a table at the food stand and he gets her an American beer and muffin and a coffee for himself. She says "Why so pensive? Anything wrong?" "Nothing." "Your marriage?" "Couldn't be better." "She's a wonderful girl and your daughters are the delight of my life. But they're all healthy, nothing wrong at home?" "Everything's fine and dandy, as Dad used to say." "You remember?" "I think so, or else you told me." "So if everything's good, what's bothering you? Because something is." "Just the same old thing. That I can't see you as often as I want to. I wish I lived in the city so I could pop in on you almost every day. I would, too, if I lived close enough. In fact, I'd make sure to get an apartment no more than a few subway stops from yours." "That's nice," she says.

"It's enough just that you said it. But you have a good steady job—tenure, now, so no chance of losing it—and your life is somewhere else. Maybe one day you'll get a good teaching job here. I hope it happens while I'm still around." "Come on, you're indestructible. If the opportunity ever arises where I can get a comparable job here—even one with a little less money—I'll jump at it, because Sandra also feels lousy she can't see her folks as much as she wants to." "I live for that day." "You look so pensive," she says, after he puts on their foodstand table a sandwich and beer for her and coffee for him. "Believe me," he says, "it has nothing to do with anything troubling me." "Then what does it have to do with, because it doesn't look like nothing." "It's just my face. It looks pensive when I'm not. I'm all right and my family's all right and everything's going well: job, my writing, even the car." "Good," she says, "that's what I want to hear." She smiles and he takes her hand and kisses it and says "It's wonderful being out with you. I'm glad I came in. I only wish I could do it more," and she says "You do what you have to do. I don't make demands because I know your situation. Just being with you today will last me till your next visit." "That's so nice of you to say." "It's the truth. I meant every word," and she takes a bite of her sandwich and sips her beer. "This has nothing to do with anything we were talking about," he says, "but I was thinking about it on the train in, so I'll ask. How many years did you dance in George White's Scandals?" "Please, don't get me started." "No, tell me. I'm interested." "Just two, but they were the two best years of my life—so much fun and excitement and such nice people to work with—till I met your father and had you kids." "Wasn't there something once, where the Prince of Wales took a fancy to you on stage and you almost became the Duchess of Windsor?" "Oh, you're a funny guy."

13

He thinks: It's odd how he thinks of her at least once a week. Dreams a lot about her too, and the last time they slept together was forty-one years ago. He'd come back from France. She went to the dock to meet him. They'd exchanged letters around every other week the last two months. He'd gone to Paris to learn French fluently and get a news or some other writing job there, but he won a university fellowship in California and returned. He'd met her at a New Year's Eve party in New York five years before. She's so beautiful, he thought, staring at her sitting on a couch and talking to some people. He waited till she got up and was alone, and introduced himself. They talked. After about an hour, he said "Like to go out for a sandwich?" She said she came with someone—"just a friend, and I don't want to desert him." "We'll come back." They held hands in the restaurant, kissed on the street on their way back to the party. All very fast. She gave him her phone number. They became lovers a week after they began seeing each other. Two months later, after staying at her apartment almost every night—he lived at home—she wasn't answering her phone. Went to her building and rang her downstairs bell; nobody rang back. There were no lights on in her third-floor windows. Got into her building and knocked on her door. Called her two best friends and both said they didn't know where she was. Called her folks in New Jersey and said "Could you have Rebecca call me?" and her father said "She's right here, I'll put her on." She told him she's sorry she hasn't spoken to him for so long and he said "It's another guy, isn't it? I should have known something was wrong when you asked for my key back last week because you said yours was getting stuck," and she said it was getting stuck, and yes, the man she dated for a year before she met Meyer and almost married and they're going to get re-engaged. They met at a coffee shop the next day. She gave him a bag of his things and some books she'd borrowed from him and said she hoped they'd remain friends, but it was better for them both he not try to contact her for a while. He got a news job in Washington. Two years later he moved back to New York and bumped into a friend of hers, who said Rebecca got divorced. Why doesn't he call her? She isn't with anyone, and she still speaks of him highly, and is sorry for the way she broke up with him then. "Well, we were both very young, but I took it okay." "She appreciated that too. Confidentially, it made it a lot easier for her. She admired your maturity." He called. They met for dinner. He walked her back to her building, made sure not to try to kiss her. "Like to do this again?" he said. "If you don't want to, for whatever reason, fine." "No, this was fun. It'd be nice." They became lovers in a week. Got engaged two months after that. A few weeks before the wedding, which was to be a small one at her parents' house—around thirty guests—she said she wanted to postpone it for a while, half a year, maybe a year. "Nah, it's the same old thing. We'll never get married. You'll meet another guy and stop seeing me altogether." "I would like a complete break," she said, "but no more than a couple months. I just don't want to rush into another marriage so soon after the last bust." "All right, a couple of months isn't so long." He called in a month and she said she's decided it's better if he holds no hope of their getting back together again. "Screw you," he said, and hung up. Then he was in Paris and got a letter from her, three years after she broke up with him the last time. She'd got his address from his mother. "She was reluctant to give it to me, and who could blame her? Why am I writing? Oh, been thinking of you and wondered how you were." She met him at the ship. He was immediately attracted to her at the party. An actress, gorgeous face and body. Once, after they'd made love every day for about two weeks straight, she said "Can't we give it a rest one night? Let's see if we can just go to sleep with our arms around each other." "We can do that after making love." "Meyer, my crotch is beginning to hurt." When they were engaged he liked introducing her to people he knew as "my fiancée, Rebecca Hill." After a couple of times, she said "Please don't introduce me as your fiancée. I like being it, but

I don't want to be designated as such to other people. If someone asks you 'Are you two serious?' then of course you can say we're engaged or getting married in a month." Sometimes, when they separated on the street and went opposite ways, she'd keep stopping and turning around and wave to him. He liked going to her parents' house and sleeping over, though he was always put up in the guest room, even the month before they were supposed to get married. A big comfortable house, lots of fireplaces and old furniture, two dogs, mother a terrific cook, father a playwright of some note. Romantic, having a father who made a decent living writing plays and mother who was once a celebrated actress. They'd take long walks in the woodsy neighborhood. Hold hands, stop to kiss and hug. "I'm so in love with you," she said. "I can't wait for the wedding so we can sleep together in your old room," he said. They planned to go to Europe on their honeymoon. Spend a month there, travel by train. Cheap hotels and inexpensive wine and food. They didn't have much money and didn't want to borrow any. Maybe rent bikes for a week and stay in youth hostels during that time. He was working for a radio news outfit and got a month's vacation. She had a bit part on a TV soap opera and in October would have a good role in a Broadway play. He looked forward to picking her up at the theater after the show and walking home. They'd got a one-bedroom apartment on the West Side in the fifties. She kept the apartment. He told her to keep everything they bought for it: furniture, kitchen utensils, bamboo blinds, artwork by friends. He got a studio apartment on East 88th near the river. When the news show he wrote for went off the air, he got a severance package that enabled him, if he lived frugally, to just write fiction and one-act plays for a year. He had a few jobs the next two years: teen magazine editor, advertising copywriter, ghostwriter for two Holocaust memoirs he could never get published, permanent sub for one term in a tough Brooklyn junior high school. He dialed her phone number once in those three years, heard her voice and hung up. He was slightly drunk, calling from a bar late at night, and had no intention of speaking to her. Walked past her building just at the chance she might be leaving it or on the block. Then he went to Paris and soon after he settled there got the first letter she ever sent him. His sister had invited him to the New Year's Eve party but told him to come late, around twelve, since it wasn't her party and she'd already invited too many friends to it. "It'll be a big boisterous affair, lots of artistic and scholarly types, and some of them very successful, I understand. You'll easily fit in." She said "Who's the pretty blond you cornered for a while?" "An actress. She's lively, funny, intelligent, not to say good-looking, and if you can believe it, she seems interested in me too. She went to get her coat. We're going out for a sandwich. What can I say? Sometimes, in minutes, things just click." "You're going to a restaurant when there's so much good food here?" "I want to get her alone. Too many guys sniffing around her. We'll be back." When he started seeing her again after her divorce, his sister said "You're making a big, big mistake. Nice a person as I always found her, she's not to be trusted." She yelled to him from the dock "Meyer, Meyer, over here," and waved. He waved back from the ship and yelled "It's going to take a while. Something with Customs. Maybe you shouldn't wait for me." "That's all right," she yelled. "I've brought a book." "What are you reading?" he yelled. They slept together that night. It was the middle of July and very hot. She was apartment-sitting till she got her own place, and all they had to cool them was a small desk fan. She fell asleep after they made love. She had no sheet over her and he stared at her body for about an hour. Her forehead and breasts were wet with sweat and he dabbed them with a paper towel. Then he stroked her thigh. With her eyes still shut, she said "Don't." "I love you," he said. "Have since that party my sister invited me to." "I know. I've loved you too. I don't now." All this with her eyes closed. "I like you a lot, though." "So we'll see what happens?" he said. "I'm game." "I might be too. Go to sleep. The room will seem cooler if it's dark. And don't paw me. It's too hot for it. I wish I'd apartment-sat a place that had an air-conditioner." "Could we make love once more?" he said. "If you don't want to, that's fine." "I'm very tired, and uncomfortable from the heat. But if you want to and you're quick and you don't mind my dozing off during it, all right, but let me shower first to cool off." She showered, came back, said "Why don't we just go to sleep." "Not exactly what I'd like doing, but okay with me. I said I wouldn't push." Next morning she woke him up and was already dressed. She was going to spend the weekend with a friend in New Haven and would drop him off along the way. She drove him to his parents' building, double-parked in front and said "We shouldn't have slept together last night. I shouldn't have met your boat. Shouldn't, even, have written you, but I wanted to make amends for all my awful treatment of you, but should have done it some other way. Now I've made matters worse. It's not going to work, Meyer." "Why?" Three years letter he got a letter from her care of his mother, who forwarded it. "I understand you're in California. So am I, in L.A., working on a movie (a small part but a beaut). If you're anywhere near here, I'd love for us to meet. You're one of my dearest old friends and I miss our straight talks and rapport." He was working as a technical writer for a systems analysis company just outside L.A. They met for lunch, had a good conversation. She'd got an annulment the year before of a marriage that lasted five days. "Talk about errors one can make? I must've been nuts. I knew he was crazy. My last actor ever." He shook her hand goodbye in the restaurant parking lot. She said "Get off it, smart guy," and kissed his cheek and gave him a bear hug. He wanted to give her a big kiss on the lips, see what her reaction would be, but then felt she wouldn't like it. "I'm so glad we're still friends," she said. "You're someone special to me." They corresponded a few times—she was back in New York—and then stopped. Years later, when he was living in New York again, she called him from her hotel. "You're the only Meyer Ostrower in the phone book. Oh, to be so singular. I know there must be at least a dozen Rebecca or R. Hills. I'm only in town for a few days, doing two TV commercials. Don't ask, but both have to do with things cloacal, one of your pet words, I recall. Anyways, my dear, I thought we could catch up on each other." They met around three in her hotel's coffee shop. "I'm off the rest of the day," she said, "so why don't we spend it together? Go to the Modern as we used to, have dinner at a snazzy place. I'll pay. I'm making a ton of money on this trip." "Wish I could," he said, "but I have to take care of my stepfather in an hour. I'm the one who exercises him and gives him his shots." "He's still alive. I'm glad." She returned to Chicago, where she was in a repertory company. He got married, had two children. She married a third time, had two children. He once visited her in Princeton where she lived with the man who became her husband and whom she had her kids with. The guy was very nice but dull. Had no interest, and said so, in literature and theater or anything like that. His main interests, when he wasn't working at the video production company he co-owned, were flying, fishing and hunting. Rebecca and Meyer sat in the backyard on the grass an hour before the guy came home from work. He forgets what prompted him to visit her and stay the night in their house. Did she contact him, or he, her? He does remember she had dark sunglasses on, which made her look even more beautiful, and was wearing culottes and a blue-and-white-striped tank top. When she met him at the ship, she wore khaki Bermuda shorts and a blue-and-white-striped tank top, maybe the same one. Both her folks were dead. Her father from drink, her mother in a fire in her bedroom that the fire department said was started with a lit cigarette she forgot to put out before she turned off the light and went to sleep. She was sitting with her legs spread sometimes, and he tried to get a peek at her panties and upper part of her thighs and maybe her crotch or some hair there. She'd also been a modern dancer and mime and her body was still in great shape. She stretched while they talked and drank wine. She'd given up theater and was now studying French literature and language at a community college. Next year, she said, she'd transfer to a regular four-year college and get her B.A. and then a master's in French literature. "My ambition, although you might think this ridiculous"—"No," he said; "anything you do is fine with me"—"is to become a full-fledged professor at a college around here or within an hour's drive, though of course not Princeton. That one's way out of my reach and you need a Ph.D., which is a little late for me to get." "You never know," he said, "how far something can take you." Last time he saw her was when they bumped into each other at the 77th Street entrance to the Museum of Natural History. He was with his daughters, she with her younger son. The boy was a couple years older than his older daughter. They walked around the museum awhile and then he suggested they get lunch in the cafeteria. She said "Why don't we go to a nice place on Columbus. This is a special day for me, meeting you." "If we leave then we'll have to pay again to come back in, because I know my kids aren't through yet." Her face and body seemed the same. He'd lost lots of hair and was about fifteen pounds heavier than when she last saw him, but she said "Look at you; you never change." She was now teaching acting, movement and mime at a drama school in Trenton. She never got her B.A. in French literature. She said she'd written several plays but has had no luck with them. "You've done rather well," she said. "I don't know if your books sell, but they certainly get reviewed. How many do you have now, five, six?" "Eleven." At the party, she said, "If I seem out of sorts a little, it's because I've a headache." "Let me get you some aspirins." "Oh, would you? That's so sweet, and I could really use them." He found out who the host was and got two aspirins from him. He brought them to her with a glass of water. She took them, drank a little water. "Drink it all," he said. "Better for your stomach lining if you drink a full glass of water with aspirins." "Is that so? You know so much. My poor stomach lining; it's probably destroyed by now. You know," she said a minute later, "the headache's gone." "Then want to go out for a bite?" "There'd be a place open this late?" "Sure. C & L. I used to work there as a delivery boy for their catering department when I was in high school. Very convenient; just two blocks from me." "You lived around here? So did I, in The Dakota." "Did you go to P.S. 87?" "No. Dalton through the fifth grade. Then the Young Professional School for budding actors." "You're an actress? In any plays I might've seen? But let's go out. I want to be in a relatively quiet place so I can hear what you're saying." "Okay, but I have to come back. I came with a friend, you realize." "I know," he said. "I like it that you're loyal." "And I like it that you think I'm loyal. I really am." Never did see her in a play. One that was supposed to open on Broadway closed on the road. Soon after he first met her he had this fantasy of sitting in a theater audience and seeing her on stage and after the show they'd go to someplace like Joe Allen's to eat and drink and then go to her apartment and make love. Another fantasy he had was traveling around Europe with her, going to cathedrals and museums, walking through old streets and eating in cheap bistros and having so much fun. He did go to Europe with his wife before they got married. His wife also dropped him a couple of times, but things eventually worked out. He intentionally didn't call her for three months after she dropped him the second time, and then she called and they met for coffee and have been together since. Sometimes he dreams—no, he's dreamed of Rebecca a lot, but sometimes he's made love to her in the dreams. He'd wake up with an erection and if is wife wasn't asleep—even if she was asleep—he'd stroke and kiss her and try to get her interested in making love, and sometimes she would. He once even came in a dream with Rebecca, something he thinks only happened in all his dreams of making love with women that one time. He walked into a room and she was on a bed naked. She was reading, looked up at him, put her arms out and said "I haven't seen you in twenty-five years. You look the same. I know I've changed. Come to me, please." He took his clothes off and got on top of her. While they were making love—it was only for about ten seconds—he said to himself "I know I'm not going to have an orgasm because I never do in my dreams." Then he had one and woke up with an erection and kissed his wife's shoulder and rubbed her back and behind. She opened her eyes—it was early morning and there was a little daylight—and said "You must have had a sex dream. I'd love to say yes to your overtures, but what I want more now is to sleep. Later, sweetie," and shut her eyes. He has photos of Rebecca he used to keep in an old billfold but he's not sure where they are now. The one she looks best in was taken at a friend's wedding reception in the late sixties. The couple has since broken up. He'd flown in for the wedding but mainly to see his mother and stepfather and sisters. He suspected Rebecca would be there since she was a friend of the bride, so that could have been another reason he'd flown in. It was at someone's apartment; fifteen or twenty guests. He's sitting in an easy chair with his tie undone and jacket in his lap; it was a warm summer day and there was no air conditioning. She's sitting on the padded arm of his chair and looks happy to be with him. Both are holding plastic champagne glasses. After the reception—or before it was over; "We gotta get out of here," he said. "This place is an oven and I'm boiling," and he also, like at the New Year's Eve party, wanted to get her alone—they walked across the park to the Met, thinking it was open, but it had just closed. "I'm sorry," he said. "I thought six, not five." They went to a coffee shop for iced tea and then to a restaurant for dinner. Chez Jacques, or a name like it, the French one on West 55th or 56th they used to go to during their second time around, where you could get an inexpensive price fixe and wine in carafes. It had been there for years—in fact, his family had gone to it when he was in his teens—but folded before he met his wife. He said when they were having dessert—crème caramel, he remembers; they always ordered it—"I'm still hooked on you, it must be obvious, and would love to sleep with you tonight." "No, that's not in the cards," she said. "Don't ruin a wonderful day, Meyer." "I'm going to ruin it," he said, and asked the waiter for the check, paid it, said "I'd like to put you in a cab and never see you again." "If that's what you want, although I can put myself in a cab or take the bus. Listen to me. We've known each other so long and well and have so much to say to each other when we do get together, it'd be a pity if we couldn't continue as just good friends." "We can't because I don't want to." He hailed a cab, said "I want to pay for it too," and gave her a ten-dollar bill. "That's too much," she said. "Give him a big tip," and he walked off. He saw her a few times after that. She once showed up at a reading he gave in a Trenton bookstore. He'd thought of telling her about it and then decided not to. He wanted to just do the reading and head home. It was in '93, for his omnibus story collection, so that might have been the last time he saw her, not the Museum of Natural History. They had coffee in the store's café and then she drove him to the train. "Next time, tell me when you're giving a reading this close, even if it's in Philly. I'll try to come." Another photo he has of her but right now doesn't know where it is, is actually a negative. For a long time he wanted to get it developed but didn't know how to go about it. He found it in an envelope of photos in her apartment when they were engaged and took it without telling her. Holding it up to the light, he could see her on her knees on what looks to be a deserted sandy beach or cove, probably the Caribbean island she and her first husband went to for their honeymoon. She's facing the camera, and her arms are stretched out, she's topless and only seems to have on a skimpy bikini bottom or panties. He masturbated to it a number of times the year or two after they broke up. For the last ten years or so he's been speaking to her on the phone about once every four months. She's now working in Connecticut, mostly in Hartford, teaching speech and body movement to elderly people at several nursing homes and assisted-living places and she also stages scenes from plays with the residents as the actors. "It's not much of a living," she said. "But it's enough, with my Social Security, if I live on the cheap, and it keeps me busy and feeling good about myself in what I do for these people." She once called him at home—he usually called her from work and sometimes after she left a message on his answering machine there. His wife answered it and gave him the phone and Rebecca said "Is it all right to call you here?" "Sure, why not?" he said. "Then Sandra doesn't mind? Good." "No, she knows there's nothing romantic between us and that all that sort of stuff was in the past. What's up?" "I haven't heard from you for so long, I thought something might be wrong."

14

The phone rings and he yells out to his wife "I'll get it"—he's been resting enough—and gets off the bed and picks up the receiver and says hello. "Dr. Ostrower?" a man says, and he says "You want Dr. Ostrower? You must mean my wife. She's got a Ph.D., although never calls herself doctor." "No. Dr. Ostrower the dentist, a man." "You don't mean my stepfather, Irwin Ostrower," and the man says, "I wanted Myron Ostrower, but that must be the guy. It's been a long time. He did some work on me—put in a new bridge—and it's come loose and I want him to fix it up." "First of all—well, lots of things. But first, my name's Meyer Ostrower, not Myron, but that's probably why you called here, or Information gave you this number—the names are very close. Where you calling from?" "Baltimore, same as you." "Okay. As for Irwin Ostrower—I took his last name when my mother married him—he was a dentist but died in '72. If he were alive today—and I'm not saying it's out of the realm of possibility but it sure borders on it—he'd be a hundred-ten." "Dr. Ostrower died? When I went to him, he was such a young, big strapping guy, looked like he worked out, though that was about twenty years ago I had the bridge made, maybe thirty. He was also, I remember, a sculptor on the side—as a hobby. Had statues all over his office, mostly of nude figures." "My stepfather was anything but big and strapping. Around five-seven, sort of heavyset, and his only interest was dentistry. It's obvious you've a different Dr. Ostrower in mind, and his name is probably Myron." "Myron. It could be Meyer. I forget. But this Ostrower dentist I'm looking for isn't related to you, where'd you know where to reach him so I can get my bridge fixed?" "Never heard of him, and as I said, or maybe I didn't, my stepfather practiced in New York and lived there his entire life, so another reason he couldn't have been your dentist." "Then it's a sure thing he's the wrong Dr. Ostrower. Why would I want to go to New York for my teeth when some of the best dentists in the world are right here. Sorry for bothering you," and hangs up. Just out of curiosity, he thinks, and goes into his wife's study—she's at the computer and he says "Just came in for the Yellow Pages"—and gets the book off the floor and looks under "Dentists." No Ostrower or Ostrauer. Maybe the guy retired or moved to another city or died. Puts the book back on top of the White Pages and then looks in that book and he's the only Ostrower or Ostrauer there. Says "That call before? Some guy, at first asking for Dr. Ostrower the dentist. He meant someone else but my

stepfather, but it was so strange. Twenty years after Irwin died—
remember, he'd be in his nineties by then if he were alive—my
mother was still getting calls at home from former patients wanting
him to adjust a plate of theirs he made, or something. You know, he
specialized in plates and bridges, which made this call even stranger,
for that's what the guy wanted too: his bridge adjusted. Oh, well,"
and he goes back to the bedroom, lies on the bed with his hands
under his head, not to nap but to think. First thing that comes to
mind is the long staircase up to the second floor of the two-story
building his stepfather's office was in. Fortieth Street, subway
entrance right below. Building's probably torn down by now. Must
have been fifteen steps up, though the way he visualizes it now,
seems like more. Steep, and no landing halfway up, either. Then
left, in the dimly lit hallway, and third or fourth door down was his
office. Front door with a bubbly smoked-glass window; nameplate—
"Dr. Irwin E. Ostrower, DDS"—under the mail slot in the door, or
maybe above it; he forgets. "Ring bell and walk in," a small plaque
said on the doorframe at around eye level. Sometimes a patient or
two or a couple of his stepfather's cronies in the waiting room. No
receptionist, dental hygienist or dental assistant to help him—he
did all that work himself: bookkeeping, patient-scheduling, teeth-
cleaning, tidying up the office. Every other month or so a cleaning
woman came in to really give the place a go-over. There was one
toilet for the entire floor of about eight offices. If his father was in
the treatment room—it had a fancier name, "operatory," but his
stepfather never used it: "If I did, nobody would know what I was

talking about except another dentist—he'd stick his head out to see who'd just come in. Between the treatment and waiting room was an alcove big enough for a desk, chair and two filing cabinets; it was where his stepfather did his paperwork and ate the lunch he'd brought in a paper bag from home. Framed photos on one alcove wall of his mother and father, taken around 1920. Another one on the desk of Meyer's mother. Huge photo on the wall of him in cap and gown, which he sat for shortly before graduating dental school. Another huge framed composite or whatever it's called of his entire class in individual graduation photos—his was a small version of the large framed one—and below one of those his diploma. Sometimes he'd be alone in the waiting room, sitting in one of the shabby chairs and reading a newspaper or dental journal. "Oh, hi there," he'd say when Meyer came in, and a number of times: "Not much business this afternoon" or "No scheduled appointments the next hour, and if there's a walk-in, I'll leave a sign on the door to come back in twenty minutes, so what do you say we go downstairs for a bite?" If he was busy, he'd say "Anything you especially came to see me for, and I'm not giving you the bum's rush, sonny boy, but I got a patient in the chair," or "a plate" or "bridge to work on for a patient coming to get it fitted any minute." "No, nothing," he'd say. "Just I had a few minutes to kill"—he worked afternoons in the Garment Center his last two years of high school—"and thought I'd stop by," and always kiss his cheek before he left. Going up the stairs one time and seeing him coming down. "What are you doing here so early, playing hooky?" and he said "I got a bad toothache in school and wanted you to take care of it," and his stepfather said "I was on my way out for a quick bite, but let's go upstairs." Another time, tooth started aching late at night. His stepfather handed him a shot glass of scotch, said "Don't swallow it; it'll burn and make you sick. Just let it sit on the tooth. That and the Anacin should hold you till tomorrow, when I'll give you a note to leave school an hour early to see me." "Why can't I go to the office with you in the morning and then go to school?" and his stepfather said "I got a busy schedule—one patient I got to work on for two hours—and I can't postpone. Do that once with someone in pain or discomfort, they never come back." He'd learned in his teens his stepfather was a lousy dentist. Or maybe he was only that way with his family— cut corners, worked on them in a hurry—because in the waiting room his patients used to swear by him. "Your pop. A magician at dentistry. He can pull out the deepest rotted tooth without anesthetic or it hurting and his fillings stay in for life." His mother started going to another dentist years before. His stepfather once said at the dinner table "I saw our check statement how much you gave that dentist of yours. You're a fool for wasting good money on him, when I can do the same work for nothing. We all learn the same techniques in school, so one dentist's as good as the other if he stays awake while treating you. You want to make me look bad in front of the kids, do so, but they're coming to me till I give up my practice or they move to another city, and even then they can come in for checkups and treatment when they visit." His stepfather would tell him to sit in the dental chair, "Relax, relax," and pick around the tooth that hurt and then start drilling, usually without taking x-rays or using Novocain. "This won't hurt—the area around the tooth's not inflamed—and why should I waste x-ray film and risk you getting roentgen poisoning when I can see with my own eyes what the problem is. If the drilling for a second starts hurting you, I'll give you a needle." When Meyer was in college and several of the teeth his stepfather had worked on ended up needing root canal, he switched to his mother's dentist and paid for it with money he earned. His stepfather must have known because he never told him to come in for checkups anymore or asked him about his teeth and gums, which he used to do around every six months. His sister still went to him for her teeth, even after she got married, but took her kids to her husband's dentist. "Someone in the family's got to use him or he'll feel completely rejected," she said. Going upstairs for a quick visit with him when Meyer was in night school and working days near his office and seeing him sitting on one of the middle steps. "What're you doing?—you'll dirty your pants," and his stepfather said "I don't know what happened. I was feeling good, went down for a Danish and coffee, and couldn't make it all the way back up. Suddenly felt too weak to, and I got a patient coming in ten minutes." Meyer helped him upstairs. It was the first sign of Parkinson's. Worked on patients with his hands shaking for about two years. Gradually lost all of them except those wanting just a cleaning or for him to send their plates and bridgework to the dental lab for repairs. Finally had to close his practice when he was falling down a lot and couldn't get up the stairs or home without assistance. Going upstairs with his sister and mother to clear out the office, mark what furniture and equipment was to be thrown out, given to a place like Goodwill or delivered to their apartment. His sister took both dental cabinets. "They're antiques," she said, "selling in some stores for a thousand each." Lots of the stuff—dental chair and table, treatment room lamps, instruments, even the mortar and pestle he used to mix the silver for fillings—were picked up by an organization that furnished clinics in Africa and Asia with old American equipment. Meyer, after his stepfather died, kept one of the mouth mirrors, which he'd never used for anything, a curette for his nails, and two forceps, which he uses sometimes as pliers or to retrieve things like paperclips that have fallen under the space bar or keys on his typewriter.

15

He dozes off and dreams. He gets a call. "Yes?" he says, and a man says "Officer Dunnigan of the Fifth Station, sir. Am I speaking to Meyer Ostrower?" and he says "You are. What's wrong? Where's the Fifth Station, here or in Providence where my daughters are?" "Here, sir. I have some very bad news for you. It's your wife. A car accident." "It can't be. She's home. I just saw her a few minutes ago, working at her computer. Hold on," and he yells out "Sandra?" No answer. "Sandra, are you there?" Picks up the phone and says "Hold on—I'm going to look for her." "You don't have to, sir. She's here." "And where's that? And just tell me if she's dead." Next he's in a hospital. It was like a movie-scene cut. He's holding the phone and talking into it and then he's standing outside a hospital room with his wife's name on the wall by the door. "You know, she's dying," a doctor says. "Excuse me? Are you talking to me?" he says, turning to the doctor. "She won't last the night, I'm afraid. Her disease ripped through her like a rocket before we could do anything for her." "I'm sorry, you're not talking about my wife, are you?" "It was that quick, I'm saying, though that's how it often is with what she had. It was, what?—only two weeks ago that she came into my office and I examined her and sent her to Dr. Newcome, the specialist." "You don't expect me to listen to these lies," he says, "do you? First one guy says it's an auto accident, now you're saying it's a disease. Get out of here," and goes inside the room. His wife's on the bed, tubes in her body, a breathing mask over her face. A television's on above the foot of her bed, and he turns it off. He whispers "Sandra?" Then he's at a cemetery, same one his mother and father and younger sister are buried at, holding his daughter's hands and standing in front of an open grave. Some men are about to lower a casket in. A rabbi's mumbling prayers. He says to his older daughter "What are they doing? We had her cremated. Why are we here?" "Shh," she says. "Stay calm, Daddy. Mom will be all right." "But why are they lowering her into the grave? I wanted none of this. I specifically asked for her to be given to science. When you girls insisted she be cremated, after the better parts of her went to science, I went along with it. We were going to bury the box of ashes under a tree we'd plant—a star magnolia, your mommy's favorite—in the island in the circular driveway in front of the house. I have the box of ashes in the car." "The coffin's not for her," his younger daughter says, "but someone else." "Who?" and his older daughter says "She's right, Daddy. Stay calm. It'll all be over in a few minutes and then we can drive home." Then he's home, on his bed, and the phone rings. It's his older daughter. "How are you, Daddy?" "I'm awful. There's no life for me without your mother." "Yes, there is. It'll take time. You have us. You have friends. You have your work. And in the future, you might meet another woman you'll fall in love with." "No, only your mother would put up with me. I'm going outside. Goodbye, my darling." "I love you, Daddy." "I love you too," he says, and hangs up. Then he's in the kitchen and hears noises outside. He goes outside and sees a forklift lowering a coffin into the ground in the place he was going to bury the box of ashes and plant a tree on top of it. "Hey, what're you doing? This is private property, not a cemetery." A man comes over to him and says "Maybe we got the address wrong. Is this 1205 Pacific Drive?" "No, not even close. You're probably a whole continent away." "Oh boy, what a mistake. But don't worry. We'll leave your garden in better shape than we found it," and he blows a whistle and the forklift lifts the coffin out of the ground. "Is there a body in that?" "No, just a tomb," the man says. "'Just a tomb'? What on earth do you mean?" Then he's walking to his neighborhood food market with a dog on a leash. Where'd I get this dog? he thinks. I don't like dogs. I mean, I don't hate them, and when I was a kid I loved them, but I'd never want to own one now. Or even be seen with one. People look ridiculous, walking dogs. Worse. Cleaning up their crap. Their terrible smells and breath and pissing in the house. And their barking, which can go on for hours and bring the neighbors down on me. And if the dog gets loose? Fines, summonses. And if he gets loose again? Double fines, more summonses. This can't be my dog. Then he remembers. His daughters gave it to him as a companion after his wife died. But I don't need companionship or a companion, he thinks. Certainly not a dog. Certainly not something I have to take care of every day and who keeps me from getting away when I want to. I don't want to travel with a dog. I don't want to bathe it or pay for the cost of feeding it or a vet treating it or have it lick my face or start humping my leg or having anything else to do with it. It can't replace my wife. Nothing can. I am destitute for the rest of my life. Not "destitute," but something to do with despair. That's what I am. In that state. "Go, dog, find another owner," he says, and takes the leash off the collar. The dog looks up at him and whines. He gets down on one knee and pets its head and says "I'm letting you go. You're a pretty dog. Some people might even say 'beautiful.' You'll find someone else. And I promise not to put up posters around the neighborhood saying you're lost." The dog licks his hand and runs off. A car speeding on the road—"Hey, you're going too fast," he yells; "55 in a 25"—hits the dog. "Oh, God, what did I do?" he says. "No dog could survive being hit like that," and puts his hands over his face. Then says "You have to face it, so face it now," and walks to what he's sure is a dead dog. The car's backed up to about ten feet of him and the driver says from his window "I'm sorry. But that dog ran right in front of me and should have been leashed. Send me the burial bill," and drives off. "Murderer, killer," he yells at the car, shaking his fist at it. He feels the dog's nose and chest. It's dead. Looks at its genitalia. She is, he thinks. Carries her back to the house, digs a hole in the same area he buried his wife's ashes in, and lays the dog in it and covers her up with dirt. Then he's lying on his bed when the phone rings. "Officer Dunnigan again," a man says. "Is this Mr. Fostrower?" "Otstrower, not Fostrower." "That's what I mean, sir. Anyway, I called to tell you your wife is sorry for all the sadness she's caused you." "She's never caused me any sadness. Oh, once early on in our relationship when she broke up with me when I didn't see it coming. That hit me hard. But we got together a few months later and it was mostly wonderful to glorious after that and with very little sadness from her to me. I'm the one who should apologize to her for the sadness I caused. At times, I could be kind of despicable to her." "Well, that's what she told me to tell you." "When," he says, "before she died? Don't tell me she's alive. No, do tell me. This is the best news I could possibly get," and he wakes up. What a dream, he thinks. Let me see if I can remember all of it so I can tell it to Sandra. He remembers the scenes as they happened. Better write these down, he thinks, before he forgets them. He jots down the highlights of each scene. Thinks he got all of the dream, but what the hell does it mean? She might have insights into it, and he goes to her study with the paper with the dream on it. "Got a moment?" he says. "Sure, what is it? And what do you have there, something you've written you want to show me?" Better not, he thinks. Because would I want to hear someone relate a dream in which I died? Actually, it wouldn't bother me, but this dream might bother her, even though she ends up alive in it, or it seemed she did. "Oh, gosh," he says, "I forgot what I came in here to tell you. And this paper? Has nothing to do with it. I was holding it when I thought to come in to speak with you, and forgot to put it down. I'll remember what it was I wanted to tell you and come back. Or maybe I won't remember. You know me." He goes back to the bedroom, sits at his worktable, puts the paper with the dream on it next to his typewriter, thinks Maybe I can make something out of all this. For instance, how would a character feel if his wife, whom he loves, suddenly dies? He'd be destitute. Not "destitute." God, that's odd, but what is the damn word? As in the dream, something like "despair." If I were the guy, my life would be over. Because how could I live without her? I couldn't. Or maybe I could but only after a long period of despondency. No, it'd be over. Don't write about it now, though. Not in the right mood, or it's not the right time for it, or something. Put the paper away and for the time being forget it. He slips it into the dictionary on the table. Big dictionary too, so it's already lost in it. Someday I might get back to it when I open the dictionary to look up a word and accidentally come across it.

16

Hears the electric motor of the mail truck, looks out his bedroom window and sees the truck stop at his neighbor's mailbox, mailman take some mail out of it, put some in, close the box, pull down its flag, and drive on to his. He goes outside to get the mail. By the time he gets to the mailbox, truck's pulling away. He waves at the driver, but maybe the guy didn't see him, because he usually waves back. He takes the mail out of the box and skims through it as he walks back to the house. Bill, bill, *New York Review of Books*, which his wife started subscribing to before he met her when she was a grad student, medical insurance statement with possibly a check, college alumni magazine for his older daughter, art opening postcard for his younger daughter, several pieces of junk mail and two contribution letters to his wife he'll junk before she sees them—she gives to just about any organization that asks—and a letter from a friend in Boston they've known for twenty-five years but only see in Maine with his wife a few times every summer. Three times, to be exact, unless they run into them in two of the main towns in the area—and Hank and Elsa are always together—at places like the Saturday farmer's market in Blue Hill or the Sunday afternoon chamber music concerts there or the movie theater in Ellsworth that mostly shows foreign films. Envelope's thick, he thinks, or thicker than just a one- or two-page letter. Could be the photos Hank took of them in his house last summer. He's been sending them for around twenty years, and if their daughters were with them, which they always were till about seven years ago when they started going on bicycle tours or to Europe together or to CTY camp and then working at these camps or in Baltimore, then one of each of them too. Hank usually took the photos inside when they were having drinks before dinner. Though the two most memorable photos, which Meyer framed and hung in the bedroom, are of his daughters flying, or of the younger one—she was not quite two then—trying to fly balsa wood gliders Hank and Elsa had given them and helped them assemble. They always invite Hank and Elsa to their rented house for dinner a week after they get up. Several weeks later they'd be invited for dinner at their house in a beautiful isolated spot overlooking the water, half hour's drive from their place. And end of August, last week of their stay, they'd all meet for lunch at a French restaurant in Blue Hill. Hank and Elsa, retired college teachers, stay through October, when it gets too cold for them. Their house isn't insulated and two of the rooms aren't even electrified; they use candles and kerosene lamps for light in these rooms and fireplaces for heat. Goes into the kitchen, junks the junk mail and contribution letters into the paper-recycling bag by the trash container, puts the other mail but Hank's on a counter. "Letter from Hank Messer," he says to his wife, who's in her study. "I bet it's his annual summer photos." "We got those a couple of months ago," she says. "We did? And I saw them?" "You showed them to me and then put them away someplace." "Then they're probably lost forever, for I've no recollection of them. What were they of?" "You holding a martini glass and looking as if you didn't want to be photographed. Me looking equally uneasy, but also ugly." "Nonsense. What this one could be about, I don't know. News, most likely." "Since when does he write us anything other than the holiday greetings that come with the photos?" she says. "But show it to me later. I'm in the middle of something, sweetheart." Goes into the living room and opens the envelope. A letter—he can see it's typewritten through the folded-up sheet of paper—and what looks like a photocopy of a newspaper article. His wife's wrong; Hank's sent them a couple of letters or notes, other than with the photos. One: "Caught this in our paper. Thought your publisher might not have sent it to you or is taking its sweet time, as they're prone to do"—and included a photocopy of a review of Meyer's last book. Another time it was an article where one of Meyer's books was mentioned. But it wouldn't be either of those, because why would he want to keep the original? He'd just cut it out of the paper as he did before and send it. It could be an obituary. Thinks that because something like it happened twenty-three years ago. Knows it was twenty-three because it was several months after he and Sandra got married—Janet and Leon had flown down from Maine for the wedding—and Sandra was pregnant with their first child. She was teaching in New York and living in their apartment, he was teaching in Baltimore and lived half the week there. He trained to New York every Thursday afternoon after his last class of the week, returned Monday by noon in time for his first class. He got a letter from "Mrs. Leon Brownstien," the return address said. Odd, he thought. Before then, the return address had always been "Mr. and Mrs. Leon Brownstien." Looks again at the envelope Hank's letter came in. Just "Hank Messer" and the return address, written in ink. Before, he thinks it was always a printed return address tab that said "Mr. and Mrs. Henry Messer." Janet's envelope was also thick. Didn't know what it could be. And why would she be writing him? Sandra's the one who first became friendly with them, and she and Janet exchanged letters a few times a year. They had a summer home on the same Penobscot Bay peninsula Meyer and Sandra rented a cottage on then. A big place, not especially attractive, furnished like the interior of a huge expensive yacht, he said— Sandra thought that inaccurate and a bit mean—but right on the water instead of just overlooking it, with a private cove and dock, and winterized: They'd go there for a weekend or week in the coldest months. Their married kids and married grandchildren now spend summers in it. Maybe, he thought, it's a letter with some news of the area she thought he'd find interesting, or which he could use in his writing, or an ad for a house they might look into buying. She knew they wanted to buy a small simple place on or overlooking the ocean or bay on the same peninsula their cottage was, but something affordable for them because they didn't have much money and couldn't borrow much from her folks or the bank. But that couldn't be it, he thought, because again, why would she send it to him? He opened the envelope and first thing he pulled out was an obituary of Leon. One of two, the other being in the weekly that covered much of that Bay area. The *Bangor Times* obituary was long and had a photo of him; Leon was a prominent businessman and philanthropist there and was once mayor of the city. Died at sixty-one. Heart attack. Janet's letter said something like "I felt this was the best way to tell you and Sandra. I would have sent this directly to her, but because she's pregnant, I didn't want to startle her, and thought the news would be easier on her coming from you." How'd she get his address? he later thought. He could never figure it out, and didn't ask her the following summer. Now he thinks she could have got it from the real estate agent Leon had fixed them up with, who around that time was sending him listings of houses for sale. He called Sandra a half hour after he opened Janet's letter—took him that long to get over the shock of Leon's death. A year later, Janet's older daughter told Sandra that her mother had died of a stroke a few days before. She was also sixty-one. Sandra became good friends with the daughter, and now they regularly e-mail each other. The way she met the family is interesting. She'd gone to the peninsula to spend a week with her doctoral advisor and his family.

They also had a house and dock on the shore, but on the bay side, the Brownstiens' was on the ocean, and did a lot of sailing. Leon had a thirty- or forty-foot motorboat that he rarely used. She liked the area so much that she contacted local real estate agencies to see if there was anything within her means on the peninsula or closeby that she could rent for the rest of July and all of August. There wasn't, so she drove along the peninsula road to the point to stop and ask several locals if they knew of a place to rent. The gas station owner, who was also a farmer and the caretaker of the small cemetery next to his station, said that the Brownstiens were tucked away at the end of a side road near the point and had a guesthouse next to their main house they might want to rent. She knocked on their door and they immediately took a shine to her, as Leon said. One reason, she thought, was because it was obvious by her last name she was Jewish—maybe the same reason the gas station owner sent her to them—and the Brownstiens were the only Jews on this six-mile-long peninsula. They invited her in for coffee, said their kids come up throughout the summer and stay in the guesthouse with their families, otherwise they'd rent it to her, and told her of a cottage with shore property on the peninsula that hadn't been lived in since the original owner, a Nobel laureate in physics, died ten years ago chopping wood for the cookstove in his cottage. It was now owned by the man's nephew, who was a bit of an eccentric, they said. He summered with his elderly mother and six Chihuahuas in a much larger but equally beautiful house down the same road. They seemed to be well off, so he might agree to rent the cottage cheap just to keep it from deteriorating and being vandalized further, if she didn't mind putting some work into cleaning it up and bringing in electricity again and getting the water pump working and clearing some of the grounds. She rented it for very little money, fixed it up, planted a garden, rented it the next two summers, met Meyer and they rented it together for six summers before it was sold for a price they would have by then been able to afford if they hadn't just bought a small simple house in Baltimore. He goes into Sandra's study—she looks up and says "What's wrong? You look like something bad's happened"—and tells her about Elsa. "Oh, dear," she says, and starts crying. "What a wonderful person, what a terrible loss, and they were so close, one never went anywhere without the other. What will Hank do now? And it comes just the way we heard about Leon, and both good friends from Maine," and he says "Just what I thought—all of it—when I opened the letter and saw what was inside."

17

Goes into the kitchen. What'd he come in here for? he thinks. Something; forgot. Starts to leave the kitchen, when he remembers: carrot. Likes to chomp on one or a celery stalk when he's frustrated about something or needs to take a break to think about something he's working on. Turns around to open the refrigerator to get a carrot, or maybe a celery stalk, and notices how dirty the counter near the refrigerator is. Crumbs and such. Touches the counter; greasy. Touches the other counters; same. And the floor. Pieces of things, scuff marks, food and beverage stains, pine needles from outside, Kibble around the cat's dish. Sink, too. Hasn't been cleaned in days, and the cleaning woman, who really knows how to do it, was here last week. Needs a good scouring, not just water sprayed on it and washed down with a sponge, where he collects all the scraps in the sink stopper and dumps them. Entire kitchen needs a cleaning. He's got time; nothing that he's doing now that can't wait, and often good ideas come to him when he's doing something else. He'll get the carrot or celery after he's done, although celery is what he now thinks he wants. Sprinkles cleanser into the sink. When he cleans the kitchen he always starts with the sink. Doesn't know why. But there must be a reason. Maybe because... well, to get the easiest part of the cleaning out of the way. He certainly can't clean it after he cleans the floor. Floor would be wet and he'd just track it up. So why does he do it before he cleans the counters? Doesn't know; habit. Or doesn't know for sure. He gets the scrubbing pad from the soap dish. While he's at it, clean the soap dish, he thinks. There are pieces of food on it and old soap water in the dish. Cleans it with running water and the scrubbing pad. Then sprinkles more cleanser into the sink because the water washed most of it away, and scrubs the sink till it's clean. Not as clean as the cleaning woman gets it, though she's told him her method. Practically covers the sink with cleanser, comes back to it half an hour later and scrubs the cleanser away. But he hasn't the time for that. He gets from the cabinet under the sink the household cleaner and the quart jar he uses for his water-household cleaner mix and pours about two inches of the cleaner into the jar and starts filling it up with warm water. Damn, forgot again what he told himself to do after the last few times he made this mix: put water in first and leave a few inches at the top for the cleaner. That way he gets a full jar of the mix. Putting the cleanser in first and then adding water creates a lot of bubbles, and he can only get half the jar filled with water before the bubbles start pouring out. Remember next time, but really remember: water first, then cleaner. Water, cleaner. Waits half a minute for the bubbles to subside and then tilts the jar against the tap and slowly adds water. "What are you doing," his wife says from her study, "cleaning the whole house?" and he says "Why would you think that? Just the kitchen. I'll close your door so the smells don't get to you." "You don't have to. I don't mind them. I even like the one you're using, lemon," and he says "No, they can get too strong and might disturb your work; they would mine," and shuts her door. He really shut the door because he didn't want her to see him on his knees cleaning the floor when he gets around to it. Got the jar three-quarters filled before the bubbles started pouring out. Forget it, just use what you have, he thinks, and spills some of the mix on each counter and the stove. Gets the dishtowel off the refrigerator door handle and wipes the counter to the left of the refrigerator—he always starts there and works his way counterclockwise to the dishrack mat, cleans that and the counter under it, then the area around the sink, next the short counter between the sink and stove, and finally the stove, front and top. If his wife saw him—another reason he shut the door—she'd ask why he's using a good dishtowel for that? "As I told you a couple of times, even after it's washed in the washing machine, it still stinks from the disinfectant." Last time she said it, he said "You're only imagining it smells from it," but he knows she's right. Since he uses two clean dishtowels to dry his washed salad—one below, other on top, then pats the top one and rolls the towels up with the salad inside—he should use rags for the cleaning mix. Too late; next time. Rags instead of towels. And it's not he forgot what she said. Just it would have meant knocking on her door, going into her study and opening the door there to the stairs leading to the unfinished attic, place he's been to only twice: when they were looking at the house to buy it twelve years ago and she asked him to see what was up there; she didn't want to, for you had to push open a trap door at the top of the stairs to get to it and then crawl around, as there isn't enough room to stand up; and when there suddenly was water coming through the dining and living room ceilings in several places a few years back, which turned out to be caused by ice jams on the roof, or dams, he thinks they're called. So these stairs used only for storing things: window screens, multipacks of paper towels, light bulbs, laundry detergent, cleaning supplies the cleaning woman uses. Anyway, wants to get the job over with fast as he can. Wipes down all the counters with the dishtowel. Then the stove, and with the now-soaked towel, washing machine and dryer. He doesn't always clean the washing machine and dryer when he's cleaning the counters and stove. Usually too many things on them: mail to go, mail that came, newspapers, books, magazines, and always the radio on the dryer, and they just don't get that dirty. Now the floor, the hardest part, partly because of the preparations. Puts the cat's water and food bowls on a counter and the recycling bag of paper on the trash container. Trash container; forgot to clean that, and wipes the lid and sides of it with the towel and puts the towel into the washing machine and the bag back on the container.

Sweeps the floor and wonders what he's going to wipe it with. Wife
hasn't complained so far about the cleaning-mix smell on their bath
towels, which are the best things to use—big and thick—so one or
two of those if any are in the washer. Except for their sheets and
pillowcases, which they wash every other week on the day the
cleaning women comes so she can make the bed—she does it much
better than either of them—and which practically take up a wash
alone, they throw clothes and towels and such into the washer over
a period of two to three days and only put detergent in and start it
when it's full or beginning to smell. Opens the washer. No towels
inside; just clothes, cloth napkins and the dishtowel. Not going to
use the napkins—too thin, and like face towels, his wife would
probably smell the cleaning mix when she held them up to her
face—and dishtowel's too soaked and thin. Takes out two of his
long-sleeve T-shirts and a flannel undershorts and two pairs of
cotton socks. Runs more water into the jar and splashes half of it on
the floor. Gets on his knees with the shirts in one hand and shorts
and socks in the other and starts cleaning the floor with them, both
hands sometimes wiping at once as he goes around the room. First
around the refrigerator, then the small space between the refrigerator
and cabinet where the cat's bowls were. Then around the study
door, trash container—should have brought it into the dining
room, but was on his knees when he thought of it and didn't want
to get up and then down again—dishwasher, sink, stove and kitchen
door. Then he cleans the center of the room and backs his way to
the dining room entrance on the other side of the refrigerator,

making sure to get a part of the shirt an inch or two under the dryer and washer, as he did with the refrigerator, and a little ways into the narrow spaces between the dryer and washer and washer and wall, where they keep the broom and dustpan and detergent, before he backs himself out of the room. Stands. Knees hurt from being on them so long, especially the right one, which has become sort of soft and lumpy in the last two years. Meant to ask his doctor, at his annual checkup couple of months ago, what it was, but forgot to, though doesn't think it's anything serious. Forty years of running two to three miles a day, probably, which he gave up entirely last year because he was told it was making the arthritis in his legs worse. Anyway, good, kitchen's clean, he thinks, dropping without stepping into the room, the shirts, shorts and socks into the washer, and then putting detergent in and starting it, even if it isn't full. Doesn't want his wife coming in and opening the washer and seeing the wet dishtowel and possibly the cloth napkins now wet from the dishtowel and his soaked clothes. How could he explain it? "I started to use the towel, immediately knew it was wrong and not what you wanted me to do, but then figured, hell, cleaning mix is already on the towel, so finish wiping the counters with it. As for the napkins, I was too dumb not to think they could get wet too, although they can't be that wet and I didn't use them to clean anything. But last time, I promise. From now on, just cleaning rags." He goes into the bedroom, sits in front of his typewriter, but he really doesn't feel like writing—doesn't know why, but recognizes the feeling—so doesn't even take the typewriter cover off. Stays there another minute just to give it a chance. Nothing. Kitchen floor must be dry now, he thinks, so he goes into the kitchen, puts the paper recycling bag on the floor next to the trash container and the cat's bowls on the floor in the same lineup he found them. The carrot; or celery. Either. First one he sees he'll eat. Opens the refrigerator. Five-pound bag of organic carrots he bought the other day is on the bottom shelf—too big to fit in the vegetable bin. Doesn't see the celery—must be in the bin—and tears a hole in the carrot bag without removing it from the shelf, takes a carrot out, washes it and bites off a piece. Thinks: Should have told his wife not to come out while the floor was wet. Or did he? Anyway, she didn't come out, unless she did when he was in back. Doesn't think so. No tracks, although she might have wiped them up. Knocks on the study door. "Yes?" she says, and he says "Floor's dry now, so you can come out anytime you want." "Thanks." He goes into the living room, sits in the Morris chair, turns on the floor lamp, takes his book off the side table and reads while he eats the carrot. Few minutes later his wife yells from the kitchen or study "Oh, no," and he yells from the chair "What is it?" "Don't come into the kitchen. You're going to be very mad. You cleaned it so nicely and I dropped a carton of grapefruit juice on the counter and half of it went on the floor." Thinks: Don't get mad. You get mad every time something like this happens, but this time don't. It's just grapefruit juice. Surprise her. Even say that. "It's just grapefruit juice. Don't worry, I'll clean it up." Goes into the kitchen and sees juice on the counter near the toaster—did he get under the toaster with the dishtowel?

He didn't, and there are always crumbs there, but will this time—and a lot of it on the floor. No juice carton, so she must have put it back in the refrigerator. "Quite the mess," he says, "but it's all right. It'll just take a couple of rags to wipe it up and then some of the cleaner. So more than a couple of rags, but that's what the washing machine's for. And if I clean it up quickly I can get the rags in the load I'm doing now." "You can shut the washer off and restart it when the rags are in." "Good thinking," he says, and presses the knob to shut the washer off. "Anyway, it isn't a problem." "Actually," she says, "isn't it a bit late in the washing cycle to put dirty rags in?" "You're right," and turns the washer back on. "I'll help you clean up," she says, and he says "No, go back to your work." "You must have really worked on yourself to exert such self-control over your anger." "No, I didn't." "You've got to be lying." "No, I'm not."

18

Says to his wife "I'm going to the health food store," and she says "What are you getting?" "Oh, a number of things. Need anything?" and she says "Package of salt-free rice cakes, please. I'm all out." "Will do," and he goes. Store's about three miles away. There's a cheaper health food store, where he could save himself five or more dollars on what he's planning to buy, but it's about eight miles away. Figured once: ten more miles roundtrip and gas now two-thirty a gallon: that's more than a buck extra spent right there. It's also the extra time it takes driving there. And this one he gets through quickly: It's one-fifth the size of the other and there are usually two cashiers, or one cashier and a bagger, and no line. Besides, this one gives a ten-percent senior citizen discount on Wednesdays, so he could end up spending less than he would at the larger store. Gets there, parks in front—another plus; the bigger store has a large parking lot but he's never been able to find a space this close—and gets what he wants: vegetarian chicken salad, three packages each of tofu turkey and cheese slices, tempeh burgers, which are on sale—store doesn't give the discount on sales items—tofu, meatless Italian sausages, collard greens, which both he and his wife like and he uses the broth from it in his miso soup—apricots—a good deal on them: two-fifteen a pound—two kinds of seaweed, quinoa fettucine, several kinds of grains and nuts and a rain-forest mix and adzuki beans, which he had to fill from bins and write the bin number on a white sticker and stick it on each bag—kukicha teabags for his wife, and also wheat- and gluten-free cookies and biscotti for her. Heads to the checkout counter. Soy yogurt, and he goes back for it and while there gets an imitation cream cheese and goes to the checkout counter. No customers there and no one at the register, so he says fairly loud "Anyone handling checkout?" A voice from somewhere in the store he can't see says "Be right there." When the man comes, a young guy who's taken care of him a number of times, and gets behind the counter, Meyer says "Senior citizen discount," and starts unloading his basket. "That's Wednesday," the man says. "Today's Thursday." "No, what are you talking? Today's Wednesday." Man looks at his watch. "Thursday." "Jesus, where'd the day go?" and the man says "Don't ask me." "I can't believe it. You sure? I could've sworn I read the dateline of today's newspaper—not the dateline; that's something else in the paper—but the top of the front page where today's date is," and the man says "Believe me, it's Thursday. How are you doing, by the way?" and he says "Fine, thanks, you?" and the man nods and starts ringing him up. Wonders should he take back some of the more expensive items—both seaweeds, for instance; too late for the miso; and the biscotti; the cookies will be enough—and get them the next Wednesday he comes, because he almost always shops here on a Wednesday because of the discount? Ah, once in your life don't be such a cheapo, he thinks. "But Thursday. I still can't believe it's today," and the man says "All day." "That's what my father used to say. Same expression. I'd say to him 'Today's Thursday?' or whatever day it was, and he'd say 'All day.' Where'd you hear it? I mean you're much younger than I, so from your father, who might have heard it from his father, or straight from one of your grandparents?" and the man says "No, they never said it. It just came into my head. I guess you can say, even if it might have been around pretty commonly once, that I made it up. Paper okay with you? They've handles on them now," and he says "Paper's fine." Pays, leaves, gets in the car and starts home. "Damn, forgot the rice cakes," he says. But I don't want to go back, he thinks. And I've other things for her she didn't ask me to get but I know she likes. Chocolate chip cookies and biscotti she can eat and kukicha tea. That one is at least 50 cents cheaper in the other store. Then: But where'd that damn Wednesday go? Start back. No, go a few days back and then work forward. Saturday. Gym, some writing, did all his reading for his Monday and Tuesday classes, went to the liquor store for vodka and dry vermouth, since he was almost out of both and the store would be closed Sunday. That night they went to a concert at the symphony hall, and after it, to a restaurant for some light food and a glass of wine; he had two. Sunday, they did what? Again, lots of things. Took a walk together in the neighborhood. He read a lot, newspapers and a book, and lit a fire that took a long time to get started. Wood was wet. Rented a movie she wanted to see, and they haven't seen it yet. Has to find out if it's a two- or seven-day rental and say to her when he gets home "Let's see the movie tonight or give it up for the time being and I'll drop it off tomorrow." Probably spoke by phone with the kids, which they try to do every second of third day. He got Chinese takeout, which they also had—he always gets one or two dishes more than they can eat in one sitting—the next night. Monday and Tuesday he taught and had office hours. Remembers driving home from school Tuesday and thinking he should go to the health food store the next day because they were out of several things. And next day would be Wednesday, which he thought was today. So what'd he do Wednesday? Went to the gym before his wife woke up, but he did that Saturday through today. No doubt wrote, which he tries to do every day between nine and twelve unless he's bogged down with schoolwork. Can't think of anything he did Wednesday that sets apart that day. Food? Monday they had Chinese leftovers and he made a spicy cole slaw to go with it. Tuesday he got fish because his wife said that's what she'd like that night—"In fact, I'd like to have a fresh white fish like flounder or sole two to three times a week and maybe not Chinese takeout so often. I'm getting tired of it." Wednesday. Can't think what they had. Fish leftovers? No, they finished it. He remembers saying, when he was collecting the dirty dishes, "Boy, you really liked it." A salad to go with whatever they had—and it couldn't have been any kind of takeout because they only get it about once every other week—but one big enough that he can have the rest of it for lunch the next day. But what else Wednesday? Doesn't remember. And his wife, like him, does almost the same thing every day: works on her book and articles in her study, but from around ten to four or five, since she doesn't teach this semester, and breaks it up two to three times a day with a short run or long walk or to go to the market or drugstore or their school's library or a bookstore. Wednesday, he thinks, Wednesday. He had to have done something that day that he didn't do on any of the others. And if today is Thursday, it means he has to hold individual tutorials with some of his grad students tomorrow when he thought he'd be free. Plans have to be changed. He always rereads the grad students' manuscripts that'll be discussed, so he'll do that tonight instead of tomorrow. He was going to go to Target tomorrow afternoon to get bulk supplies of things they're short of: toilet paper, paper towels, trash bags, and a few other thing he has on a list somewhere, and two long-sleeve T-shirts; all of his are old and have little holes in them or are frayed. He'll put that off till Saturday, or next Wednesday because the store and its parking lot are so crowded on Saturday. It still, though, feels as if he taught yesterday, drove back from school, told himself in the car to go to the health food store the next day, picked up fish and some other things at the market, read the *Times* before dinner while having two martinis—something, the drinks, he always does unless they're going out or he has to drive that night—and made dinner. But if yesterday was Wednesday, then he still can't think what they had for dinner other than a salad. Fish again? No, he knows they didn't have it two days in a row. Tofu and veggie dish? Something from the freezer? Did he open a new bottle of wine? No, they've been drinking the same 1.5 liter bottle of Zinfandel since Sunday, when he remembers opening it just before he put the Chinese takeout on the table. Wife asked for saki and he said they were all out and he forgot to get some when he was at the liquor store the day before. So maybe the health food store guy was wrong. His watch might have been a day off. Or he was saying it was Thursday to stop him from taking advantage of the discount. But he seems like a nice guy, and he wouldn't do that on his own. Storeowner or the manager told him to? Nah, some of the older customers would get wise to it after a while and stop coming to the store. But if today's newspaper at home does say it's Wednesday, he's driving back with it and the store's sales slip—it's in one of the two shopping bags, or did he stick it in his wallet when he took back his credit card? Card he knows he has. That's the thing he's most afraid of losing, other than the whole wallet, so he says the same thing to himself every time he uses it: "Keep your eye on the card." Or he'll call the store—the phone number will be on the slip—and say to whomever answers "The young man at the checkout counter made a mistake with my bill before and I didn't get my senior citizen discount. Today's Wednesday, when he said it was Thursday. Maybe his watch was wrong." He won't say the last. But he will say he thinks he deserves to be reimbursed ten percent of all the items he bought that weren't on sale and that they can deal with it next time he's in the store if he remembers to save today's sales slip. Won't say the last either. Gets home, sets the bags down and looks at the newspaper on the dryer. Thursday, and the sales slip, he now realizes, probably has the date on it too. Looks in both bags for it. Not there. It's in his wallet, wrapped around the credit card, which he doesn't remember doing. Looks at it; no date. Just item by item and the total. Says to his wife as he starts unloading the bags "A funny thing happened at the health food store. Well, I don't know about 'funny,' but certainly odd. I was convinced today was Wednesday—that's the only day they give the senior citizen discount, which, naturally, I take if I happen to be there that day—and I thought about it all the way home and still don't know where the day could have gone, because I've no memory of it." "You know what my father used to say," she says, and he says "Interesting you say that. Because the cashier at the store said something my father used to say." "What was that?" and he says "No, you first; I interrupted you." "He used to say, when I'd say something like, 'I don't know where the time went,' 'Look in your pocket, it might be there.' He was teasing me, of course. He was never sarcastic or critical of me. What did your father used to say?" "I don't know if I can get it right, but I'd ask him what day is today and he'd say, for my story's sake, 'Thursday,' and I'd say 'Today's Thursday?'—I was a little kid, you understand— and he'd say 'All day.' He said it over and over again, which is how I'm able to remember it so many years later. I thought it curious that this cashier said the exact same thing to the exact same question today, although he said he'd never heard the line before or had ever used it. Oh, I forgot your rice cakes, I'm sorry, but I did get you a box of kukicha teabags and gluten- and wheat-free cookies and biscotti." "Thanks."

19

Says to his wife "Today's the birthday of someone I know, but I don't know who." "Someone in the family?" she says, and he says "Maybe, or a friend. I know it's not anyone well known—a literary or historical figure, or in music or anything like that. I only thought of it when I saw today's date in the paper: three-three. That's how I used to remember this person's birthday, so it's more than likely someone I knew for a while but haven't been in contact with for years. It feels like long ago, is what I'm saying." "One of your old girlfriends?" and he says "Rebecca's was also in March, the twenty-first, the first day of spring, which is how I still remember it, or the day that's usually the first day of spring. And Adele, the one I lived with later in New York—but you know all about her; I don't have to tell you—hers I forget, although I know it was around Christmas, since she said she always got shortchanged on gifts as a kid because her birthday and the holiday were so close. And it's not my niece or nephew either. One of them—I think Charlotte—is April first, another easy one to remember. And the other one has the same birthday as their mother, which is in August—the eighteenth or nineteenth; I always forget which, and it could even be some other teen day in August close to those. Good thing my sister's not sensitive about it when I call to wish her a happy birthday on the wrong day. I'll get it, but you know how these things torment me— trying to remember a name or book title or the definition of a word, when it's right there, sitting on my tongue." He goes into the living room and sits in his reading chair and says to himself "As a test to prove your memory's not completely going, think whose birthday it could be." Runs through the alphabet till W. No name comes. Goes over the names of the several good friends he's had. But he never knew the birthdates of his adult male friends. A close friend when he was a boy? Doesn't think it's that far back. Women, then. Did Adele and Rebecca. Marilyn. Doesn't think they celebrated it, short time she moved in with him, though she must have told him it or he must have asked. People always know the age and birth date of the person they're living with. Lily's was the same month as his, but somewhere at the front of the month. Anyway, they never lived together and she said she hated birthdays and the infantilism, she called it, of making a big deal over them, and the idiocy, another quote, of people being anxious at entering a new decade when they've already been in it a year. Forgot Karla. Her son, that's it. Ryan wasn't even three when Meyer met her, so maybe another reason for the three business. Week or so after he moved into her house, he helped set up her enclosed porch for Ryan's first birthday party. Should he call him? It's been more than eight years since they spoke, when Ryan called him on his sixtieth birthday. Ryan was working as an investment counselor or financial advisor—whatever they're called, but making lots of money, he said—and still living in Sunnyvale, a few streets from his mother. Took down his address and phone number and put them in his address book and transferred them to his new address book a few years later. Promised, in that last phone conversation, to stay in touch by letter and phone. Last time he saw him was in '77, when Ryan was... met Karla in '65, so he was fifteen then and is forty-three today. He was in San Francisco, not on a book tour but to sit at a table at the ABA convention with the husband and wife owners of the small press that was publishing his first novel that month. They went halves with him on his airfare, put all his dinners on their bill, and he slept on a cot in their hotel room. Their table was on a balcony overlooking the main convention floor, not many booksellers stopped at it to meet the author and have him sign a free copy of his book, which was the reason for his being there and to man the table when the owners went to lunch, but they did get a few orders for his novel and a couple of their other books. No, last time he saw Ryan was in '78, summer before he met Sandra. Ryan had called him and said "You said you'd come out to see me in a year and you're breaking your promise again. Please come, please, and I'll never ask you again." He said "Put your mother on," and said to her "Why's the kid so dependent on me?" and she said "Because his real father has nothing to do with him or treats him like dirt." "I don't want to hurt him and I would like to see him, but it's expensive, the flight and staying there, and I'm just about broke." She said "He'll be heartbroken if you don't come. He's been talking of your visit for the past year. And we can pick you up at the San Jose airport and you can stay with us if you want. Borrow from your mother. She must have a little stashed away, and you're her flawless son. And you can have the guestroom instead of the couch, as my lodger disappeared last week owing me two months' rent." He thought staying with them means he can sleep with her, since she also said she'd busted up with her boyfriend a while back so it was now only Ryan and she in the house. That's what he did the one night he was there last year, and it's been months since he slept with anyone and their sex was always good. So he flew out, knew he wouldn't have if it was just to see Ryan, slept with her for a week but always left her bedroom for the guestroom early in the morning so Ryan wouldn't think he came out mainly to sleep with his mom. When he left he said to him "If I can, and I make no promises, since I don't know what my circumstances will be and I might even be more strapped for cash than I am now, I'll try to come out next year around this time," and Ryan said "I understand; just so long as we talk on the phone or write." Dials the number in his address book, a man says "Yes?" and he says "Is this still Ryan Hansell's number?" and the man says no. Dials Information for a Ryan Hansell in Sunnyvale and then anyplace in Santa Clara County or the Bay area. None. Maybe

Karla's still living in Sunnyvale or around there, he thinks. Her number he probably had in the old address book but didn't transfer to the new one. Dials Information, gets her number, thinks Does he really want to speak to her after all these years? Goes to the study door and says "Knock knock? Excuse me, but it's Ryan's birthday, the three-three," and she says "Who?" "Karla's son… the woman I lived with in California for more than three years, and Ryan, who I was the surrogate father for all that time. Read to him before sleep, taught him how to read and play sports… did everything a father would; picked him up after nursery and then kindergarten, and so on," and she says "I remember now. You haven't spoken of them in a long time." "And I thought—tell me what you think of this idea—I'd call to wish him a happy birthday, or not so much that but to reciprocate the call he made to me on my sixtieth birthday. Do you remember when he did that?" and she says "No, but I'm sure he'd appreciate your call." "The problem is, I don't have his number and can't get it from Information. Karla's I have—she's still in the same house—but that'd mean speaking to her, unless Ryan's living with her or visiting her at the time of the call and picks up the phone. Chances of either are slight." "I don't see the problem. If she had any lingering bad feelings to you over something, I'm sure she's forgotten them by now. Just call and ask for his number. It's that simple. 'Hello, how are you? Today's Ryan's birthday' and you'd like to call him but don't have his number." "Maybe you're right. Thanks." Goes into their bedroom and dials Karla's number. She says hello and he says "Hi, a voice from the past," and she says

"What do you want?" "First, how are you?" and she says "I said what do you want?" "Today's Ryan's birthday. Forty-three. Can't believe he wasn't even three when I first saw him. I thought I'd get his phone number from you—I lost my address book with his number and had no success getting it from Information—and I'd call him to wish him a happy birthday." "He died four years ago. Car accident," and hangs up. "What?" he says. "Oh, my goodness." Wait a minute, he thinks. It can't be. He would have heard about it, and calls back. "I knew you'd call back," she says. "What is it this time? The news I gave wasn't bad enough? You want details? I'm not giving them." "Look, I don't mean to be disrespectful, but I just can't believe Ryan could have died. Someone would have told me. Kirt. He always sends me a Christmas card with a note on what's happening with him and his family and sometimes that he's seen Ryan or you at some Bay area event. If something had happened to Ryan, he would have told me." "It's not something you put in a Christmas card. Besides, I specifically asked him not to say anything to you about it." "Why?" and she says "I have my reasons which I don't think I have to divulge to you. But I'll tell you anyway. One is that you haven't been part of this family for thirty-five years, so you've no right to know. Two, you made no attempt, outside of that brief visit long ago, which he had to plead with you to do, to stay in touch with him. If you don't think that hurt him, you're greatly mistaken." "Karla, I'm so sorry; so sorry for everything. What a wonderful boy," and she says "I know," and hangs up. Now he doesn't know what to think. The way she said it, matter-of-factly, not bitterly, an accident, told Kirt not to tell him—it all could make sense. And she knows he's going to call Kirt right away to ask if Ryan's dead… she'd go through such an elaborate life just to make him feel horrible for a few minutes? Calls Kirt. Gets his wife and she says "He's out; I'll have him call you," and he says "Actually, what I'm calling about, you'd know as much as he. I just spoke to Karla and she said Ryan's dead. Car accident four years ago." "What is she talking about? Though I know what she means. Ryan, about four years ago, married a very sweet much younger woman whom Karla hates. The woman has her flaws; extremely religious, in the fundamentalist sense. Doesn't drink, swear or read dirty books. Nothing but the Bible and her religious newspapers and magazines. Karla thinks the girl's a perfect square, dull and uptight and also conniving and manipulative as can be, and tried convincing Ryan that marrying somebody so unsuitable for him would be a disaster. She said she wouldn't go to the wedding or have the bride in her house. She'd rant on about her to Ryan every chance she got and wouldn't let up even after they were married. Ryan finally had to tell her he was cutting himself off from her till she stopped insulting his wife. That was about two years ago. Soon after that, Ryan and his wife moved to Oregon—mostly, I think, to be away from Karla—and she hasn't seen or heard from him since." "Good, he's alive," he says; "what a relief. Do you have his phone number or know what city or town he's in so I can get it from Information? It's his birthday today and I'd like to call him." "No idea, and I know Kirt doesn't either. Ryan got an unlisted number so Karla wouldn't be able to call him, or that's Kirt's interpretation. I'm sure, though, Karla knows the name of the girl's parents and where they live, and you can get him that way." Goes into his wife's study and says "You wouldn't believe what I've just been through." She turns around in her chair to him and says "What's wrong? You've been crying," and he says "Have I? I didn't know. It's Karla. She told me Ryan was dead when he wasn't. How can anybody hate me so much?"

20

"Says to his wife "Like a tea or Yanno? I'm boiling water," and she says "No, thanks, but thanks for asking," and kisses him on the lips and goes into her study. What a doll, he thinks. Boy, was I lucky. Beauty, brains, a great body, a wonderful person and mother, and she loves making love. Water boils, he gets a Prince of Wales teabag, then thinks Why not green tea? It's healthier. Or maybe it isn't; the caffeinated tea's supposed to do some good for the body too. Anyway, it seems healthier. Drops the green-tea bag into the mug of boiled water and goes out to the glassed-in porch with it. It's cold, and he turns on the electric radiator—it'll take a good ten minutes before the porch warms up—and sits in the comfortable chair there. Should he get his jacket? Ah, the tea will warm him. Sipping the tea and looking out the porch at a passing car, he thinks Suppose he first met his wife when she was the age she was when he first met her and he was the age he is now? Interesting idea. How would it go?

It's at a party similar to the one in a Washington Square row house where he really did first meet her. She came with a man, he came alone. Is he married? No, he never married or had kids. He was engaged several times, even came within a few weeks of getting married, but the women all broke it off. Why? One decided they were too young to get married; they hadn't experienced enough on their own yet. Another didn't think he could provide for them if they had a baby, which she wanted, and she had to take time off. Another didn't think he loved her enough, and another said she suddenly realized she didn't love him enough to marry him. Another bumped into the man she was engaged to years earlier and fell in love with him again. Five times. A lot. Makes him wonder if he ever really did want to get married. He did, at least twice, judging by how hurt he was after they dumped him. Does he regret now never getting married and having a kid? Yes. If he could, he'd have a kid now, despite his age, in or out of marriage, but preferably in. He's healthy, active, more like hyperactive, energetic, works out, loves sex, looks, most people say when they learn his age, ten to fifteen years younger than he is. "Good genes," he always says, but thinks it's also because he never smoked, stays out of the sun, watches his weight, has all his hair and keeps himself in shape. Sees her sitting in the living room talking to someone. A woman closer to his age. He's attracted to her, looks at her. Stares, really. She catches him staring, which is what he wants: to show his interest in her. Is he making a fool of himself? Sort of. But there's a chance something will come of it. Is there? A slight chance, perhaps very slight. She smiles, he smiles. She goes back to her conversation with the woman. Could it be she's interested in him, too? No, just curious why he stared at her. Lovely looks, nice body from what he can see of it, beautiful smile, intelligent face. But everyone at the party is intelligent. Everyone he's talked to so far. It's that kind of crowd. Host is a writer and book reviewer for *Newsweek*, and at the art colony he met her at this summer was writing a book on Isaac Babel. A biography. There still hasn't been one written in or translated into English, she said. She's the magazine's Russian expert and does all the book reviews of Slavic writers and writes long articles on things about Russia and the former Soviet Union. They had rooms next to each other, shared a bathroom "and soap dish," he liked to say, and became friends. So far tonight he's talked to a successful Russian émigré painter, a well-known Czech novelist, several American writers and academics and a filmmaker and their wives and husbands and women and men friends. All were intelligent and articulate. Woman he's interested in stands up, shakes hands with the woman she was talking to, turns his way and looks at him, he smiles, she smiles back, turns away and goes into the living room where the buffet and drink tables are. The other woman remains seated, drinking a glass of wine and surveying the room. She suddenly whips her head around to him, catches him looking at her, smiles, he smiles and turns away. Is she interested in him? Even if she is, and she's not bad looking for her age, he'd want to hook up with someone fifteen to twenty years younger than he. Woman he's interested in is probably thirty to thirty-five years younger than he—maybe more. Definitely more than thirty. Or the woman just wanted to know who the younger woman was glancing and smiling at when they were talking. If only this woman, who's now surveying the room again and seems to be avoiding looking at him, had got up and left and the younger woman had stayed seated. Then what? He'd go over—he'd be nervous doing this but he'd do it—and say something, he doesn't know what. Maybe "Is the woman who was sitting here coming back?" If she said "Yes" or "Why?" he'd say "Because I was thinking of sitting down here, if that'd be all right with you." If she said no to the question is the woman coming back, he'd say "Then mind if I sit down?" She'd say something like "No, of course not," and he'd sit and they'd be facing each other, he with a glass in his hand, she didn't seem to be drinking anything and he doesn't remember her walking away with a glass, nor is there a glass on the side table by the two chairs, not that it couldn't have been somebody else's if there was one there, and he'd start a conversation. What would he say? Something like "I know this is what people always say at parties when they first meet each other, or often, anyway, but how do you know Lois, the host?" She'd say how and probably ask him how he knows her. But suppose she said something like "She's a colleague of my husband," what would he say? He should have looked to see if she was wearing a wedding band, not that all wives do or that he would have spotted it from where he stood. She looks like someone who'd have a very thin wedding band, barely visible from even fairly close, and being gold it'd sort of blend in with her skin, and also no engagement ring. But if she mentioned a husband or fiancé, what would he say? "Oh, that so? Does he also write book reviews for the magazine, because by your saying 'colleague,' I'm assuming that he's also at *Newsweek*?" and they'd talk a little more, she'd get up or they both would— certainly he'd stand if she got up first—and leave him, and that'd be that, end of any possibility of having anything more to do with her. If she didn't mention a husband or fiancé, and she doesn't seem the type to say "my boyfriend"—instead she'd say "my friend" or "a friend"—and asked him how he knows Lois, he'd tell her about the art colony. She's no doubt heard of it—she could even have been to it, for poetry it'd seem—and she'd probably ask him what he was up there for. He'd tell her and she might say she's sorry, she hasn't heard of him, and he'd say "Not even from Lois?... only kidding, and I don't know why I said it. Believe me, though, in not hearing of me, you're far from being alone." Anyway, she's in the dining room. Sees her from this room talking to a man who's about her age, maybe a few years younger. Maybe she came with him. Or she only first met him here—a few minutes ago, even, right after she went into that room—and he's single, or married, but his wife isn't with him or is in another room and he likes to flirt or play around, and eyed her awhile from the dining room, when she was talking to the older woman, before making his move on her, or else is a friend but someone she's not involved with. When he was much younger— he's saying, forty-five to fifty years ago, when he was in college or soon after he got out—they called it a platonic relationship, which seems such an outdated or just pretentious way of saying it now. He wants to introduce himself to her and find out if she's married or seriously attached to someone and of course other things about her—What does she do? Where does she live? How does she know Lois? Did she also study Russian literature?—and then if there's any chance he can see her again, if their conversation goes well and she shows some interest in him, if just intellectual, and he doesn't find her superficial or dull. Doubts from her expression she could be. But someone her age and so attractive and with such a bright face, she's probably married or attached or between men. Go into the next room, he tells himself. Why, to make an ass of himself? No, pursue it; you get nothing from holding back. Just your having exchanged looks, that'll be it, and then she'll be gone. If for anything, go in to see if she has a wedding band on, not that that should stop him. She could be separated from her husband but still wears the band and will till the divorce. A woman told him this. Something her lawyer advised her about the settlement of the couple's holdings, but he could be wrong. Goes into the dining room. She's talking to the man. By the way they talk—their expressions, as if at times they know what the other's about to say—they seem to have known each other awhile. Gets to about fifteen feet of her, couple of people between them, and glances at her left hand. Or is it the right that has the band? The left; Russians wear it on the right. No wedding band on either hand or any kind of ring, so she's almost surely single. And she could be Russian, the blond hair and high forehead and something about the clothes: a peasant blouse, he thinks, with a ruffled collar, and hair combed into a chignon. Would her being Russian stop him? Why would it? Her English is probably perfect, or if she's a scholar, she knows several languages and they could speak in German or French. Never got near enough to the woman and her in the living room to hear if they were speaking English, and there are so many people talking in this one, he can't tell which voices are hers and the man's. Steps back, almost into the living room, feeling he got too near her. She might think he's being too obvious, a move he now doesn't think is a good one. Still talking to the man, she looks at him. He smiles, she doesn't, and turns back to the man. Uh-oh. If only she had smiled, but she probably thinks he's following her, and doesn't like it. What he doesn't want is for her to think him creepy, which could make anything that could possibly happen between them impossible from the start. Well, nothing will happen, but it'd make the chances of that better. The man looks at him for a second and then back at her, and resumes talking. Seems he's saying "Can I get you something—a drink?" She shakes her head and says no. But it's also possible he said "Do you know the old guy in the blue shirt to your left? Don't look now, he's looking at us," and without looking his way she shook her head and said no. They spoke English; he tried very hard to listen and heard the words "to" and "you" and "know" or "no." He shrugs and goes into the living room. Seems impossible now to meet her or that she'd want to meet him, he thinks. It'd be wonderful, though, if she came into the living room and started a conversation with him. Birdbrain, get real for a second; why in hell would she? In fact, it'd seem she'd do anything but. Though maybe she's curious why he kept looking at her and followed her into the dining room, if that's what he did. It doesn't have to be what she thinks, she could think. He might think he knows her from somewhere, as a teacher in the college or grad school she went to. Or someone at a party somewhere introduced them a while back and she's forgotten his face—their conversation could have been brief and it's possible he's aged a great deal since then, she could think—but he hasn't forgotten hers and he's just been looking for a good opportunity to speak to her here, ask how she's been, or ask after the mutual acquaintance or friend who introduced them. The chairs where the two women talked are empty. He sits in the chair she sat in. Maybe, if she comes into the room and sees him sitting there, she'll get the hint. He's sitting where she sat. He could turn it into something, but nothing that wasn't stupid or juvenile. But he's alone and with his back to the room—that could mean something to her. Other chair's the better one for surveying the entire room and part of the dining room, so his sitting in this one might suggest he's not going out of his way to look at her. But maybe she'd sit in the other chair and say something to him. Keep dreaming, slugger, because what could she say? "Excuse me, but you keep looking at me—or you did before— as if you know me. Do you? We've met?" Wait, before she'd sit she'd probably say something like "Excuse me, but is this chair taken?" He'd look up, try to hide his delight, and say "No, please sit, if that's what you meant, or maybe you just want to take the chair away," and smile and she'd smile and sit and say "Excuse me again, but you keep looking at me—or did before—as if you know me or we once met. Have we? I'll have to apologize if we had and I forgot it." No, she'd never say that. Forget about her thinking they once possibly met and she's forgotten his face and he hasn't forgotten hers and that business about the possible change in his face because of age. She knows he doesn't know her and they've never met. Knows he keeps looking at her because he's attracted to her. Knows he wants her to situate herself in a place where she's not with anyone so he can go over to her and start a conversation. Gets up and sits in the other chair so he can look out at the party. Not especially for her, for he knows nothing's going to happen there, or the chance of it is so slight that it might as well be nothing, but more to do something and not look like an oddball with his back to everyone while sitting opposite an empty chair. Just then—he wasn't in the chair for more than a few seconds—she comes into the room with a different man than the one before. Or maybe they came into the room in the last few minutes while he was in the other chair and he didn't see them because his back was to them. They're holding hands. She lets go of the man's hand, or he lets go of hers, and says something to him and they go over to two women standing by the fireplace. There was a fire going when he first got to the party, but it's now just sparkling cinder. He'd like to put more wood on while the cinders are still hot—there's a split log and kindling in what looks like an old peach basket to the side of the fireplace. But that might seem too obvious a move to get near her, when the truth is that watching a fire from the chair he's in is something he really wants to do. She hasn't looked his way since she came into the room. Could be she doesn't know he's there or has had it with having to respond in some way to his glances and smiles. She was holding hands with the man, he thinks. They're married or seriously attached. Looks at them talking to the women. All of them start laughing at something one of them said. Then she looks at her watch and says something to the man and women—one of the women, who's been the loudest of the group, says "Oh, that's too bad"—looks at him, he smiles, she smiles back and turns to the women and says something and goes into the dining room. Now what's that supposed to mean? Just when he thinks his chances with her are hopeless, she smiles at him and goes into another room, leaving the man talking to the women. The watch and that "Oh, that's too bad." She's leaving. He leans partly out of his chair past the entry to the dining room and sees her shaking a man's hand, not the man she was talking to there. Then she goes down the hall off the dining room to either the bedroom at the end of it—he left his coat on the bed—or the bathroom hallway down the hall. If you're going to act, you got to act now, he thinks. She went down the hall alone, she'll come back alone. Go to the dining room, make yourself a Bloody Mary, but just the juice and vodka and ice, no time for the squeezed lemon and Tabasco sauce as you did with your first two drinks, and wait till she returns from either back room and say something. What will he say? Something. But what? He doesn't know. Yes he does. "Excuse me, but you've obviously seen me staring at you, and let me first say that I apologize for that. It's not that I think I know you and I certainly didn't want to make you feel uncomfortable. I just wanted to talk to you, and if you're in a rush and would rather not talk to me, or for any reason, please say so and I'll stop. I know I'm being a bit pushy or even aggressive here in cornering you like this, but I thought it worth it." No, he wouldn't say that. But something like it. Not even something like it. "Excuse me, but I'd like to introduce myself if I may." Not that, either. Too fuddy-duddy and stiff. Something, though. When it comes out, he's sure it'll be all right. If he shows his nervousness, that might be okay too. But make yourself a drink. It'll fortify you. He almost feels dizzy at the prospect of talking to her. Hasn't done anything like this for years. Goes to the drink table and makes the drink. What the hell, he has more time than he thought, and squeezes a lemon wedge in— Tabasco sauce might smell up his breath—stirs the drink with his finger and starts sipping it. But what're you doing? he thinks. She was holding hands with the man. Maybe he's just a good friend and there's nothing between them. Then why would they hold hands? Maybe they weren't. Maybe they only had their hands very close without realizing it. That what it looked like? Could've. His eyes are so bad sometimes that he often makes mistakes seeing things. Also his glasses. He's needed a stronger prescription for a year. The man could be another one she met here and who wants to have something to do with her, or someone she met before but who isn't anything to her. Slugs down the rest of the drink and puts the glass on the buffet table. "Meyer," a woman says, and he says "Not now, please," and turns back to the hallway. She's coming from the bedroom. Has her coat on and is holding her gloves. He goes over to her just as she enters the dining room. She's looking at him and he says "Excuse me, I know I've been a little obvious, but it's for an explainable reason. I didn't want to be rude. I thought I recognized you, is what I'm trying to say, and have racked my brains trying to figure out where. Were you ever a student of mine at NYU?" "I didn't go there." "Then we could even live in the same large apartment building on Riverside Drive. Four-twenty-five." "No, but I do live uptown." "Then maybe I've seen you at University Market on a Hundred-fifteenth or in a local restaurant or bookstore or walking on Broadway a few times, and that's it." "It's possible, but not the market. I live in the West Eighties, a long way from Four-twenty-five. I know the building, though. I've friends there." "Everyone seems to know someone who lives there. It's a pretty remarkable building. Loaded with academics and writers and musicians and even a couple of painters and filmmakers. Do your friends live in the front?" "No, in the rear." "Oh, I thought maybe I'd seen you in the front elevator, going up or coming down from your friends." "No, in the rear." "Anyway, I really did think you looked familiar. I know it could sound like a line, but it's true. That's why I said I didn't want to be rude. I didn't want you to think I was avoiding you or didn't recognize you. Person I have in mind must be someone who looks or looked a little like you. A former student. I've had so many of them." "What do you teach?" "Oh, it's not important," he says. "If you don't think so, then it probably isn't, but you'll have to excuse me. I was on my way out, and someone's waiting for me." "The fellow in the living room?" "If you mean the one I was standing beside just before, yes." "He's your husband?" "Why would that be of any concern to you, but I'll answer it anyway. No." "I'm sorry, did I ask something I shouldn't have?" "Listen, I don't mean to be rude either, but I saw you looking at me a number of times tonight, and it didn't appear to be the way you said it was—the do-I-know-her story—and I just have to say I'm not interested." "You mean in me?" and she says "Come on; really." "Okay, you're right. My story is bullshit, though I am a teacher and I have had a couple thousand students, half of them women, and I admit I was and am interested in you. But the age difference, not to say my stupidity in acting out, and I don't even know if I have the expression right, my absurd fantasies sometimes— too much for you, true?" "To be honest, the age difference is huge. Even if I wasn't with someone now, I'd never consider seeing a man so much older than I. I would, though, if I thought him interesting, and I'm not saying I think you are, except for your honesty, and that could be a part of the whole act too, have a coffee with that person or meet him for a harmless lunch." "So have coffee with me one day or a harmless lunch." "Too late for that now. Excuse me, and good talking to you," and she sticks out her hand to shake. "My name's Meyer, by the way. Meyer Dumbo Ostrower," he says, shaking her hand, and she says "Funny," smiles as if she did think what he said was funny, and goes into the living room. She and the man she was with there leave a few minutes later. The man wasn't wearing a coat. It's cold out, below freezing, but some men don't wear coats in the cold. He had a sweater on underneath his sport jacket, so maybe that's enough for him.

He gets up, goes to the door of his wife's study and says "Got a moment?" "Yes, come in." "This won't take long. I just had this very strange idea for a story and practically wrote it out in my head. Shouldn't be too difficult to put on paper if I do it in the next few days. Want to hear?" "Go on." "In it, I have this man and woman meet for the first time at a party on Washington Square—in a four-story row house just like the one Lois Sachs lived in and where we first met. I've done this as a story and long scene in a novel a couple of times, so maybe altogether four or five times. That evening was obviously, you might like to hear, though I've probably told you already, the most eventful or momentous—you know what I'm trying to say—in my life." "No, you never told me, although I sort of guessed by how many times you've written of it." "But in this one, maybe to make it different from the others and to bring it up to date or deal with themes I've been dealing with in my work lately… anyway, the woman's the same age you were when we met at Lois's and the man's the age I am now." "So what happens? He makes a pass at her?" "Just about. Fumbles. He's nervous. He hasn't done anything like this in years." "He's slept with women, though?" "Slept with them, though I hadn't thought about it, but hasn't tried to pick anyone up. But she rejects him more because of his age than because she came to the party with another guy—someone more around her age—which you didn't that evening, did you? You came and left with Sveta." "Marlene. She was in town staying with me for a week." "In what I concocted, the older guy knew—he could just tell. You get to have some quick, astute insights, living that long and going through so many experiences—that she and the man weren't tight as a couple, but were probably sleeping with each other, and their relationship wasn't going to last. Or maybe I'm making some of that up now. He was a bit stiff, the younger guy, seemed cold and uninteresting—a banker or broker, interested in money or trading and little else, or maybe he didn't have time for much else, while she seemed the opposite. And the older guy felt that if he were much younger he'd have a chance with her, because she seemed interested in what he had to say and amused by his behavior. That she would have given him her phone number, despite the other guy being there in the next room waiting to leave with her, or told him how to reach her, which is what you did with me that night—spelling your name and giving your street number so I could look you up in the phone book if I was still interested in doing so after the party, you said." "I think your take on the situation is right. You're already almost ten years older than I, so it would be too great an age difference, don't you agree? Although I would, if you were like you are today and unmarried, consent to meeting you for coffee or a simple lunch if it was obvious that that would be enough for you." "Just what she said, but it must have been obvious it wouldn't be."

21

Grabs the arts section of the newspaper, goes into the bathroom off their bedroom, lets his pants down and sits on the toilet and starts to read a movie review, when he thinks that he and his wife were just talking about Lois, woman whose party they first met at, and never said a thing about her being dead. She died around fifteen years ago. They were eating dinner, kids probably at the table with them, he remembers especially a sad Corelli concerto grosso playing on the record-player, or sad movement of one, when the phone rang. He got up and answered it in the kitchen—it was in the house before the one they have now—and an unfamiliar woman's voice said "Is Sandra Rosen there?" He said "This is her husband, we're eating dinner. If this call is to sell us something or ask us to contribute to some organization, we don't take solicitations or respond to telemarketing of any kind over the phone." "I'm Lois

Sach's aunt. Her mother's given me a list of close friends to call, but I suppose you know Lois also, so I can just as well tell you."

His sister called. "I've very bad news. There's no way I can break it to you without it being disturbing, so I'll just come right out with it. Mom died of a stroke this afternoon. If this is any consolation, the doctor said she never felt anything and was probably dead before she hit the floor." Later in the call, he said "I'll get on a train right away." She said "No need to rush. Mom gave me written instructions a while back, saying she just wanted to be cremated, no funeral or memorial or any fuss, so we don't have to deal with it for another couple of days. Meanwhile, I'll take care of everything from here."

His sister called from the hospital. "Mom told me to tell you you'll have to move up your plans on coming to see Irwin tonight, if you're still planning to. He took a turn for the worse this morning, and when we got here, they told us he was failing." "Why didn't you call me about it sooner?" and she said "At the time we didn't know how bad off he was, and I also didn't want to wake you." "Do I have enough time to see him before he dies?" "When I first got the call, I would have said yes. Now I don't think so. But if you hop on the next train up here, maybe you'll make it in time." "I'll have to go home first and have Sandra drive with me to the station, so she can have the car. The other one's on the fritz." He was parking the car in front of their house when Sandra came out and said "Your sister just called. I'm sorry. She said your stepfather died fifteen minutes ago."

He'd just come back from his lunch hour at work when his sister called. Their younger sister was riding her bike on their block when she got hit by a car. She and the bike were dragged to the corner before the car stopped for the light. The driver thought the clanking under the car was a muffler dragging on the pavement. If he'd stopped right after he hit her, she said, the doctors say the injuries wouldn't have been so bad. If it hadn't been a school holiday, she wouldn't have been on her bike. And if there wasn't a city law that bikers can't ride on the sidewalk, the accident wouldn't have happened. "And if I hadn't convinced the folks to buy her a two-wheeler so she'd get some physical exercise and be outdoors more," she said, "and then taught her to ride, she'd be alive this minute. Her body was so mangled that nothing of it can be used for transplants. The folks are at the hospital with me and we've already been told to choose a funeral home to send her to. We should be here another hour, so come right over to help me with them and then to take care of me." He cabbed to the hospital. They'd already gone to the funeral home. He guessed which one and cabbed there and his mother said all the funeral arrangements had been made. "The casket will be closed for good, once they finally get her in it, because her beautiful face was almost completely destroyed. I had to see it—Irwin and Naomi wouldn't go in to identify her—and I don't want anyone else to experience what I saw." "But the people here can fix her up," he said, "make her look like she did before, only sleeping." "We also decided it doesn't pay," his stepfather said, "for just a quick look."

He was sleeping at his girlfriend's apartment—it was around 10 a.m., Sunday—when his mother called. "Your Aunt Emma died in her sleep last night," she said. "It wasn't easy tracking you down, but your sister thought you'd be here. You were Emma's favorite, and she seemed your favorite aunt too, so I thought you'd want to know right away and later meet us at the funeral home." After he put down the phone, his girlfriend lit a cigarette and said "I heard what your mother said. This would be an ideal time for you to have a cigarette, if you smoked." She finished the cigarette—they were still in bed—and said "I suppose this means we're not going to make love. Last night you were too smashed to, if you remember, and I was looking forward to it this morning. Was she really that close to you?" "She always, when she saw me, gave me these big slobbering kisses on my cheek, so wet that right in front of her I'd have to wipe them off. She got a big kick out of that, but I didn't think it funny. I'd then go to the bathroom to wash my face. Otherwise, she was terrific, but I always disappeared when she came to avoid those kisses, though eventually had to come out to greet her."

He was writing the first draft of a short story, when the phone rang. Don't answer it, he thought. You do and you're on the phone for more than thirty seconds, you'll lose your train of thought and possibly the story. He typed while the phone continued to ring. After about eight times, it stopped. The phone rang about ten seconds later. Has to be the same caller, he thought. If he gets two calls a day, that's a lot, and never one right after the other. He picked up the receiver and said "I'm sorry, can't talk now, very important business, please call back later, thank you," and hung up and went back to his writing. Phone rang about ten seconds later. It's important, he thought. Could be something about his mother or someone else in the family. He answered it with a hello. It was the brother of a close friend. "All these years, as many times I was over Walter's apartment, we never met, but I knew what great buddies you were and I got your phone number from the address book I found on his night table."

He went to his office, after being away from it all summer, and got his telephone voice messages. The first was from his department's administrative assistant downstairs, who, after she left the message, called him in Maine with what she'd wanted to ask him. The next was from a student asking if he was going to be around the last two weeks of August, as she wants to come in to see him about an internship she's doing this summer. "I know you don't do e-mail, so here's my phone number," and she said it so fast he couldn't get it. A message from a former grad student of his he had no recollection of, asking for a job reference. "I'll call back later or try to reach you some other way." Next a woman, saying "Hi, it's Kate, I've very important news to tell you. I've been calling your home for days. You don't seem to have an answering machine there and the phone rings and rings till I give up. Call me. I need to speak to you. Time is very important in all this, and it's not something that I want you to find out on your answering machine," and gave her home and business numbers. He wrote them down and thought Which Kate is it? He must know a half-dozen of them, and all the Kates he had as students, but they would have given their last names and said they were former students. And he didn't know what she was talking about regarding his home answering machine. They have one and it was on all summer. It might have been filled when she called, but then the automated voice would have said so to her. But he didn't remember there being that many messages on the machine when they got back. She was probably dialing the wrong number or maybe some other person. Anyway, neither he nor his wife know how to retrieve answering machine messages to their home from another phone. The next message was from her and said "Meyer, it's Kate again. Did you get my message? If you did, why haven't you called? I told you, it's very important and not something I can tell you on your answering machine. Please call," and gave her phone numbers again. He still didn't know who it was or what it could be about. The next message said "It's me again. I've awful news and it seems I'll have to tell you it on your answering machine. Lily died. A quick-killing liver disease. I took care of her at my place her last few weeks—she didn't want to go to a hospice. She suffered a lot, painkillers barely helped, and now she's mercifully gone. She didn't want you to know she was dying, when I told her I wanted to forewarn you. She didn't want your sympathy now, she said, when you gave no moral support and little feeling before. Money, she said, strapped as she was, she never wanted from you. I told her wasn't she being a bit unfair to you? For didn't you once want to marry her and adopt, if that's the right word for me, both children? No matter. She was given to science—

her wish, and a big relief to me, since I never could have afforded a funeral and cemetery plot or cremation. I'm having a memorial for her on Pescadero Beach, a week from Sunday, the fourteenth, at three p.m."—two weeks ago, he thought. "I'd like you to come to it. Need, is more like it. I have no one but you now. My brother's a drug addict and shit and couldn't spare a single tear or an 'I'm sorry' for her when I told him Lily had died. All my relatives on her side are either religious zealots or right-wing fascists, and I don't want any of them at the memorial or to ever see them again. They already so much as told me that the disease my mother got was retribution for giving birth to two bastards from two different men. So, just friends of Lily's and mine there, and you. Fly out. I know it's expensive, but it's the last thing you'll have to do for me, I promise. I don't think, after more than thirty-five years of not having seen me since I was less than two, it's asking too much from you." She gave her phone numbers again and directions to the memorial site from the San Francisco and San Jose airports and said "Call me anytime, day or night, but call. Incidentally, I'd pick you up at either airport, but with everything I have to do for the memorial—I want to make it special—it seems you'll have to rent a car. If you don't mind being in the air for so long, you can do the whole thing in one day. Bye-bye. I love you. Please call." The next message was from her. "Yours truly again. I just want to remind you about the memorial on the fourteenth. Please don't disappoint me. Thanks." The next message said "Where are you? Why haven't you called. Most importantly, why weren't you at the memorial? You could even have come without calling me; I wasn't going to change the time and date. I'm all alone now. Never a real father, now no mother, and my one sibling is all but dead to me, as I'm definitely dead to him. You have a family. What you did by not coming to the memorial was bad enough, but now please don't ignore me. That's all I'm going to say. If I don't hear from you, then you're all but dead to me too." It was a little past noon in California when he played back her messages, so he called her at work. Her answering machine said "Hi, you've reached Katherine Squires. I'll be away from my sloppy desk for unspecified but very personal reasons till after Labor Day, so please leave a message." He hung up and called her at home and got her answering machine. He said "Kate, or Katherine, it's Meyer. We only got back from Maine two days ago and I got your messages on my office phone today, the 29th. I've no idea why my answering machine at home didn't come on for you. There were quite a lot of messages on it after almost two months of our being away, so it was probably full when you called. I'm sorry, very sorry, for Lily, and sorry for your loss. She was a lovely person, in every way, and it's true I did want to marry her, but she refused. She said I wouldn't make a good father or faithful, or whatever she said, devoted husband. I'm faithful and devoted and I think a good father, but that's what she thought. All right, long ago. She no doubt saw something in me that I didn't, and she was probably right at the time. Please accept my deepest condolences. I know how tough it must be for you and I admire--" The beep sounded, and he called her again. "Meyer again. I admire you for all you've done for your mother. As for the memorial, I couldn't have come out for it even if I'd wanted to, and to be honest, I know I wouldn't have wanted to. Too arduous a trip for me to do in a day or two, and I was in Maine, which would have made it even harder. And look, despite what Lily told you, it was never a sure thing that you and I are biologically related, and now that Lily's gone, it can't be proven. I wanted blood tests for the three of us a year or so after you were born. I would have done mine in New York and you and Lily in California, and I would have paid for all our tests too, somehow. But again, she refused. Said she didn't want to put you through it—that it could be physically painful. And besides--" The beep sounded, and he called her again. "It's me. Besides, Lily said, and this was just part of her rampant paranoia about the system then, blood tests can lie to the favor of the person paying for them when it comes to establishing paternity and that being cleared of any responsibility in that matter was what I was looking for. That wasn't how I felt, but what can I say? I would love speaking to you, though, and if I ever get to California, and there's always a chance, or you get to Washington or Baltimore or somewhere East, to see you. Call me. I'll be in my office another hour—it's now twenty past noon California-time—and then I'm heading home," and gave his office and home phone numbers. He left those messages around two years ago. Hasn't heard from or called her since.

He was in the bedroom of the cottage they were renting in Maine, unpinning his first child's diapers, when the phone rang. "Sandra, you there?" he yelled downstairs. "I'm changing Lynette's diapers, so get the phone." No answer. Must have gone for a run or is down by the water. The ringing continued. "All right, all right, I'm coming, but you'd think after seven or eight rings you'd give up," and lifted Lynette out of her crib, wrapped a towel around her bottom and carried her downstairs and answered the phone. It was his wife's mother. "Were you napping?" and he said "No, why would I be napping so early? It's not even two." "You didn't answer the phone for such a long time. And it's probably nice and breezy up there, unlike this miserable hot city, that it's what I'd be doing, napping or resting." "I was in the middle of changing Lynette's diapers. She was wet and has a diaper rash, which we're taking care of, so not to worry, but she's very irritable because of it. I'm sure she'll start crying before we stop talking. Here, Lynette, give a good wail for Grandma Haline." "Please don't encourage her. I kiss you, my darling; I kiss her. Could you now get me Sandra?" and he said "She must be out somewhere. I called for her before but she didn't answer." "Ask her to phone me as soon as she gets back. I'm afraid she's going to be extremely upset with what I have to tell her. One of her two old Siamese—you know we're taking care of them because she didn't think them strong enough to travel--" "Yes, yes, of course. What happened to her, or what'd she do?" "I can't tell which is which, they look so alike, but Boris thinks it's Natasha. She suddenly had a seizure this morning, foam coming out of her mouth and everything. We took her to the vet immediately, but she had to be put away."

Phone rang at home. He was at his worktable in the bedroom and picked up the receiver and said hello. "Good morning. May I speak to Sandra," his father-in-law said. "I have very bad news for her." "What is it?" and he said "I have to tell Sandra first." "She can't come to the phone right now. And we left the portable handset off the receiver all night and it won't be working for another hour." "You can't drag the phone you're talking to me on to wherever she is?" "Cord doesn't reach the bathroom." "Her mother killed herself a half-hour ago. I'm waiting for the police and firemen now. That's what they said would come when I called 911. I discovered her in her bathroom. She took pills and vodka and put a bag over her head and left a note with how she did it, I suppose to make certain everyone knew I had nothing to do with it. Tell Sandra to stop whatever she's doing and come to the phone. She has to for me. I'm in so much shock I can barely move." "I'm so sorry, Boris, so sorry. I don't know what else I can say. Just a moment. I'll get her, or maybe the handset's working now." He picked it up and pressed the Talk button. No dial tone and the window didn't light up. "It's still not working. Needs more recharging. I'll get her, don't worry. Hold on." He went to the bathroom door, knocked on it and said "Sandra, your dad's on the phone. It's about your mother. He has to speak to you right away." "It sounds bad. What happened?" and he said "He wants to tell you himself." "He must have told you, so tell me." "Can I open the door?" "Yes." He opened it and said "I'm sorry, sweetheart. Your mother killed herself half an hour ago, or he probably means that's when he found her." "Portable still not working?" "Yeah." She got off the toilet, flushed it and went to the phone.

Phone rang, waking him. Room was dark. Must be very late, he thought. Felt for his watch on his night table and pressed the face-light button on it. Ten to four. Can't be anything but bad news. Phone kept ringing. "What's going on?" Sandra said. "What time is it?" "The phone. It's ten to four. It must be about your father. It's bad news, I'm sure." "Answer it." "You don't want to? I'll bring over the portable." "Just answer it." He went to the phone and picked up the receiver and said "Yes?" "This is Dr. Cory at Lenox Hill Hospital in New York. Is Sandra Rosen there?" "It's about her father. He died this morning, didn't he?" "May I speak to her, please?"

22

Sits down at his worktable in the bedroom, takes the cover off the typewriter and is about to throw it on the bed behind him, but fits it over the back of his chair, stares at the typewriter awhile and then at the wall to his right where there's a small rainbow from his wife's prism on the windowsill in front of him, looks outside when a bird flies through the trees, then reaches for the pile of typing paper on the table. His wife comes into the room before he can grab two sheets of paper and says she's not feeling well and wants to lie down—would he mind very much not working here, or she can go into one of the kids' rooms? and he says "I'll take the typewriter into the dining room. So far, not much has come. Dry time. In between pieces you can say. Just ideas, but none of them materializing into anything. Sorry. Talking about myself. What do you think's wrong with you? You look okay." "Headache, stiffness in the limbs and my fingers are all tingly and feel less nimble. Not the flu, though; I know those signs. Maybe I'm getting arthritic. I'll feel better after a little rest." She takes off her sneakers and lies on the bed, folds her hands together on her chest and closes her eyes. "Want me to cover you?" and he holds up a light cotton blanket he keeps on one of the chairs and uses for his naps. "The house is plenty warm already, but thanks." "Too warm? I can turn it down," and she says "No, just right for lying without a blanket," and closes her eyes again, hands stay folded on her chest. "Draw the curtains?" and she says "Not worth the bother. And if they're closed, the room will be dark and I might sleep through dinnertime and I've too many things to do," all said without opening her eyes or moving, it seems, any part of her body. She looks like someone on view in a coffin. Put that thought straight out of your head, he thinks, and picks up the typewriter, goes into the dining room and puts it on the table. Forgot paper. Getting it will disturb her and he knows he's disturbed her enough with his questions. But he needs paper— should really keep some in this room, since he works here so much—and goes back to the bedroom, says "Excuse me, I forgot typing paper." "You could have taken some from my printer. We use the same kind." "I also need Ko-Rec-Type. Still not feeling so hot?" and she looks at him and says "No. Could you shut the door when you go and also take the portable phone? That way, you can get the phone quickly if it rings. If it's for me—someone I know," shutting her eyes, "tell them I'm not feeling up to par and am resting and can't come to the phone. Just 'She can't come to the phone.'

The whole world doesn't have to know the reason and I don't want to sound like an invalid or sicker than I am and alarm anyone." "Will do. Rest well," and he bends over her and kisses her forehead. She smiles but her eyes stay closed. He gets a batch of paper and a clean tab of Ko-Rec-Type and the typewriter cover, looks at her as he leaves the room—she's still in the same position, hands together, eyes closed—and shuts the door quietly and goes into the dining room and fits the cover over the back of the chair next to the one he sits in. Puts two sheets into the typewriter, aligns them with the paper holder. Easier to write here or in the bedroom? Same, really, if there's no noise and nobody's flitting in and out of the room. And to start something new? Who the hell knows. Oh crap, these goddamn interferences. Not that he's blaming her. She isn't feeling well, and anyway, it's also her room. Way she was lying on the bed, though. If he had a flower with a long stem and she was in a good mood—not sick—he would have stuck it between her hands. No, he wouldn't. Wouldn't want her to think of herself as a corpse or that he was thinking of her as one. She must really be feeling lousy, because she'd never interrupt his work unless for a good reason— interrupt it with more than a question or two, as he does with her—especially when she knows, though she could have forgot, he's trying to start something new. He didn't bring it up but same thing happened a few weeks ago. She came into the room, had to lie down—did he mind very much not working here? She could always go into one of the kids' rooms, she said—but he knew she'd feel better on their bed and on her side of it. "Sure," he said. "I'll move into the dining room. No trouble at all. I can work as well there as much as any place." He was at the end of a piece, which is always the easiest part for him, working off a quick first draft he'd done a couple weeks before. "But what's wrong," he said, "specifically?" Headache, stiffness is one leg, then spasms in the other that she couldn't get rid of for a while. Spasms were painful, worse than a charley horse, which she's had plenty of, she said, but nothing as bad as this. And lethargy, which she didn't complain of this time. She was feeling great, then suddenly got tired. Also, she said, a funny icy feeling in her fingers, but actually not so funny. He said "Maybe you should call Angelino and he'll want to see you," and she said Not necessary; it'll go away. And they have their annual checkups in two months; she'll talk it over with him then. She got on the bed, thanked him for being so considerate, said she knows how he hates his work to be interfered with but this was important, closed her eyes but didn't fold her hands together on her chest. Just laid them out alongside her. From that time to this, she was healthy, energetic, occasionally peppy, worked long hours with no difficulty, it seemed; nothing seemed wrong. She left the bedroom that day an hour later, saying she felt fine now; the rest—she even dozed off for fifteen minutes—was all she needed. Scary in a way, he thinks. More so this time than last because almost the same thing's happened twice. In fact, wasn't scary at all the last time. He thought it was a one-time occurrence and that she'd get over it fairly quickly, which she did: faster than he'd thought. Scary now because two women she knows, one a close friend in New York and the other a high school classmate she's recently become chummy with online, have MS, and both, in the early stages of the disease, had symptoms similar to what she complained of the last time and today, something he didn't think of until now. In around five years, the one she's online with was confined to a wheelchair; can't walk, can't get out of the chair without someone helping her up and then holding her, and can barely use her hands. She's able to chat online through a voice-activation system. The close friend in New York was first diagnosed ten years ago and can only walk with the aid of a walker now and slowly seems to be getting worse. And the wife of an editor acquaintance of his got ALS and in a year couldn't leave her bed unless she was lifted into a special hospital chair—was partially paralyzed and had a hard time swallowing and couldn't breathe on her own and needed round-the-clock caregivers—and in two years was dead. That wasn't unusually fast for that disease, he read in a science article. Her symptoms early on were something like his wife's today and the last time, but not as much so as the MS women's. Scary, too, because what if she has MS or something as bad and deteriorates as quickly as the online woman? Because of the expense and that he doesn't like having strangers around, he thinks he'd have minimal professional caregiving for her. He'd cut back on his teaching so he could do most of the work himself. Could he do it? He's an old guy—that's how he sees himself, or feeling his age, is more like it. That's not altogether true. He's still pretty strong, works hard at staying in shape, although he's definitely slowed down—doesn't walk with the same bounce or lift heavy objects as easily as he used to, so a lot of that staying in shape is just to look better. But certain things about his health haven't been too good lately. Shortness of breath the last few years. He really feels it when he climbs stairs to his office on the top floor instead of taking the elevator or when the elevator's not working, which it isn't a lot. A year ago, three flights did him in; now it's two and he has to rest about thirty seconds before climbing the third flight to his floor. Angelino said last time he wanted to put him on a treadmill as part of his next checkup. He's afraid of what they might find; blocked arteries, for instance, leading to a double or triple bypass. He knows what's involved in those operations; his father-in-law when he was in his eighties and a guy he knows from Maine who's ten years younger than he. Where they cut your chest open and it takes a year to fully recover. He's also had a strange almost nauseating feeling on the left side of his head every time he brushes there and even when he runs his hand through the hair. Okay, he's being slightly hypochondriacal, but what he's saying is that because of his age, things could suddenly go very wrong with him too. What if his wife does get sick with something—that these last two times were the first signs of it—and is eventually confined to a wheelchair like her online friend and like her can't get in or out of bed without help. Certainly, if they had caregivers, they wouldn't have them at night. This woman—he forgets her name; Leonore, he thinks—is physically completely dependent on her husband between six at night and nine in the morning, when he goes to work, Sandra's said. Caregivers are there the rest of the time, and it's costing a small fortune: fifteen to twenty dollars an hour five days a week. Medical insurance doesn't cover a penny of it. Weekends, friends and relatives sometimes come in for an hour or two to relieve him. What if Sandra is sick and becomes totally incapacitated, and they're in bed—he lifted her onto it and got her into the sleeping position she wanted, as this woman's husband does—and sometime at night he gets a fatal heart attack or stroke? As he said, he's sixty-eight and hasn't been feeling great, so it's possible. What would she do if she thought he was dead or in a coma and couldn't get help for either of them? They'd have a phone of some kind on her night table, as they don't now—the portable and regular phone are on the dresser—but suppose she reached for it and because of her condition knocked it to the floor or she had trouble with her hands, as her online friend does, and couldn't even hold or use a phone. He pictures it: She wakes up, the room's dark, she says his name a few times and asks him to turn her onto her other side or on her back, something Sandra's said the woman's husband does at least twice a night to prevent her from getting bedsores. Would she, after pushing and poking him and then after she stops screaming, or whatever she'd do once she realized he was dead or in a coma, try to roll herself off the bed, risk hurting herself when she falls, and crawl to where the phone receiver or handset or cellphone is, if she's able to use any of those and also able to crawl? If she couldn't use the phone and nobody came for days, and even if someone came, couldn't get in the house because no one answered the door, would she just languish in bed alongside his body or on the floor? If someone did ring the doorbell, maybe she'd hear it and yell for help as loud as she could. Though because their room's in back and her voice by then, because of all the yelling she's already done, might be weak, the person at the door might not hear her. Eventually, the caregiver, because of a number of reasons, might sense something was wrong—he didn't come to the door in days, nor answer the phone why he didn't, and his car was still in the carport—and call the police. Or one of their daughters, in some other city, after calling for days and only getting a busy signal or the answering machine or voice mail, would call a friend of theirs or the police to come over. But that might take a week or so and Sandra wouldn't be able to survive that long—no food or water and already so sick and maybe even a couple of broken bones now from the fall. But why's he thinking all this? It goes way beyond preparing himself for the worst. And why would he even prepare himself for the worst? It's something he's done a lot of—he worries, just about always has, especially for his daughters. Prepared himself for a phone call of one or the other's death or serious injury half the times they took the car at night or went out with some guy or went to one of those twelve-hour marathon concerts with lots of drugs around and camped out. And when they went off to college and just a year ago when they traveled around Italy together for a month and, despite his warnings—Sandra urged him not to worry; they're capable and smart, she said—hitched part of the way. Nothing ever happened to them—a few dents and scratches on the bumpers—or nothing they ever told him and Sandra, or they told her and she never told him, and the dents and such he noticed himself and had to question his daughters about them. And when Sandra had trouble in the hospital delivering their first child, he worried she'd die. He thought, as he did with his daughters lots of times, though much worse with them, how would he be able to go on after that? And when he was young he worried about his mother when she was so sick she had to stay in bed for a couple of days. It was only the flu or a bad cold most of those times, but he'd jump to the worst possible thing that could happen to her, and be so relieved when she came into the kitchen and said she was feeling up to a little coffee and toast. His father never seemed to be sick until he had that heart attack on the street. And his stepfather also seemed in perfect health—never missed a day of work till he started showing signs of Parkinson's when he was seventy and in a year had to give up his dental practice—though he probably came down with something now and then but still went to the office. Sandra will be okay. For sure she has nothing like the beginnings of MS or ALS or any other disease. She's been like this, or something close to it, a number of times since he's known her—weak, bones ache (that's what the tingly fingers and stiffness in her legs could mean), maybe sweating and a temperature, which she didn't seem to be doing or have today or the last time, and her face flushed, and so on. As for his own health, the shortness of breath just comes with age, he supposes. Angelino would have put him on a treadmill right after his last checkup if he thought there was anything wrong with his heart, or whatever one goes on a treadmill for. As for the strange nauseating feeling he gets on the left side of his head when he brushes his hair there, it probably comes from having banged his head too many times on the opened kitchen cabinet doors here and also on the bottom of the high cupboard above the kitchen counter in the house they rent in Maine every summer, and it'll heal in time if he can avoid hitting his head there again. But why no similar feeling on the right side? Well, for a number of reasons he could come up with if he thought further about it, he just seems to hit the left side more. He goes to the bedroom to see how his wife is, opens the door slowly. She's sleeping on her back, one hand across her waist and the other by her side. She looks as if she's smiling. The kind of smile from bed, though those times with her eyes open, when she wants to signal him she wouldn't mind making love if he was also interested. Is she awake, then, and knows he's in the room? Then why are the eyes closed? "Sandra," he whispers. "Sandra." She doesn't move, eyes stayed closed, she continues to look as if she's smiling. He puts his hand over her mouth and feels her breathing on it. Leaves the room, shutting the door to within an inch of the jamb. Should he have covered her with the cotton blanket? The room was a little chilly. He starts back to the door. No, don't bother her; she'll sleep fine.

23

Puts on his muffler, jacket and watch cap and leaves the house. Anything to do something, he thinks. His gloves! Not again. What the hell's wrong with his brains? Starts back to the house when he remembers the gloves are in the jacket's side pockets, and puts them on. Resumes his walk, gets to the mailbox and wonders which direction should he go, then thinks he doesn't want to take a walk. It's not laziness or fatigue. After a lot of resting today and a nap and now out in the cold, he feels energetic. So what is it then? Does he need a reason for everything? He just doesn't feel like taking a walk now of any length, and goes back to the house. Sit outside, he thinks, as he's about to open the kitchen's storm door. Why? Just because how often does he do it when it's cold, and maybe a few good ideas will come to him that wouldn't in the house. But he doesn't even like sitting out here alone when the weather's mild.

Prefers sitting in the Morris chair in the living room, feet up on the ottoman sometimes, some quiet music on while he reads a newspaper or book. Used to like sitting outside and reading when it was warm out and, if it was past six, having a drink, but doesn't anymore. Reason? Again, doesn't know; it's just a feeling he gets. Every time he thinks to sit on the patio and read or have a drink or both or just stare at the tall trees around the house or at the sky, he tells himself what's he going to see that he hasn't seen, and not only that, all the chairs are uncomfortable out there, and he'd rather be sitting on the soft Morris one inside. Gets one of the patio table's bistro chairs out of the toolshed, opens it, wipes the cobwebs off with his handkerchief, will have to remember to put the handkerchief in the washer when he goes into the house, and sits in the carport, facing the patio. Less wind here. Nothing much to look at, though, the patio surrounded by bushes with leaves on them and an opening in them with more bushes past it, and turns the chair around so he now looks out the carport the other way: the long steep lawn leading up to his nearest neighbor's house. But all he can see, from where he's sitting, is the lawn, and he brings the chair to the edge of the carport and sits. Not bad out, he thinks. He's got the right clothes on for this weather. And lucky to have a carport for his car and himself when it snows or rains. Good, good, he's comfortable. So, does his wanting to sit and not walk have something to do with age? His health, age, slowing down and increasing desire for comfort and all that are old stuff with him as topics and a bit dull. Sky's dull too, single shade of gray, and trees around his neighbor's house are all bare. Interesting, though, is the lit Christmas tree he can faintly see from here in her living room, more than two months after Christmas. Why doesn't she get rid of it? Must be completely dry by now, needles making a daily mess on the floor. He knows he wouldn't want it. But she's young, around twenty-eight, divorced, two small children—so that could be why she keeps the tree, though it'd be a fire hazard, he'd think—lives alone with them and their nursemaid. Very rich, house cost a fortune when she bought it two years ago— price was given in the "houses sold" listing in the Sunday real estate section of the *Sun*—and must have cost another fortune to remodel—a neighbor was in it and told him what had been done to the interior—but all that's her concern. He and his wife have little to do with her. One reason: her age. But mainly because she drives her car too fast on the driveway they share. He's left a couple of notes in her mailbox about it and a message on her answering machine and never got a response. Also, she has three huge dead trees on her side of the driveway. If they fall—and they could because the roots are probably shot—they could land on his house, so he sent her a certified letter saying all that and asking her to have the trees removed. A note in his mailbox from her went something like: "Dear Mr. Ostrower. What you request regarding the old trees would be extremely expensive. But, even though a friend of mine who knows about these things said there's still some life in those trees and with enough fertilizer they might come back and flourish, I'll cut them down if you'll go halves with me, and tree removal service of your choice. Most sincerely, Victoria Norton." He put a note in her mailbox: "Excuse me, Vicki, and certainly no offense intended, but why should I share the cost? I can sympathize with the expense of cutting down and taking away such large trees, but they are on your property. Most sincerely, Meyer." Maybe he's making a mistake by not going in with her-- his wife thinks so. In their county, he's learned—something his neighbor probably doesn't know yet, but her friend, if that person exists, might find out—if a tree falls from someone else's property, you're responsible for the damage to your house and grounds, the tree owner's only responsible for removing the tree. Has to remember to send her another certified letter, this one a little stronger—how would she feel, for instance, if one of her trees fell on his house while his wife and he were in it?—or just call her tonight with that argument. But something there for an idea? Dried Christmas tree all lit up and bleak dead ones outside. Squabble over the dead trees, narrator refusing to pay half, neighbor saying "Spite your nose, then," he saying "What the heck's that supposed to mean? Besides, it's anachronistic—something I used to say as a kid. Ah, forget it," and turning his back on her and walking away. Or saying "While you're at it, you should get rid of your Christmas tree too, not that it's my business. But we're closing in on Easter," and then walking away, and a few days later during a storm, or shortly after one, the ground saturated with several inches of rain, one or two of the trees falling on his house. His wife working on her computer at the time, he taking a nap in the bedroom and suddenly awakened by the crash and rain coming through a hole in the roof—so it'd still have to be raining—or through broken windows, but both of them getting out of the house unhurt. Could be something, but just doesn't feel it's the right one now. Then what? Would love for there to be something. Gets nervous and irritable if a dry period goes on for more than a couple of days, and it's almost been a week. Shuts his eyes. Maybe an idea will come. Has before that way. Image of their cat walking across his neighbor's lawn with a live frog between his teeth. Where the hell that come from? He pulls it out of the cat's mouth and drops it in the creek that runs past his house. It still makes no sense. Opens his eyes, blinks the image away, shuts them. Woman he lived with for two years before she broke up with him, and some months later he met his wife. Throwing her head back and laughing, then angrily wagging her finger at something. Well, she was always laughing, it seemed, and loudly, when she wasn't criticizing him for one thing or another. Wasn't that bad, and "she laughed a lot" would be a more accurate description of her, but how'd he stand all that fault-finding? Rather, why'd he take it? Again, the sex was good, and he'd gone through a long period of loneliness before he met her, and she was very smart, funny, pretty, and literary, and for a while he thought they'd work things out and marry and have a kid, for he was by then in his early forties, but done her enough. Last time she read a story of his with a couple like them in it, she sent him a postcard care of his publisher: "Saw your new collection; browsed through it but didn't buy. Not that I'm cheap; I just don't like wasting money. It's unfair of you to continue to depict me as a witch. From now on, keep me out of your execrable, puerile, revengeful shit." Blinks, but she's already gone, then shuts his eyes again. His best friend, who has Alzheimer's and has been in a New Jersey nursing home for four years. In fact, it was that woman who'd introduced them: They were teaching English in the same high school. His guilt over not seeing him for almost two years? Used to drive up to visit him around every third month. His friend was getting increasingly worse, had trouble placing him, but once he knew it was Meyer, was glad he'd come. Last visit, his friend hadn't a clue who he was. "Give me time. A-B, C-D, E-B-G. I'm going through the merry-go-round. I'll get your name before I leave, and once I have it, I'll get your face. But I've always been bad with time, hand mirrors and giving flowers. You a visitor here too? I've come to see my dead brother." He never had one. But as a possible piece? More emotional and complete as an idea than the tree one. Narrator goes up to see his best friend in a nursing home in New York. Friend's lost lots of weight and hair and never recognizes him, doesn't even try to, and almost continuously speaks gibberish, but nothing the narrator can get any meaning out of. "One-two, button your nose... I'm learning the alphabet all over. Three-four, close your face. Give me a minute. I'll get it." Okay, it's now clear he was trying to remember where he knows the narrator from. Thinks on his drive back to Philadelphia that he'll probably never go see him again. Could be that he went with some hope. Friend's wife had said on the phone the previous night "There's been no deterioration in his condition since you last saw him and he may even have improved a little." No, that wouldn't work. She'd said "Believe me (and his first name), it's not worth the trip. He won't know you from a hole in a wall and you won't make out most of what he says." He said "Oh, I feel I can get him to recognize me. Certain touchstones or milestones or whatever they're called that we did together and he'll eventually remember, or at least one of them, and that can be a start. I'll just persist, but not to the point where it's obviously disturbing him." "You're kidding yourself," she said, "but let me know how it goes." A strong possibility, that one. Almost the whole thing's there. He goes, friend goes into a rage because of something the narrator said or falls and breaks a bone because of something the narrator did—and he later calls the wife to confess his arrogant and harmful self-assurance. Will include that contraption his friend was in last time Meyer was there: part walker/part wheelchair, with a tray in front of it for food and to rest his arms on. When the narrator's friend wants to get out of it—"Let's go for a walking tour of the museum, Mr. Visitor," he says, "but not while I'm still trapped inside this torture machine"—an aide rushes over and says "Please don't help him out of the chair. He's gotta stay in it till we change him or get him on the potty. Since he refuses to exercise or undergo any physical therapy, his leg muscles have atrophied and he'll collapse if he tries standing on his own. —Let this be a lesson to you, Herman," an aide said to his friend the last time. "You do what we say here and not always what you want to and you'll be much better off." "Another time," Herman said to Meyer. And then, doesn't know why, he thinks of an incident he hadn't thought of since around the time it happened... '77, so twenty-eight years ago. Of course, now he knows why. Herman, when Meyer told him of it, said to write it down—"I'm sure you can make a great story out of it"—and he tried but could never come up with a good ending. He was working as a bartender at a restaurant-bar on 38th Street and 7th Avenue. During the week there were two bartenders working the long bar, but on Saturdays, because business was light—the place was closed Sundays—he worked the eleven-to-eight shift alone and helped the manager close up. Every other Saturday around noon these two guys, brothers, would come in and sit at the bar and have a glass of wine—never more than one, and the bar was usually empty except for them—and something to eat: cheeseburgers and a big salad between them when it was warm out, soup and a roll each and a slice of heated-up apple pie between them when the weather turned cold. After that, and they tipped generously, they'd go to three different movie theaters in the city, they said, and later have dinner and discuss the movies. This went on for about a half a year. One came in from Westchester, he remembers, the other from Long Island, and they'd meet in Penn Station and walk to the restaurant. Then he didn't see them for a while, and he was on a subway after work, heading downtown to his girlfriend's apartment, when he saw one of the men at the other end of the car. The man waved, he waved back, he was going to leave it at that, but the man walked over to him. "You remember me, don't you? Used to come into your restaurant with my brother every second Saturday." "Sure, how could I forget you guys? You were among my few regulars.

How you doing? I've been wondering why I haven't seen you. What happened, find a better joint? And how's your brother?" and the man said "He died only two weeks ago. Got sick a few months back, which is why our Saturday ritual stopped. And then, when we all thought he was getting better, he had a stroke in his sleep. I haven't been the same since. That's why I'm riding these trains. I don't know what to do or where to go without him. We were very close. As close as two brothers have a right to be. Our wives are sisters. I suppose that makes us even closer. My brother knew you'd worry that you haven't seen us or think we deserted you. Just a few weeks ago he said I ought to stop in to tell you we're okay and we'll be seeing you soon, when we continue our Saturday moviegoing. That's how thoughtful he was. Always concerned with the feelings of the next guy." "He was a nice man. I'm so sorry. And it was obvious to me that you two were real pals." "We've been like that all our lives. There was never an 'older brother' and 'younger brother' with us. We were equals and compatible from the start," and he said "I'm sure you were. But look, I really don't want to leave you, but my stop's coming up now and I have to change trains." The man started sobbing as the train was pulling into the station. Meyer patted his arm and said "Please come to the restaurant again and we'll talk some more. Saturdays around eleven or noon's the best time, when the place isn't busy. Actually, anytime, Saturday, and no matter how busy I am, and I really shouldn't be, because it's just empty office buildings and factories in the neighborhood on weekends, I'll make time to talk," and the doors opened and he got off the train. When the train pulled out, he looked through the windows and saw the man walking back to the other end of the car. It's a good incident, he wrote several drafts about the brothers and then meeting the man on the subway, but he still can't see a way how to end it. He can't just have the man walking through the car, maybe with his hands over his eyes or a handkerchief to his face, which he thinks is what the man did. Maybe the narrator can stay on the train with the man past his own stop, going to wherever the man's going, downtown to the Battery, or across town at 14th Street, which is where Meyer was going. Talking to the man for an hour or two. Maybe going in for coffee with him someplace. Then the man saying he feels a bit better now, talking to him helped, and the narrator should go home or to wherever he was going when they met—"I bet to your girlfriend," and the narrator saying "You're right." And the man smiling for the first time that night and shaking his hand and the narrator hugging him and the man hugging him back and saying he's going to take him up on his offer of coming into the restaurant for another nice long talk and the narrator saying "Please do; I meant every word of it." Then, month or so later, the narrator quitting the job for a better one at another restaurant—Meyer actually was forced to leave when he fell off a stepladder at the bar while reaching for a liquor bottle in a cabinet and broke his shoulder—and saying to the manager "If a guy comes in wanting to speak to me—sort of a pudgy fellow, around fifty, short, lots of curly gray hair, name's"—and he gives it—"tell him to phone me and we'll get together for coffee or a drink." And giving the manager his phone number, though he'd already have it, and the phone number of the new place, but he never hears from the man. He could even call the manager at the old place a few weeks after that and the manager says "Nobody like you described came in for you," or that manager's left and the new one doesn't know what he's talking about and hasn't got time to talk, and hangs up, and he could end it there. He'll think about it. It's certainly the best idea how to end the piece yet. But try for one more. Shuts his eyes. Nothing comes. Opens them, shuts them. Just darkness with flashes of light through it and then his mother's face emerges from the dark. Bad line if he ever thought of using it. The word "emerges" and then "from the dark." Near the end of her life, looks like. Face very much like it is in the last photos he took of her and has looked at a number of times, sleeping in her wheelchair in Central Park. Same area—Strawberry Fields—where he and his sister bought a bench plaque with her name on it and "in memoriam from her loving children"—his sister's idea and wording, which he felt he had to go along with, though it was very expensive, and even if she hadn't sat on a park bench in years; just the wheelchair. Was afraid she'd wake up and say "Getting your last shot of me before I croak? What are you going to use them for, material?" Looked so frail and weak and her breathing was bad, that he thought she might die before he got her home. She stayed asleep. Slept until they reached her brownstone. Then he woke her, because he had to walk her down the steps to the building's areaway, and she said "That was a good nap, but I wasn't much of a talking partner. Please don't say I slept part of the time with my mouth open." Perked up awhile once he got her in a comfortable chair, said "See how sick I am? I'm not even asking for a drink." He said "You want one?" and she said "I'm a bad host; we don't have any. Your sister got rid of my one bottle of Jack Daniels because she doesn't want me to drink. Said, 'doctor said so,' "and he said "I brought a bottle just in case you had run out. I'll have one with you," and she said "Thanks, but I've no taste for liquor anymore. That's good, I suppose, but to me it's just one more tip-off I'm at the end of my road." Caregiver gave her dinner. She didn't talk while she ate; between bites she stared past him or at her empty fork. "What are you looking at?" he asked, and other questions to get her talking, but she didn't seem to hear him. "Mom?" and she put her fork into the food, bit a little off it and again stared past him. She's never done that before, he thought. What's it a sign of? When he was getting ready to go, he said he was leaving the bottle and if she ever felt like it again, she should have a glass but with lots of ice and water. "Sort of a compromise between you and the doc." She said, first words since she started eating, "Take it with you. The girl here will only drink it, which must be another reason your sister doesn't want any liquor around, and then she'll drop me when she's putting me to bed." Kissed her, said "Do you remember not talking to me while you ate and sort of staring into space? It concerned me," and she said "Of course I talked to you. I've always been a talker, maybe too much, and eating's never stopped me from talking either. As for staring, maybe for a few seconds I was tired, that's all." "Good," he said, and then how sorry he is to go. He'll come back next week for a day, take her out to lunch, anything she wants, and she said "I don't like lunch anymore. People will see how ugly I've become and take pity on me and also on themselves. I'd be spoiling their lunch. Nobody wants to eat near a corpse. And next week you'll be here? The same? Sunday? I hope so and that I'll live that long. Seeing you always gives me the incentive to stick around longer, but it's becoming harder and harder to; I just don't have it in me anymore." "Come on, that's nonsense," and he kissed her, smiled, trying to get a smile out of her. She said "You always had a nice smile. It can get you places. I once did, too, and look where it got me." "What do you mean?" and she said "Nothing. I don't want to concern you about me any further." Just before he left, he said he'll call her when he gets home. "Don't bother," she said. "I'll be asleep," and he said "Then tomorrow morning," and kissed her goodbye. Cried when he walked to the subway. Just about always cried right after he left her. If this were part of something he was writing, would he drag out the apartment scene so long? Doesn't think so. He'd cut some of the dialog and one or two of the kisses. He'd leave, feel lousy for her as he walked to the subway, then would start running to the subway station because he stayed with her longer than he'd planned to and he didn't want to miss the next train to Baltimore from Penn Station. A few days later, his sister calls to say their mother died that morning. Or, his sister calls the next day just before he was going to call his mother. "If you want to see Mom alive again, and there's no guarantee, get on the train right away. She's home in a coma. We're not taking her to the hospital this time. She hates those places, and after the last time, made me promise she can die at home." "But if going to the hospital can save her?" and she says "Leave; now!" and hangs up. But he's covered her death plenty and sometimes the same way. An hour after he gets there, two hours, three: his mother dies while he's holding her sitting up in bed, her head resting on his shoulder or slung over it, throwing up white fluid, eyes opening a few seconds and looking at him, or seeming to look at him, and then closing for good. Caregiver saying "That's it, she's gone; I've seen it before." Caregiver saying "What happened; she dead?" His sister hurrying into the room from her old bedroom where she went to nap. Hurrying in from the kitchen where she went to make tea, saying "What is it? Tell me!" "Oh, Mommy, Mommy, oh, Mommy" he says, still holding her and patting her back, first time he can remember calling her that in more than fifty years. "So childish to say 'Mommy,'" his sister said when we was around fourteen. "It's Mom or Mother. Grow up!" Saying to his mother "I got ya; don't be afraid; you'll be all right," though she was probably already dead. His sister insisting they wait three hours before dialing 911. "I want her to be cold. I don't want an entire fire brigade barging in here and breaking her bones when they futilely pound on her chest to revive her." Also done a number of pieces of taking her to Central Park in her wheelchair or to one restaurant in particular on Columbus Avenue. His mother, before the last few months of her life, always asking to be transferred to a regular chair at a table by the patio window so she can look out at the street. "I love seeing people passing, walking dogs or stopping to talk, especially young people with little children, and when they pass they do it quickly without really noticing me. I'm an inveterate observer of life," she once said at one of these tables. "That's why I'd never allow you and your sister to put me in a nursing home. Nothing enjoyable to see there, and the screams and the stink. Sitting by the window here and observing also helps me to pass the time if you're in one of those silent moods you've sporadically fallen into since you were a boy. Remember? Always when you came back from a Saturday afternoon movie." "Those were headaches I got there; the silent moods were probably caused by other things." This time—it's the last time he takes her to a restaurant—it's she who doesn't want to speak. Trains in from Baltimore, gets to her apartment—she's still in bed, blinds are closed, she doesn't want to get up and shower, the caregiver tells him—and he raises the blinds of one window and says "Hey, what's going on, Mom? How do you feel? You look great. Want to get up now so we can get started?" She shakes her head. "Why not?" "Not hungry today." "Come on, you have to shower and eat. Or eat, at least." She looks away. "You want to tell me why? Then you want to tell me how you're going to keep your health up if you don't eat?" "Don't force me." "I'm not. But I'm starving and have been looking forward to this lunch all week. Same old place? Nice cheese omelette, home fries, spinach with capers, the rest? Not exactly the best first meal of the day, but in some countries it could be considered breakfast. And though I don't like nipping before six, and that's six at night, we'll each get a drink." She smiles and says

"I can never say no to you. It's not the drink enticement that changed my mind, either," and he says "Good," and leaves the room. Caregiver showers and dresses her and they both get her into the wheelchair. "Comfortable?" he says, and she says "As well as can be expected." "Is anything hurting you, then?" and she says "Even if it was, I don't like to complain." "Like a pillow for your back?" and she says "Then I'll look like a real invalid." On the street, he says "Nice day out, huh?" and she shrugs. "Lots of people on the street. Well, it's New York, nothing like where I live," and she says "Where's that again?" "Right outside Baltimore," and she says "So move back. I'd like that." "When I retire, maybe," and she says "When's that?" "When both kids have graduated college," and she says "That's too far away. I'll be long gone by then." "Nonsense. You'll come to their graduations," and she says "Wouldn't that be nice." At the restaurant, he asks the hostess for a table by the patio window, and his mother says "No, at the banquette along the wall, my back to everyone so nobody can see me. I look like an old hag." "Not so," he says. "You're still very glamorous-looking, but we'll do what you say and go in back." At the table, he says "Want to sit in a regular chair?" and she says "I'll stay where I am. It hurts every time I'm moved from this chair to another one, though I hope I'm in nobody's way." He pushes her closer to the table and says "Wheelchair in far enough?" and she says "For my purposes, yes." "Like your customary Jack Daniels on the rocks, twist of lemon peel, pinch of water?" and she shakes her head. "Now this is something. First time you ever refused one when you were out with me. And you should have it because it'll stimulate your appetite. But if you don't drink, I won't," and she says "Do what you want; you're a big boy. I simply don't feel like drinking or eating or doing anything or even saying much. It's how I'm feeling today and felt yesterday and all the other days this week." "Mom, you're exaggerating again. I'm going to order one for you anyway, and if you don't drink it, I'll do it for you." She shrugs. He orders the drink the way she always has it and a glass of wine for himself. She doesn't touch hers. He orders her a plain omelette—"Something light," he says, "if it's your stomach that's bothering you"—and cuts half of it into slices for her, but she doesn't eat. "I told you," she says, pushing the plate away. "You're wasting good money, and an omelette's nothing you can put in a doggy bag and take home." He pushes the plate back, sticks her fork into a piece of the omelette and holds it out for her to take. "Stop it," she says. "I'm not a baby. I'm only helpless like one." "Then the hash browns and tomato wedges. They look good." He eats the omelette piece off her fork, sticks his unused fork into the potatoes and puts it on her plate. She looks away from it, sees someone at the next table smiling at her and then mouthing a hello, smiles back and looks at her plate but doesn't touch her fork. "Maybe you want a tablespoon for the potatoes. That's how I usually eat them. It's easier." "Please," she says very low, "this is embarrassing me. I told you I'm not hungry and I hate the way I look. This outfit the girl put on me is all wrong too. Can we go home?" "But I haven't bit into my sandwich yet or drunk your Jack Daniels." "You'll get drunk, wine and liquor both."

"That's all right. I'll be more fun to be with," and she laughs. "Good," he says, "I made you laugh. Now if I can get you to eat, I'll be even happier... Okay, so only I'll eat, and then we'll go," and he bites into his sandwich, chews a little, says "Want half?" and she shakes her head, and he says "So what have you been doing the past week since I last saw you?" and she says "Nothing." "Surely you've done something," and she says "What I'm saying is what could I be doing in my present condition? Letting myself get showered and ready for breakfast, and twelve hours later, ready for bed. Telling the girls I'm tired of eating their awful cooking and to take the food away. Other dull and irritating things. The toilet. Pills. If I'm not hungry it could be because I fill up on so many of them. Wasting my time with too many naps. But I'm bored, so I sleep. I said it before and I'll tell you it again: This is existing, not living," and he says "I'm sorry. I wish there was something I could do. But despite their cooking, and that's another reason you should take advantage of this restaurant food—the omelette piece I had was damn good— the women who look after you are competent and nice?" "They're pleasant enough, but they don't speak much English. That'd be a problem if I wanted to talk, but I don't. Or the weekend girl— today's—her English is so-so to okay, but because of her accent I can't understand most of what she says. The television programs they watch are loud and dumb and hurt my ears and are often in Spanish. I suppose I should be thankful that my hearing's still that good. But I let them watch when I'm sitting in the same room. If I don't, they might leave me, and the agency's short of girls. What would I do then? I don't even want to think about it. Besides, there's no other place for me to go in the apartment but one of the bedrooms or the toilet, and that just means sitting for an hour with little to no success—I'm sure you don't want to hear about it—or more naps, and I'm sick of both those. Also the kitchen, but there's nothing I want to do there or could." "What about cable? Or I'd get you a VCR so you could see movies you've missed," and she says "I've no interest anymore in movies or television or being thrilled or swept away or entertained." "Books? I got you those large-print ones of a couple of new novels by writers you've always liked. They working?" and she says "I've lost my taste not just for literature but all reading, newspapers included. And no matter how large the print is, I have trouble concentrating and making out the words. Glaucoma? Cataracts? One of those or even the double whammy— I forget what the doctor said—but I'm not going in for any more operations. It's not worth the expense or anybody's effort." "Books on tape? You don't even have to turn the pages, and some of them are read by very fine actors," and she says "Thank you, but none of it interests me. You must be tired of my griping, after I said I don't like to. I was never like that, though it's not hard to see why I've changed," and looks away, catches herself in the wall-length mirror behind him, and looks down at her lap. "Eat, Mom... a couple of bites?" but her eyes close and face relaxes. She going to doze off here? he thinks. Well, let her; it'll give him time to think of things to talk about that might interest her. After a few minutes—he's done eating, finished her hash browns and tomato wedges; didn't eat anymore of the omelette because of the egg yolks in it; should have had it made with just the whites—and drunk his wine and a little of her drink and the waiter's taken away their plates and glasses—he says "Mom? Mom? You can open your eyes now; food's gone. How about a dessert and coffee?" She opens her eyes, straightens up in the chair and says "Now that I'll have, but just the coffee, black. It'll pep me up, for the last thing I want is to fall asleep." They have coffee and he asks lots of questions, most of them he's asked before. "Was your father really so strict that you crossed the street when you saw him outside, to avoid talking to him? Was your mother really a dress and lingerie model for a fashionable New York department store, and later, after she married at seventeen, considered the most beautiful woman on the Lower East Side? Was my real dad's father as much of a *shiker* as you've made him out to be—Dad, you said, always denied it—that he couldn't put in two days' work straight? What line did the future king of England use when he tried dating you when you were dancing in the Scandals? Your father actually walked on stage during a number and pulled you off? Or is that what you thought he'd do if he knew you were dancing half-nude? And Dad's mother. How come he was the only child in his family not to be repeatedly chased around the house by her or beaten with a broomstick? Was he really slim when you first knew him? Because I've never seen a photo of him, and some going back to before you met, where he wasn't at least slightly chubby. Admit it. I was a pain in the poop when growing up, right? And weren't you and Dad Number Two a little frightened—and if it's true, I'm sorry for the worry I caused you both—that I'd become a junkie or alcoholic by the time I was thirty?" To all his questions she mostly nods or stares at him or smiles when it's obvious she doesn't want to smile, or says "I know… You're right… I'd rather hold judgment… It's exactly what you said," as if she hasn't heard or listened to what he said but doesn't want to be thought inattentive or completely out of it, and finally "Enough of these questions, already. We've finished our coffee. Unless you want a refill—I know I'd love another, but my bladder wouldn't tolerate it—let's go home. I'm getting tired." Took her out to lunch only if the weather was good. If it was raining or very cold, snowing or ice on the street, he'd get takeout for them on his way to her building from Penn Station. Mostly for her, though. He wasn't much for lunch except at a restaurant, so would pick at his food a little in her apartment and save the rest for her dinner that night. "Why aren't you eating?" she'd say, and he always said "You know me. Not much of a lunch muncher, but I'll finish it before I go." "Don't talk about going; you just got here, and it makes me sad when you leave." Should have got takeout for whatever caregiver was looking after her those weekends, but too late for that now. And Irwin, his stepfather. Anything there? Wheeled him plenty of times outside for almost three years, mostly to Central Park. He was still living in the city then, up the block from their building. Moved there from a much nicer and less expensive place downtown so he could help his mother with him. Went to their apartment every day and in the evening to have a drink or two with his mother.

He was the one who gave him his daily insulin shot in the morning. His mother tried to but couldn't—"I'm petrified of needles"— though she did just about everything else for him. Cleaned him up after he messed in bed, which he did a lot. "Can't you hold it in till I get you on the commode?" "I try. What do you think, I'm doing it on purpose? It's not enough I got Parkinson's and diabetes both, that you gotta humiliate me too?" Cleaned his bedsores three times a day with hydrogen peroxide, even the one on the thigh near the buttock which got so big you could put a lemon in. Meyer couldn't even look at that one because the flesh was so raw and some of the bone was exposed. "I also get sick to my stomach looking at it," she said. "But what can I do? It's got to be done and there's no one else but the visiting nurse, whom I'd like to come more but can only afford twice a week." Showered, shaved, exercised, dressed and often fed him. Meyer would come by around eleven or twelve every night to change his stepfather's diaper if it needed it—by now his mother and Irwin slept in different rooms. Also to clean up the mess if he made one—he usually gagged doing it—and to stick his stepfather's prick into a plastic urinal so there'd be less chance of his wetting the bed overnight and turn him over on the side he wasn't sleeping on to prevent more bedsores. But a walk in the park with his stepfather. Doesn't think he did that one before. Wheels him out to the building's areaway, helps him stand, has him hold on to the railing on a separating wall there while he carries the wheelchair to the sidewalk, helps him up the steps and sits him back in his chair. "So where we going today?"

"I'd love to take you and Mom out for lunch, but you won't let me."

"You don't make enough to be tossing around dough like that. Besides, the food's much better and safer at home than in any restaurant. And they're all clip joints, charging half a buck for coffee when it should be, for what it costs them to make it and their overhead, a stinking dime."

"They have to make a profit, don't they?"

"What do you know about profit? You're the guy who hates money. They make too much profit as it is, is what I'm trying to explain to you, and I don't want it to be off you or me, where we're taken for complete jerks."

"Another reason for going out to lunch is Mom could use a break from taking care of you."

"She's getting one now."

"You know what I mean. A restaurant, outside the house, having a lunch she didn't have to make."

"So take her and leave me."

"I can't. You need someone to always be with you, I'm sorry."

"What, to watch me sitting in a chair and reading the paper? And if you get someone from some service to do it, it's money thrown away."

"You've fallen out of chairs."

"Once."

"More than once, and you broke your nose and another time

a finger."

"Twice, then, but at the most, and what's a little finger? I was reaching for something. So I won't reach for anything anymore when I'm sitting. I'll ask whoever's around to get it for me, and if no one is, I'll wait. Nothing's that important to get right away, anyway. But change the subject, will ya? It's hurting my ears."

"So what do you say; we going to the park? Weather's perfect for it."

"What am I going to see there that I haven't already? Trees, grass, people running or on bicycles, other old guys in wheelchairs. I'd rather sit on a bench on Central Park West and look at real life passing."

"We can do that. Though it'd be kind of dull for me, just sitting, and the car fumes are no good for you either. How about if we cut across the park to the Met? That way, we can get a bit of nature and fresh air and also culture. And I've never taken you there."

"I used to have my dental office right across the street from the Met. Opera singers would come in, mostly from the chorus. They didn't make much and they knew I worked cheap. I had to be very careful not to anesthetize their tongue, or else they couldn't sing that night."

"Oh, you used Novocain on them? You never did on me."

"I never had to with you. You rarely had a cavity and when you did I got it quick and so never had to dig down too deep."

"I had plenty of cavities. And I used to almost faint sometimes when you drilled my teeth."

"That's why you started going to another dentist so early and with your own money? Boy, you hurt me with that one."

"If you want to know the truth, and I'm sorry if I hurt your feelings then, but yes. You wouldn't even take x-rays, though you probably did for all your other patients."

"Not all. Some asked would they save money by not getting numbed and having x-rays, and I said 'Sure, I save, you save,' so they did without them. I told you, most of my patients weren't well-off."

"Let's talk about the Met Opera house, and I know, before, you knew I meant the museum. Any of the big opera singers your patients?"

"Sure. One *bulvan* was more than six and a half feet tall."

"Very funny. But seriously, I mean the ones who sang the leads."

"All of them. No, they went to Park and Fifth Avenue dentists with big names and prices and dental hygienists and receptionists. They could've saved a bundle with me. My office isn't beautiful? No bubbling fish tanks and the latest magazines? So what. We're all taught the same in dental school, so no dentist is any better than the other for the routine stuff, and I cleaned my own patients' teeth. As for the museum, why would I want to go there? Too big and far, and I read they charge admission now. Besides, I've no interest in art."

"You don't have to give them what they ask for. I usually give a quarter. And they have a decent cafeteria there."

"I ate."

"But I could use a coffee and sandwich."

"Why didn't you have them when we were home? Let's just go to the bench you usually take me to at the entrance to the park. All I want today is some peace and quiet, so not near any playground like you did the last time."

"One moment you want to sit looking at traffic, the next you want quiet? And I thought you liked kids."

"Who told you that? Maybe a long time ago when you were still a kid, but not for years, not even your sister's. They're too lively. They make me dizzy with their running around without knowing where they're going, and they yell and screech and really bust my eardrums."

"I know of a nice peaceful spot in the park we can go."

"Good. I'll take a nap there. I hope you brought something to read with you, because I'm not a good conversationalist when I'm asleep."

"I always do. It's in my back pocket."

"You'll tear your pants that way, but do what you want. You never listen to me."

He wheels him up the street to the park. But too much like the ones he did with his mother in the park and going to it. Maybe something with a younger sister. Also in a wheelchair and in a hospital. Why "also" in a hospital? Did one of the last things he thought of doing take place in one? Thinks so, but forgets. Narrator's living in California and gets a call from his older sister or his parents that his younger sister's in the hospital, possibly dying from her disease, and he should fly in. "I don't have enough money for a ticket, nor know anyone to borrow from," and his mother—either she or his father is on the phone extension in their bedroom—says "We'll buy you one from here." "Take the midnight special, I think they call it," his father says. "They're cheaper, and you'll still get here in time. She's not going anyplace quick." "Let's not be stingy about this," his mother says. "Go regular class, first plane you can get out." He sees his sister in the hospital every day, stays several hours, then comes back around six for a couple of hours. She seems to get a little better, and one night—his parents have gone home, and father's his real father—he says "I bet you've been in this bed since you got here. Wouldn't you like to get out of it and stroll around the floor? Maybe see what books and magazines are in the library down the hall." "I'd like that," she says, "though I don't know if I can read. My eyesight's gotten so bad since I got here, my glasses no longer help. And you'll have to check with the nurses if it's okay." "I don't see any harm," a nurse says, "and it might lift her spirits and air some of her bedsores." They get her in a wheelchair. He pushes her down the corridor with one hand, his other hand pulling along the rolling IV stand. "This is hard," he says. "I'm also afraid we're going to run into something or your needle will come out." "Let's just sit in the patients' lounge," she says. "In all my times in this hospital, I've never been in one." They go into it. "This is what I was hoping," she says; "nobody in here. I want to talk private." "Uh-oh, here comes the rebuke, long held in, now let out, about what a lousy brother I've always been. Shoot." "All right. Despite your trying to make me think I'm getting better, I know I'm getting worse and am going to be dead very soon. I want to ask you something, though you might find it, for reasons of not wanting to or because it's such a ridiculous question, impossible to answer." "First of all, if I can cut you off, you're not going to die. Look at you. You're up for the first time in a week. Your face has better color and your hand grip's much stronger. In every way—appetite, alertness, speech—you're better. Here, grip my hand and you'll see." "Stop it," she says. "If you want to hold my hand, that's something different." "It's the truth. Mom and Dad think so too. I'm sure you're coming home in a week or so, maybe sooner, and I'm sticking around until you do." "Listen to me, I don't want to be played with. Just answer my question. I'm the youngest, so of all the people in the family, why do I have to be the first to die?" He shakes his head. "It's simply not true." "Meyer, you rat" though he'd never use his real name, "tell me." "I have no explanations. I don't like this conversation. Please, let's change it." "Why don't you like it? I'm telling you what I think. Almost all my life. Since I was five: sick, doctors, hospitals, always more operated on, always getting worse. Yet sick as I am, worse as I'm going to get, I don't want to die." "I know. You're right. I'm sorry," and he takes her hand and kisses her fingers and starts crying. "Oh, wouldn't I love to cry also," she says. No, doesn't work. Never did her death that way before, though has used a patients' lounge as a location, but it's way off.

Dialog's stilted, situation doesn't feel real. She's too articulate for someone so sick, and he's playing for tears. How'd it really go? If he did it the way it happened, there'd be no story. She was already dead when he got the call. So try it as if he's there when she dies. Gets a call at work. There's been an accident. His younger sister was hit by a car. She was riding her bike. She's in the hospital. He flies in from California the same day. Paid for the ticket out of his own pocket. Takes a cab from the airport to the hospital and he's so broke now that he almost doesn't have enough cash to pay the fare. His folks are in her room when he gets there. She's sharing it with another patient. There's no wheelchair. It was his father who called him. There's no older sister. She's his only sibling. His folks are exhausted and go home. Or she's older than his younger sister was when she was hit on a bike and died. She was walking across the street when a car hit her. He stays that night sleeping in a chair by her bed. She's in a coma for two days. Then comes out of it and they all think she's going to recover. She's in the hospital for five days. Tubes and wires hooked up to machines and jars and a bag are on or in her. But she'd be in the intensive care unit if this was right after such a bad accident. She's dying of a disease she's had for years. When she was brought in the doctors knew she wasn't going to recover this time. He reads and draws most of the time and goes to the hospital cafeteria for coffee and a snack or to bring a coffee back. He goes home every afternoon for a few hours to shower and nap. He sleeps every night by her bed or on a couch in the visitors' lounge on her floor. She's on morphine the last two days and mostly sleeps. When she's awake she looks straight up at the ceiling or stares at him through half-closed eyes. Her eyes follow him if he goes to the other side of the bed. "What is it? You want me to do something for you or get the nurse?" She gives no sign she heard him. Nor when the patient in the next bed calls out for a nurse or says something loud in her sleep. He doesn't think the nurses and aides are looking in on her enough. He thinks they've given up on her and are spending more time with patients they think will recover. He doesn't think she's turned over enough to avoid getting bedsores. He's sure the hospital staff on her floor thinks he's a nuisance and causing more harm than help for her by demanding they do more. He pats her forehead and neck and cheeks with a damp towel when they're sweaty. Wipes her lips with glycerine swabs when they look dry or when her tongue repeatedly pops out to lick something. Twice in the last three days she's there she looks at him and says his name and "Why me? Why me?" Her eyes close both times after she says this and she seems to doze off. She doesn't make any noise while she sleeps and her chest never goes up and down or heaves. Sometimes he puts his ear next to her mouth to make sure she's still breathing. Sometimes he goes out into the corridor and cries. Or holds it back till he gets inside the visitors' restroom on the floor. Sometimes he takes her hand through the bedrail and talks to her. He wants to get her to speak. He hopes she'll suddenly open her eyes all the way and say "I'm feeling much better." Or "What day is today?" Or "How long have I been here? Can I have some water?" He sometimes thinks he's overexerting her by trying to get her to talk. "Remember when we were kids and Mom asked me to babysit you and you were adamantly against it? You said you were too old to be babysat and I was too young to babysit. Do you remember that? Remember when Mom took us to Central Park and bought us ice cream cones? For about ten years straight I only ate vanilla. I forget what flavor you liked. Maybe all. But a few minutes later she said 'I'm going to tell you both something after you finish your ice cream.' We said 'What?' She said 'Just keep eating and you'll find out.' She told us after we finished that we hadn't offered her any of our ice cream. That it was a very impolite thing to do and not what she expected of us. She also said 'Not that I would have taken any if offered.' We both felt awful and apologized. She said 'Too late. Next time act differently.' Do you remember any of that? I don't know why it's stuck in my memory so. Remember in summer camp during color war when we were on opposing sides? Camp Pokono and Ramona. I saw you going into the mess hall and you said you couldn't talk to me because I was on the maroon team and you were on the gray. I said 'Of course we can talk. This kind of war isn't one where you have enemies. We're brother and sister and when we see each other we say hi.' You said you were told by your captain that it has to be that way between relatives and friends on opposing sides if your team is going to win. Do you remember that? What I also remember is that you'd had a serious operation for your illness about six or seven months before. But you still went on to win a swimming race for your team. I think it was backstroke. Was that it? You were quite the athlete. But was I angry that you won? No. I was thrilled for you and boasted about you to my team members for the rest of the day. 'My sister! What a gal! She just finished recuperating from major surgery and she's beating the pants off everyone else.' Anything he can think of. He thinks maybe he'll at least get a smile out of her. She doesn't respond to anything he says. Then he has to pee real bad. He doesn't want to use the toilet in the room. Doesn't want to flush it and possibly disturb her and the other sleeping patient or leave the toilet unflushed. Also doesn't think he should be using their bathroom except to wash his hands and splash water on his face. He takes his hand from hers and says "Sweetie? I've got to make. I'll be right back." She just stares at him and he supposes her eyes follow him out of the room. He goes down the hall to the visitors' restroom. It's occupied. He goes to another restroom at the other end of the floor. He hurries back because he feels she's in worse shape than ever and he doesn't want to leave her alone too long. Her door's closed. He knocks and opens it. A medical team's inside and curtains have been pulled around her bed. A nurse asks him to leave. He says "But she's my sister. We're very close." "I'm sorry. You have to wait outside the room. You'll be in the way." He says "Is she going to be all right? Let me stay here and try to comfort her. It'll help if she's distressed." She shakes her head and starts to shut the door. He circles around her and pulls the curtain aside and takes his sister's hand. He knows they won't let him stay. His sister's eyes are closed. She doesn't look distressed. A doctor uncouples his hand from hers. "You're interfering in our attempts to help her." Another doctor edges him out of the room. "We'll come out to you when we're done." "But that's what I'm asking. What are you doing to her? How bad off is she?" The doctor goes into the room and shuts the door. He waits outside the room. The doctors and a nurse come out in about twenty minutes and shut the door. They walk past him without noticing him. He says "Doctor. Doctor. My sister inside the room you just left? You said you'd tell me what's happened and how she is." The doctor who edged him out of the room comes back. The other two doctors and the nurse go on. "My mistake. I forgot. Your sister passed away just now. My deepest sympathies." He says "Oh dear. The poor kid. She's been sick with that disease for so long." "She died peacefully. Never awoke. No pain or discomfort." "May I see her now?" "The nurses have some work to do on her first and then you can go in." He calls his parents and then waits outside his sister's room. Two nurses and an aide leave the room holding a few filled plastic bags and pushing a machine. He opens the door. A curtain's around her bed. A curtain's blocking off the other patient's bed and she's saying "Nurse? That you? Can I have my medicine now? The leg's killing me." He thinks: Not much different than other things he's done of other people, except for a number of details. One the narrator's wife. Another his mother. Maybe if he did three hospital episodes in a row: father, mother, sister, all of whom the narrator's with when they die, two in the same hospital ten years apart, mother at home. But chronologically as in his life: father, sister, mother. Or four of them in a row: two fathers, sister, mother, each about ten years apart and showing him in different stages of his life. He gets up and goes into the house, takes off his outside clothes and goes into his wife's study. She's not there. He calls his sister on the phone on his wife's worktable. Her answering machine comes on and he hangs up without leaving a message. Calls his older daughter. The message for her voice mailbox says she'll be in Vermont for a few days and out of cellphone range, something she probably told his wife, who forgot to tell him or didn't think she needed to. He says "Hi, it's Daddy. Just thought I'd call you, no particular reason. Much love, sweetheart, and hope you had a good trip." Should also have said "Never say on your message to callers that you're going to be away for a certain time. It's an open invite to possible burglars." Calls his other daughter. No answer and no voicemail message. Just rings and rings. Dials again. Same thing. Usually the answering device picks up if she doesn't. Maybe he's been dialing the wrong number. No, hers is easy, with that 2-3-2-3 for the last four digits and 6-5-6 for the prefix. It's his sister's and older daughter's numbers he frequently has to look up in his address book before dialing but didn't have to today. Good, his mind's working. Phone rings about ten seconds after he hangs up. He thinks: See how prescient you are. It's your younger daughter. Lifts the receiver and says hello. It's his sister. "Anything wrong?" she says—no "Hi" or "Hello." "No, why would you think that?" "Because you never call, then suddenly there you are but not leaving a message, so I thought something might be wrong with you or Sandra or one of my darling nieces." "I call; what do you mean I don't? Just that before I was feeling a bit melancholy after thinking a lot about Mom and Dad and Irwin and Rosalie, and wanted to speak to someone in the family, and who's left?" "Wish I had time to, but I'm up to my gills in work." "Wait," he says. "How'd you know it was me calling?" "Later," and she hangs up. Goes to the back to speak to his wife. She's on the bed, on her back, seems to be sleeping, arms by her sides. He leaves quietly and shuts the door. If she had opened her eyes while he was there, he might have said, but only if she had smiled at him, "Mind if I join you? I'm a little tired too." If she smiled some more once he got on the bed—this is how it usually went—he'd know he could start making love to her. Try the typewriter again. Maybe something will spin out this time. Sits down in front of it at the dining room table—would he really have said that if she had been resting on the bed with her eyes open? Thinks so, but again, only if she had given him a why-not-join-me? smile or something comparable, as she had plenty of times before. He even gets excited now—a little, he finds, touching himself through his pants. But forget it, taking his hand away after squeezing the head of his penis for a few seconds, for who knows what he'll feel like doing when they're in bed tonight? He knows he's rarely good for two ejaculations in one day if they're not separated by ten hours or so if or if he hasn't had a night's sleep in between, and puts paper in, holds his hands over the keyboard, but nothing comes. Thinks: Anything from before? Forgets what he was thinking of possibly using other than the mother-father-sister deathbeds' idea. Maybe ending it—the deathbed scenes would have to be memories now—with a phone call to the narrator's older sister—the dead sister, then, couldn't be his only sibling—who says, when he tells her what he's been thinking, "Sorry. Work; I'm way behind and gotta get back to it," and hangs up. Or ending it with the narrator calling his one daughter, getting her voice mailbox or answering machine at work or home, leaving an unalarming message— "Thought I'd call you; nothing important; and I might try you at work" or "home"—and then looking for his wife. Doesn't seem to be around. She was resting on the bed before but now isn't there or in either bathroom. Opens the basement door and yells her name down the stairs. But no lights are on, he thinks, so she can't be there. The porch? Too cold. She must have gone out for a walk. He didn't hear a car engine start up, and then she usually in this weather lets it run idle for a minute and a half till it's warmed up, so he knows she didn't take one of the cars. If she had, he can have the narrator think—he might have been in the back and didn't hear the car—she would have told him she was going. Strange, the narrator thinks. You go for a solitary walk, you don't have to tell anyone. Taking the car, even when there are two of them, you say. That right? Sounds so. And what would he have said if she was in the back and awake or in the basement? the narrator thinks. "Hi. Just wanted to know where you were. Nothing else on my mind. Go about what you were doing." And maybe "Sorry to disturb you." Actually, the narrator could think, he would have said, if she were lying on the bed with her eyes open, and only if she smiled in something like an inviting way to him, "Mind if I join you? I'm feeling a bit drowsy too." If she smiled again the same way or said something like "No, of course not" or "Sure, it'd be nice your lying beside me," then he would have known he could start making love to her once he got on the bed. But too long and complicated a piece to do a first draft of now—the four hospital scenes, phone calls, his wife. And he is a little tired—he can feel it in his fingers, which won't help his typing—so only up for something simple and short. Can't think of anything. Sometimes if he just starts typing the first thing that comes to him, it grows into something, but all he types is "I am typing, I'm typing, I typing, I type." Why not a letter, then? Whom to? His three correspondents all got answers to their last letters a few weeks ago and he hasn't got anything back from them since. To the president, maybe, something he thinks he's never done to a politician or government official, to tell him what he thinks of the job he and his blundering and dangerous administration are doing, he'll say, "and by that I don't mean to say you're not also dangerous, mendacious, incompetent, opportunistic" and some other even more critical adjectives he'll use, and give reasons why he thinks this—the war, especially. "Stand in front of another huge banner—you know the one I'm talking about: 'Mission Unconscionable'—this one saying 'For the good of the universe, I quit.'" Nah, the last part's silly, and reason's better than anger, insult and cheap shots. And even if he wrote the letter—he doubts he will—who would read it? An intern at best, and he doesn't have the address. Could just send it care of The White House, Constitution Avenue, or is it Pennsylvania? He should know. Worked as a reporter in Washington for close to three years. He knows 1776 Independence or Constitution Avenue was the DAR headquarters then, and

probably still is. His first news assignment was there, interviewing
DAR members at their annual convention, for radio stations his
news service represented in various cities and states. The local angle,
they called it, and maybe there's something here. The woman
reporter for their news service, who normally covered these kinds of
stories, was out with a broken foot. He'd done a number of
interviews on tape when the Secret Service and DC police started
asking everyone in the convention hall but DAR members to show
an official ID. Because this was his first week working for the news
service and they hadn't gotten him his press credentials yet—and
how he got the job in an elevator and the woman he met on the
streetcar his first day going to work and his own bumbling ineptitude
in the newsroom that day which almost cost him his job, is another
storylike chain of events he might try to write—he was asked to
leave. "Why?" he said. "It's just a routine convention of a bunch of
patriotic ladies, and all I'm doing is asking them a lot of banal
questions," and they told him President Eisenhower was about to
make a previously unannounced appearance on stage to greet the
convention, so anyone not authorized to be here would have to
leave. He said "I'm a bona-fide reporter, and now it's too big a story
not to cover," and they said if he didn't leave on his own they'd have
to arrest him. "Go on, arrest me; what's the difference now? I get a
big break on my first story and you're telling me to skip it? I already
screwed up enough with my news outfit, so my boss will can me.
—No, don't arrest me," when they grabbed his arms and put them
behind his back and pulled out a pair of handcuffs. "That was

dumb of me to say, I'm sorry, and I'm going like you said," and two agents walked him to the door. An AP reporter followed him outside and asked what the trouble had been. By the time he got back to his newsroom, a brief story of his being thrown out of the hall and almost arrested was on the wire. He apologized for not being able to record Eisenhower's address to the convention off one of the loudspeakers, and his boss says "What you did was way better. Ike just said howdy and keep up the good work, while you got the name of our fledgling news service all over the country. We could even pick up a few new clients from this. Forget your taped interviews for now. Write a sixty-second spot on how you nearly got arrested and being roughed up, which you'll read in our next feed in three minutes." Not bad, he could definitely keep it short, a funny piece of how adversity turns into success, but really just a vignette. But the letter to the president. They must get hundreds a day on the same subject and probably answer them all except the insane ones with the same statesmanlike response. "Your right to disagree with our policies is one of the basic tenets of what it means to be an American and what our brave soldiers…" Then maybe one to the *Times* or *Sun*_about the war. But what's he going to add that hasn't been said in the many intelligent letters he's read in those papers the last two years? Then to what or whom? Why not his wife? Hasn't written her in twenty-five years. He'll actually mail it if it isn't too stupid or sappy. "My dear wife," he types. Should the "d" and "w" be capped? What's the rule, because both ways look right. Just leave it. "I haven't written you in a long time. Since 1980, when I was teaching here and you were in New York teaching." Doesn't read well and the year's wrong. Wrote her for almost two years from Baltimore, starting in September '80, when his first semester began. Start over. Puts new paper in and writes "Dear wife." An awful salutation, even worse than the first. Puts new paper in and writes "My darling Sandra." Forget "darling"; just "Sandra." New paper in and "Dear Sandra. I haven't written you a letter since, well, probably April or May '82, more than a year and a half after I started my job here and while you were still living in New York. We were married for four months by then and you were four months pregnant with Lynette but still teaching, not that I needed to tell you any of that. Even though I came up by train almost every Thursday after my last class for a long weekend with you—some weekends I was too busy with school work to or, to be honest—I don't think I ever told you this—just tired of the weekly train trips back and forth or wanted to be alone to spend the next three days writing—I still wrote you letters at least every other week, some of which you received while I was with you in New York, and sometimes included a poem I'd written about my love for you, and in the last months of writing these letters and poems, my happiness at being married to you and that we were soon going to live together in Baltimore and, of course, have a child." Reads what he's written. What he sensed while writing it: too wordy, turgid, run-on and, in places, unclear. Puts new paper in. "My dearest Sandra. It's been 23 years since I've written you anything more than a note. You know, the kind that I leave on the dryer before you get home to tell you that I'm out and where I've gone and when I expect to be back, and so on. Right now, as I write, you're in the bedroom sleeping or resting, or you were when I last looked in on you, and if resting, maybe hearing me clack away on this machine. I hope not. I wouldn't want to disturb you with my typing or keep you awake when you wanted to sleep. Actually, I closed the bedroom door after I looked in on you. Because of that and the way sound doesn't travel well to the back, I doubt you can hear me. I used to write letters to you around every other week when I was living in Baltimore and you were still in New York. I'd often include a poem or two about you—my 'S-Poems,' I called them. Do you remember? 'S-1,' 'S-2,' etc. I think I got to around 'S-30.' I stopped writing them when I stopped writing you letters, a short time before we started living together permanently. I should've continued writing the poems but for some reason I didn't. Maybe knowing I was going to send them through the mail with a letter to you was an inducement to write them. Anyway, I made a copy of each poem before I mailed it. Did you save the originals? I know I kept my copies, but have no idea where they are now. If you did save them, I wouldn't mind seeing them and maybe making new copies. Not to try to publish them—I'm no poet; they came too easily, which I knew meant they couldn't be any good—but to bring back the early years of our relationship and what I was thinking and feeling then. By the way, this is the fifth or sixth time I've started this letter. A few of those times I got stuck on just the salutation, such as, is it 'My dearest Sandra' or 'My Dearest Sandra'? Stupid, right?" Oh, this is stupid.

One last shot, and loosen up. New paper in. "Dear Sandra. My first letter to you in 23 years. Last one was probably in April or May of '82, when I was down here and you were up there and we'd been married for 4 months and were soon going to be living permanently together. I also sent you about 30 of my 'S-Poems' with those letters, sometimes 2 at a time. I've no idea what I did with the copies of the poems—I of course sent you the originals—and you most likely did the wise thing in throwing them out. Did you? Just asking. They weren't good poems—we both knew that—but they did, you gotta admit (if you remember any of them), show my feelings for you. But let's see, what do I want to say in this? I'm so out of practice in writing anything to you but a short note. You know, the kind if you're out of the house and I'm going to leave the house before you get back and someone called you while you were gone, and so on. Last time I looked, you were in the bedroom sleeping. Did I already say that? Probably in one of my false starts. You were on your back, arms by your side, smiling. Who smiles when they sleep? Obviously, people do. Or maybe you weren't asleep. Were you? Did you hear me enter the room? I tried to be quiet. Were you awake with your eyes closed and smiling at something you were thinking and didn't hear me? Let me guess what you were thinking about—that is, if you weren't asleep. Our marriage. Though I give you a hard time now and then (I swear, you never do to me), it's a good marriage overall, isn't it?, which I think too. Anyway, what can I tell you here that I can't or don't want to say to your face? That I love your face? Too easy, and besides, I've told you that lots of times. That I love being your husband and have never regretted marrying you, not even in my angriest moments with you? Told you that, too, though not the anger part. Usually when we were alone at a restaurant for dinner and I've had, true, a coupla drinks, altho I've also said it, again usually after a drink or two, when the kids were with us, and have always said it on our wedding anniversary when we were at a restaurant for dinner, with or without the kids or drink. Then I usually took your hand, if I wasn't already holding it, and kissed it, and you said a few times, if I'd had something to drink, 'I know it's mostly the liquor in you speaking, but I feel the same about you.' If I hadn't drunk anything yet, you usually said something like 'That's always nice to hear.' 'Look at Daddy,' one of the kids once said long ago at one of these anniversary dinners, 'he's crying,' when it was really just that my eyes had watered up a bit, which was what usually happened while I told you these things. So what am I saying here? My first letter to you in 23 yrs—that, I know I've said in this letter—and here I am writing mush. But mush only because of the feeble way I'm saying it. If I were writing about two imaginary characters who are or are not standing in for us, I might be able to do it right. In other words, the love-mush could be done well but isn't being done well here. So, were you sleeping? Would've been nice if you had said, if you weren't sleeping, 'Care to join me. I'm feeling much better' or 'not as tired now.' I would've. We would've made love, I'm sure. We might even be making love at this moment. I would've taken off all your clothes but your shirt and bra. Maybe also not your kneesocks. We'd be making love on top of the bed and your feet would get cold. I would've pushed your socks halfway down your legs—I like rubbing your calves—and also pushed your bra and shirt up past your breasts. And of course—you know me; I have to be completely naked—taken off all my clothes including the socks. I must have good circulation, since my feet never get cold. But you didn't invite me to bed and I didn't want to just lie on it. That might've awakened you if you were asleep. I was thinking, as I looked at you smiling with your eyes closed—have I said this? I don't think so, not even in one of my false starts—that your smile was like the one you sometimes gave when I walked into the room and you were lying in bed with your eyes open and wouldn't mind making love if I was up for it, so I don't know what to make of your smile before. That's not a trouble. I tried something there that didn't work. What an abominable letter this is—a word I first heard from my Aunt Hershey when I was a kid and not really used well here; 'terrible' would've been so much better—altho it does confirm my love and desire for you. 'Confirm'? What a word for what I want to convey to you. 'Convey'? What a word for what I want to say. My mind sometimes, and it seems more often than ever. And I'm not so sure this letter does confirm and convey what I want to say. Anyway, that should do it. End on a low note, I say. I thought when I started this letter that I might be able to write a beautiful romantic one—a love letter, I could even call it, like most of the ones I wrote to you in New York 25 years ago—that would make you feel good and also romantic when you read it, put you in the mood for romance, is what I'm saying—where you'd say, if I was in the house when you got it—what? a day or two from now?—'Can I interrupt you for about 20 minutes or so?,' which you've said in different ways a number of times—but nothing I wrote and the way I wrote it could really do… get… inspire… oh, I'm stuck. End of letter. At least I wrote something today I could send out and gave my fingers, the five I type with—two from column A, three from column B—some exercise. My dear wife. My darling Sandra. It's a good marriage, don't you think? As one of the kids recently said, we still have a passion for each other. I wish my mother and my father and stepfather had such good marriages—I don't know about their passion for each other, but it could've been as good—and your folks too. And we have such good kids. All our folks did. Tho so many losses the last few years. But lots of happinesses too. This letter's truly getting sappy. What I was afraid of before I started it. I'll stop. I don't want to waste your time further. I don't know if I'll send it. If I don't, I might, tho, tell you I wrote a long letter to you and didn't send it and, in fact—this is what I'll do if I don't send it— destroyed it. You might then say 'It would have been nice getting a letter from you after nothing but notes for 23 yrs left on the dryer or taped to the outside of the kitchen storm door, but I'm sure you had good reasons for not sending it. Still, I would have been interested in what you said and what it was that prompted you to write me a letter after so long.' I could then—I know I said 'end of letter' and 'I'll stop,' but stay with me a few lines more—tell you some of the things in it if I could remember them, and you'd probably be glad I hadn't sent it and that you didn't have to spend so much time reading it, for the letter was very long. Anyway, all that said, whatever that expression means to what I've been saying, I'll now end this letter that might not be sent, with my love to you. So, my love to you. Meyer." Shouldn't he have signed his name rather than typed it? Scratches out the typewritten "Meyer" and signs his name under the scratched-out part, and then above his signed name, "Love." So, he thinks, you going to send it? Doesn't know; might. Read it first before deciding. Reads it, deletes some of the words and corrects all the typos with a pen. It's not that bad a letter, he thinks, and it really does show his feelings for her. Gets an envelope from the living room credenza, a stamp from the book of stamps on the shelf above the stove, stamps and addresses it, scratches out his department's address in the top left corner— doesn't want her to think he mailed it from the office and the department paid the postage—writes his name and address below the scratched-out part, sticks the folded up letter inside and seals it. Walks to the mailbox with it. Temperature must have dropped ten degrees since he sat out here, or it only feels like that because he's been in the house so long and has no jacket and cap on. No, it's much colder; he can feel it on his face and there's no wind. Puts the envelope into the mailbox, lifts the mailbox flag and runs back to the house. In the kitchen he thinks he doesn't know if he likes leaving the letter in the mailbox till tomorrow when the mail truck comes. He'll think all night should he send it or shouldn't he? Well, should he? He's not sure. Shouldn't he, then? Oh, let it stay. The marriage is safe. It's an honest loving letter, dimwitted as most of it is. And with the "marriage is safe" thought, he means the letter's not going to hurt it. First in twenty-three years? She'll probably keep it somewhere among her personal belongings till who knows when. If she's like him, till she forgets she has it or where she put it. No, it's too dumb a letter to send. Just tell her when she wakes up how much he loves her, if that's mostly what it was for. Puts on his jacket and cap, walks to the mailbox, gets the envelope out and pulls down the flag. Tears the envelope in half and goes back to the house. Should have carefully unsealed the envelope flap, got the letter out and torn it up, blacked out her name and address on the envelope and saved it for another mailing. Goes into the house and tries peeling off the stamp. Can't. Tears the envelope and letter halves into tiny pieces. Doesn't want her finding any of it. If she saw her name or their address or anything that she knew related to her, she might say "You wrote a letter and tore it up?" and he'd have to tell her what was in it. Dumps the pieces into the trash container rather than the paper recycling bag that'll be picked up this Monday with the other bags stuffed with paper and a couple of cartons. Is it this Monday? Every so often he has to check if it's mixed paper or bottles and cans. Looks at the four-year pickup schedule the county sent that's held to the refrigerator door with a magnet. This Monday's for bottles and cans. Following Monday's for mixed paper. Trash gets picked up every Thursday unless it's a holiday; then it's picked up the day after. His cap's off and he's about to take off his jacket, when his nose starts running. It's because he went out in the cold without the jacket and cap, he thinks, or maybe that he sat outside so long. Takes the handkerchief out of his jacket pocket, wipes his nose and upper lip and feels something like hair on them. Cobwebs. Damn, forgot to dump the hanky into the washer when he came in from sitting outside. Drops it in, tears a sheet from the roll of paper towels on the kitchen counter and wipes the cobwebs off his face.